# A Bloomy Head

# A Bloomy Head

*A romance: the first in the Regency Cheesemakers sequence.*

J. Winifred Butterworth

This is a work of fiction. Any resemblance to places, events, persons, or investigations real, historical, deceased, or discontinued is purely coincidental.

**Other works from this author**

*Writing as Sharon J. Gochenour*

*The Threads Quartet*
The Golden City
The Golden Empress (coming at some point)

*Writing as Juniper Butterworth*

*The Goblins and Cheese sequence*
The Changeling
Priest-Queen
The Dragon Under the Hill
The King in the Forest (coming soon)

*The Sea Goblins sequence*
Shipwrecked
Bewitched

*Writing as J. Winifred Butterworth*

*The Regency Cheesemakers sequence*
A Bloomy Head

## Table of Contents

### Content and (brief) historical notes
(from Sharon)

This book is set in 1820, shortly after the end of the Napoleonic Wars, a twelve-year period during which between three and seven million soldiers and civilians died as a result of violence, disease, or starvation. The male protagonist of this novel used the British apparatus of war to catapult himself out of a dreadful situation, in which he was forced to live as a gender not his own and sexually assaulted, and into a respected career as a doctor, operating on the battlefield and later in various British colonial possessions. He has experienced a forced pregnancy as a result of his assault, and it was a horrific experience for him, but his most traumatic experiences do not happen on the page. The name he was given at birth is never used in the text, only the name he chose for himself.

Astute historians will note an echo of the storied life and career of one James Barry, the first doctor known to have performed a caesarean section in Africa where both mother and child survived. James Barry was also assigned female at birth in 1789 and may have birthed his own child before starting his medical training. It's not possible to say what gender identity James Barry would have claimed had he lived in our century, any more than it is to guess at whether Charles Hamilton or James Howe, famous "female husbands" of the late 18<sup>th</sup> and early 19<sup>th</sup> century, might have called themselves trans men, butch lesbians, or something else entirely.

I, however, am writing this book in 2024, and I have chosen to write about historic queer people who are as confident in their identities as the trans folks I know and love now.

The female protagonist of this book is a cheesemaker and a child of a survivor of the French Revolution. I have taken the not-especially-revolutionary position that armed conflict is horribly traumatic for the most vulnerable, and the repercussions of this trauma unfold throughout the book. This protagonist also has suffered from infertility, loss of pregnancy, and emotional abuse from her first husband, including infidelity. Again, her most traumatic experiences do not appear on the page, but she grieves them, and they are alluded to by other characters. Her infertility is not healed in the text, and she does not end the book with children or the promise of children.

Lastly, this is a murder mystery. There are some murders.

As should be obvious, the responsibility for any faults in this book is fully my own.

**An even briefer note**
(from J. Winifred)

I have written about cheesemaking in the fashion to which I am accustomed. I have not bothered myself overmuch with the differences in fungal environment between my own cave and a hamlet in central Shropshire in the early part of the nineteenth century.

Do not write to me about any perceived errors in cheesemaking. I do not care.

# PROLOGUE

*February 1794, Seine-et-Marne, France*

Ophélie Martin watched her father's head fall off from the attic of the house across the square.

Jean Martin paused for a moment at the top of the stairs, blinking down at the people gathered tight around the guillotine platform. They'd already done two prelates and the owner of a shop who sold imported lace this morning, their heads now lined up on the railing at the front. After the first prelate, who was particularly loathed, the crowd had begun to disperse, but there were still at least four dozen people waiting to see a landowner get his just deserts.

Ophélie stared at her father and wondered what he was thinking. Probably he was thinking about his cows, because he was usually thinking about his cows. The Martins had once owned twenty-seven. Now, of course, they owned none.

The two executioners must have wanted their lunch. They shoved Jean down onto his knees and pushed his head into the pillory. The top of the pillory smacked into place, and before Ophélie could draw another breath the blade had dropped. Jean's head tumbled summarily into the bucket arranged for that purpose. The whole process took less than a minute.

Ophélie waited for some sort of emotion to rise over her. Grief, perhaps. Fear? Anger.

No emotions came.

Perhaps she would have felt more feelings about this event had it been the first of the horrors she had witnessed this year. First Maman had died, carried away by the grippe, along with all of Ophélie's siblings: baby Laurent and Annette, Paul, and Thérèse. Then the citizens of Meaux, inspired by the Parisian patriots, had decided they no longer cared for clerics and began methodically ridding the ville of their presence. The Martins had unfortunately been rather pious in the last century, and both Grand-mère and Arrière-grand-mère had proudly sent their youngest sons to the church. One did not like to think of what had happened to Cousin Maurice or poor old Great-Uncle Étienne or, at the last, to Uncle Henri, but it did rather put watching one's father be guillotined into perspective.

Then *they*, whoever *they* were, because Ophélie was not at all sure, had come for her father and his cows.

Jean Martin was not the sort of man one expected great things from, either great villainy or great heroism. He was tall and thin and rather faded. He believed in God in the polite sort of way that a man with two brothers who are priests believes in God, and he drank and smoked correspondingly modest amounts. He loved his cattle and he tolerated his wife and children.

After Uncle Henri had been arrested, Jean had sent Ophélie, now his only child, away to stay with friends; after Uncle Henri had met his horrible end in the cell under the city hall, suddenly the friends found that they had no room to keep Ophélie.

Ophélie did not care to sleep out-of-doors, and she had not been sure if her father's farm was safe to walk back to, so she had gone to the house across the square from the cathedral, where Uncle Henri had once lived with a dozen other priests. It stood empty and ruined now, ransacked by sans-culottes, but it remained unoccupied because of its nerve-wracking proximity to the guillotine in the square, reminder of the clerics who had died suddenly and horribly last December. She did not think anyone would come looking for one girl sleeping in the attic under a pile of old cassocks. She should have time to make a plan. It was obvious she had to leave this town, and probably this departement, if she wanted to survive. And Ophélie *did* want to survive, in spite of her family's evident lack of skill in that area.

Ophélie crawled away from the window. She had wrapped a strip of black fabric cut from one of the cassocks around her bright hair, so no one might see it glinting down below, and had stayed closed to the floor, so no one in the square might look up and recognize a human shape in the window. Ophélie supposed she was lucky she had chosen this house on this square to hide in; otherwise she might never have known what had happened to Jean. She supposed she was lucky to have woken up in her cold attic and gone to the window just in time to recognize her father's shape and bewildered face as he was marched through the crowd.

Ophélie crawled to the pile of cassocks and collapsed into it.

Yes, lucky. That had to be it. She rolled over and stared at the rafters over her head. She had her health, her hands—something she would never again take for granted, after what had been done to Uncle Henri—her intelligence, and a great deal of cheesemaking knowledge. Really, in times like these, a girl could hardly expect more. Lots of girls would be grateful to have parents until they turned sixteen. France was full of orphans, fuller now than it had ever been before, she imagined.

Ophélie blinked, and in that tenth of a second of darkness, the tenth of a second after the blade sliced down onto Jean's neck replayed behind her eyes. She had seen that expression on his face before, when Souris, the lead cow of his dairy herd, had kicked him in the knee last November. The expression was not angry, not distressed, but puzzled.

I thought we were friends, his face seemed to say. Is this how friends treat each other?

Ophélie blinked again and found that somehow, oddly, her face was wet, and her neck, and the collar of her dress and her hair. It was hard to draw a deep breath. She supposed the attic was very dusty. She jammed her hands in the pockets of her apron, because the dust seemed to be making them shake with a rattling violence. Her right hand found a small, hard object, and she drew it out, desperately thankful to have anything to look at and think about, anything at all: but the object was a whetstone Jean had given her, a piece of gray stone mounted on a small block of wood into which he had carved a running horse, represented by a few sinuous lines.

Ophélie told herself that she was lucky that she had no food in her stomach, because if she had eaten a meal today she would need to vomit it up now. She was *lucky*. None of her family had survived, but she had, and what was that if not luck? Now she needed to make a plan to escape this place, to find somewhere a girl who knew a lot about cheese could build a new life.

# CHAPTER ONE

*February 1820, Shropshire, England*

Kate Easting did not see her husband fall from the haymow in the far barn.

Ophélie Martin's daughter did not see him perched precariously at the edge, nor wonder what he thought in those last few moments before his body smashed to the earth twelve feet below, breaking his neck.

She did not know why he had been up in that mow at this time of year. They always used that hay early in the season so they wouldn't have to cart it back to the main farm for the cattle in the dead of winter. Maybe he had noticed a loose board he wanted to fix, or had seen a wasps' nest he wanted to knock down.

Kate had been home, washing clothes, not thinking too much about the fact that Will had been out for the whole day, because if she thought about it she might admit to herself what a relief it was to not have him in the house. If she admitted to herself what a pleasure it was to be away from him, she'd dread his return that much more.

She couldn't bear to think of it, so after she had scrubbed all the shirts and shifts and smallclothes and kerchiefs and dish towels and hung them up to dry in front of the hearth, she took all the sheets from all the beds and boiled them in her biggest pot and hung them up too, until the kitchen was a forest of linen hung on criss-crossing lines.

Will's wife was so busy carefully not thinking about how awful her husband was to have in the house that she did not hear the knocking at the door when it came, and only turned around with the laundry beater in her hand when Freddie Harkness, their nearest neighbor, burst in with the news.

Kate had not found Will's broken body in the yard of the far barn, his lifeless eyes staring up into the rain. That had been his brother George, who had been late to help his brother this morning do whatever he had meant to do in the far barn.

Kate had not seen Will die, had in fact been at home virtuously washing Will's shirts and cleaning Will's house, but she knew as soon as George's rage-filled eyes found her in the kitchen full of fluttering linens that this death, too, was to be her fault. Nothing could exonerate Kate for her many crimes against the Easting family, so far as George was concerned. Firstly, she had had the temerity to come into existence as the child of a farmer who fancied himself a poet and a Frenchwoman of uncertain religious background, an act that was by itself an offense against all patriotic English folk. Secondly, she had married George's brother as a desperate seventeen-year-old orphan, when Will certainly could have married someone prettier and with more money. Thirdly, and most damning, she had produced no living children in the seven years since that marriage. This, George and Will had agreed loudly while in their cups at King George's Bull, made her a most unnatural woman. They agreed often enough, and loudly enough, in that location that multiple wives of other pub-goers had felt the need to share this information with Kate.

George stormed into the kitchen, tearing down the linens and screaming. Based on Freddie's shocked expression, the Easting brothers usually comported themselves with more dignity outside the house. If Kate had not already been accustomed to being yelled at by an Easting man, perhaps George's outburst would have shocked her, too; as it was, she dodged around the lines until Freddie grabbed George, shouting.

Kate ran up the stairs to the bedroom she had, until today, shared with Will, slammed the door shut, and locked it. She dropped onto the bed, her fingers wrapped in her apron, her heart hammering against her ribs.

A minute later, another set of feet pounded up the stairs, and a fist crashed against the door of the bedroom. The latch rattled furiously, and George said a number of things that would have likely been extremely foul, if Kate could have heard him over the rushing in her ears.

After a long while of this—maybe thirty minutes? maybe an hour?—the shouting and rattling stopped, and George went away. Kate's head still rang.

Maman bore six healthy children who all outlived her, Kate thought, staring at the empty fireplace. *Perhaps I am unnatural. Perhaps I am a changeling.*

She did not think she was a changeling. She and

most of her siblings looked like taller or shorter versions of her father. John Mary, who was four years older than Kate, had adopted a great number of Edward Gravenor's mannerisms. Peter, who was a year older than Kate, was an inch taller than their father had been, but had his calm eyes and curly hair. Henry, Kate's twin, was six inches taller; Kate was six inches shorter. Jake, two years younger, was only just taller than Kate. Anne had been born another five years after Jake, and like John Mary, she was a tall, narrow person, with Edward's gift for handling cattle.

If I had been able to have a child, would they be short or tall? Kate wondered. Her head hurt. Her stomach hurt. Her heart hurt.

Would my child have had red hair, like me, or dark hair, like Will has? *Had.*

She would need to wash all those sheets George had stomped on again. How long would that take? How long would she have? The chances of George letting his brother's unnatural widow stay at the farm he had now inherited were very slim, especially when John Mary's farm was a mere five-mile walk from here. Never mind that John Mary could ill afford to support another sister, especially in the dead of winter; never mind that the Gravenor house was ancient and leaking.

Will always said it took too long for me to visit John Mary, Kate thought sadly. I suppose the joke's on him, now.

She got up and went to the window. It was not late, but in February in Shropshire the sun set by five o'clock, and the light was slanting low between the trees and the outbuildings. George was in the yard, gesturing violently as he yelled at Freddie and another neighbor, Isaac Wethers. A long, narrow shape, the size of a tall man, lay on the ground between their feet, wrapped in a tarpaulin. Kate swallowed hard. That must be Will, then, or what was left of him. She supposed she would need to go down and dress the body as soon as George had worn himself out with yelling. He was like Will in that way; his temper tantrums eventually fizzled out.

The thought of touching her dead husband was repulsive. Kate wondered if it would be different if she had still loved Will.

Kate peeked around the bedroom door, in case George had silently made his back up the staircase. She descended to the kitchen. The damp linens lay twisted and dirty on the floor, like so many giant gray slugs. Kate found a basket and began slowly collecting sheets and handkerchiefs.

Maman gave birth to six children who made it to adulthood, but I don't think she'd be very happy with any of us now, Kate mused as she dropped another shirt into the basket. John Mary no longer made cheeses, Maman's one pride and joy. Peter was the vicar in Copstone, which would have sent Maman into a rage. She had no patience for the church or churchmen. Henry had gone to the army at the same time Kate had made her ill-advised marriage, possibly the worst profession her gentle, easily-confused brother could have chosen. The same year, Jake had gone to sea as some sort of junior cabin rat. Kate had not seen either of them in seven years, which she never let herself dwell on because no task was made easier by sobbing. Only Anne had been left to rattle around with John

Mary in their ancestral, falling-down wreck of a home, because Papa had left no money, only debts and frustrated debtors.

I suppose I'm glad Maman didn't live to see this, Kate thought bleakly, turning to face Freddie and Isaac the neighbor as they bore her husband's corpse through the door. She didn't escape France so her oldest daughter could become a penniless widow. It's lucky, really.

"You can put him on the table," Kate said, aware of a certain small pride in how calm her voice sounded. "I'll get some water for washing."

# CHAPTER TWO

Henry's foot slid off a round stone in the streambed, and he stumbled. A trickle of water found the hole in his right boot. He cast a despairing glance about him, trying to gauge the terrain against his memory, but the abandoned hedges and wayward trees pressing close against the path had dramatically altered the outline he recalled. Dark, unfamiliar shadows loomed over him and wet, clawed branches snatched at his clothing.

When Henry had left Shropshire at age seventeen, he had been rather vague about where he was going or what he was doing, overwhelmed by the death of his father and the disappearance of his mother. He had no notion that he would have to retrace his steps seven years later in the barrenness of winter, with ten stone of dead weight flopped over one shoulder.

The man Henry had been carrying for three miles did not stir.

The cold rain had stopped, just in time for the February sun to dip behind the trees. A frigid wind chased down the path after Henry, shaking the oaks until their blackened boughs sluiced water down over his battered hat.

"Not much farther now, sir," Henry told the body he clutched, which he desperately hoped still contained the soul of Dr. Thomas Holyoke. "My brother's farm is just up this hill."

The doctor roused himself enough to groan, and a shudder of relief ran through Henry. He had carried more than his fair share of corpses during the war on the peninsula, but he had hoped to retire that set of skills now that he'd returned to England.

"That's right, sir," Henry said, in his most encouraging manner. "We'll just get up this hill here and have a bit of a rest, shan't we, sir?" He scrubbed his face and stared up at the bank, which looked very steep and very slick in the faint light from the clouded moon. In spite of the chill, Henry was hot and sticky under his coat. He was a head and a half taller than the doctor and five stone heavier, but though the shorter man had been gripped by fevers for the past two months, he remained a solid weight. The thought of tripping and dropping his commanding officer in the darkness, perhaps even breaking the man's femur again, sent an icy spider of fear crawling down Henry's back.

Henry took a deep breath, shuffling his feet to make sure he did not tread on any more loose stones.

Something hard jabbed into Henry's ankle, and he almost lost his grip on the doctor again. Henry tried to swear, but he was too tired, and all that came out of his mouth was a garble of cow ailments. He sighed angrily and glared down into the shallow water rushing over the tops of his feet.

There was a hand in the stream.

Henry stared at the pale shape protruding from

the scrubby alders along the bank. His own limbs felt numb, and his mind felt very empty. He looked up at the cold white blotch of clouds twisting in front of the moon, then back down at the stream. The hand was still there, lying among the stones of the bed, fingers curled in toward the palm. The thumb had been half-severed long ago and stuck straight out from the palm. This stump was what had stuck him in the ankle.

The hand was attached to an arm, and the arm disappeared beneath the alders. There was probably a body under there somewhere, though it was so dark that Henry could not even pretend to see its outline. He stood and stared at the hand for a long minute, before nudging it with his toe. The hand was as stiff as wood.

Dr. Holyoke let out a thin moan. Henry, who had been considering panicking, jammed the panic down into his heels and considered the options. On the peninsula and at Waterloo, he had seen plenty of dead bodies and indeed, rather a lot of abandoned limbs. Either the owner of this hand was under the alders, in which case they were dead, or they were somewhere else, in which case the hand was of no use to them now. Either way, the doctor was growing colder and sicker by the minute, and Henry still might get him to safety. He did not have time to bother about *hands*.

Henry renewed his grip on the doctor's ribcage, set his shoulders, and plowed up the sloping streambank, his feet slipping and skidding in the sucking mud.

The path reached again, Henry squinted into the darkness. The way split here, one route cutting through the trees and the other bending to follow the stream.

He wished he could remember which one he ought to take. But then, Henry wished for a number of things at this moment. He wished that the mail coach to Wolverhampton hadn't broken down, that the last of his money hadn't vanished with a beggar who turned out to be a cutpurse in Birmingham, and, above all, that the horse which had shattered Dr. Holyoke's leg had been hit by lightning as a colt. He would give his eyeteeth just for the clouds to move away from the moon again.

That thought made Henry glance back toward the stream. From where he now stood, a spray of ratty willows obscured the streambed, but he knew the hand was there. He shuddered and amended his last wish. He did not want to see all that was abroad on this night.

"I'd reckon we're only a half-hour's walk away now," he told the doctor, who did not respond.

Henry cast about himself for any familiar stone or stump he could use to support his optimism. He didn't really think Dr. Holyoke could hear him, but he could hear himself, and he sounded like he was lying. He didn't like lying, even by mistake. It made him terribly anxious.

Henry's eye caught on something, something small and far away. After another minute of staring, he was certain that he had not conjured up this vision out of panicked hope and fear. There was a light coming through the wood, a ghostly flicker of paleness moving toward him along the bank of the stream. Henry gasped, almost letting go of his precious burden in his relief.

"Sorry about that, sir," Henry said to the doctor,

before gently freeing one hand to wave. He bellowed, "Oy! Over here! Help! I need help! I've a sick man here!"

The light paused and jerked. Henry had only a moment to wonder if perhaps it was not, as he had hoped, a lantern held by a human being, but something significantly less tangible, before it rushed toward him, swinging from side to side. He caught his breath, regretting his shout. It could be a ghost, he thought, or it could be whoever had done for the owner of that hand in the stream, come back to make sure there were no witnesses.

Henry swallowed hard. The night pressed close.

The light drew closer, growing a little larger with every bob in the darkness. Now it was accompanied by the sound of wet footsteps, each one slapping against the puddles and soaked leaves.

Henry held his breath.

The light resolved into a tin lantern, held by a small person dressed in a dark, mud-splattered dress and cloak. Henry only had a moment to fret—he could hardly ask a woman, and a small woman at that, to carry the doctor while he rested his aching arms for a spell, though he supposed that meant she probably hadn't been the person to dump the body in the stream —which meant that someone else had dumped the body—no, he wasn't thinking about that right now— before the light caught the woman's face, and Henry entirely forgot the doctor, the frozen hand, and how that horrible thing might have arrived on this secluded path.

"*Kate!*" Henry said, stunned.

"*Henry*," Kate said, equally stunned.

"But why are you—"

"How are you—"

They had both spoken at once, then stopped speaking at once.

"I've been given my papers," Henry said.

"Will's dead," Kate said.

"Oh, no," Henry said.

"Oh, *no*," Kate said.

Two pairs of blue eyes stayed locked for a moment. Henry's mind, generally an orderly, quiet place, buzzed with feeling. People in Copstone village always commented on how odd it was that the Gravenor twins, born in the same hour of the same day in the same house, looked like they had been fathered by two different men. Henry was as huge as an ox, so pale his eyebrows were an article of faith, and Kate was dumpling-short with hair that looked it was on fire. Henry was not sure what to make of this sort of comment, as he and Kate were the most similar of all their siblings, and he did not think he would care to be twins with anyone else.

Henry looked carefully at his sister in the flickering light of her lantern. Right now, Kate looked very tired, he thought. Her eyes were puffy and red, as though she'd been crying. She oughtn't be here, wandering the wood after dark; even if her husband was dead—and how could he be dead? William Easting hadn't been old or sickly—and in any case he had a younger brother who could take care of the farm, make sure the bills were paid—

"George wouldn't let me stay," Kate said flatly.

"He said as we'd no children, I was no kind of wife to Will, and I could take myself off to my family. I held on for two weeks, but—well. Tonight he threw me out."

Henry thought of the letters Kate had sent him, and a wave of horror swept over him. "No *surviving* children," he said.

"Yes, well," Kate said, shrugging, trying to look stoic and doing a poor job of it. "I suppose it's all the same to George. Who's this, then?" she asked, peering intently at the dark shape on Henry's right shoulder.

"Oh, right, him," Henry said, and then, as his original purpose came crashing down on him, "*Him.* Oh, *foot rot.* How close are we to home? All the trees have changed since I was last here. He needs a bed, and to get warm, and a doctor. His leg—well, it's been two months since it was broken, and I thought he was healing, but the fever came back a week ago."

"This is the path to the Halverton farm," Kate said, gesturing behind her with the lantern. "Ned Bell's field is just over there. He's not kept his right-of-way clear, now that he's got that other field closer to Copstone." Henry perked up at this. Home was on the other side of Ned Bell's field.

The disembodied hand in the stream crawled over that thought. Had Ned Bell …? but no, surely not. Ned Bell was as timid as a wild sheep. And anyway, Henry wasn't thinking about that right now. There was nothing he could do for the body that belonged to that hand, wherever it might be.

"Can you carry him another quarter-mile?" Kate asked, and the hand scuttled out of his mind again. His sister was surveying his injured charge with her grave, competent eye, and Henry, even knowing how dire the doctor's situation was, felt comforted. Kate always knew what to do. He had forgotten how much he'd missed having Kate around.

"Did you come from Southbridge?"

"Wolverhampton," Henry said.

"Oh, you sweet dolt," Kate said, her voice suddenly tender and exasperated. "You must be exhausted. Let him down and I'll get under his other shoulder."

"I'll be fine," Henry said, but somehow when Kate set down the lantern on a stump and came toward him, he did what she said, letting Dr. Holyoke slide toward the ground. Kate ducked under one of his arms, and suddenly Henry was carrying significantly less weight. Kate was small, but she was strong.

"I didn't have any more money," Henry explained. "Be careful of his leg, Kate. It's splinted, but that horse took it all to pieces."

The right-of-way was just as overgrown as Kate had warned, and after a minute Henry took up a branch to clear the creeping hawthorn branches and brambles out of the way. What ought to have taken no longer than whistling "God Save the King" became ten minutes of bashing and shoving and peeling thorns out of his trousers.

Henry thought of the hand like a pale crab swimming under the water, and the arm it was attached to, and the body which had at some point possessed both of those extremities. He ought to tell Kate about it; Kate would know what ought to be done. But he found that between the effort needed to smash the brambles away from the path and not trip in the darkness and manage the weight of the doctor, he couldn't fit that nightmarish vision into words.

Nor, Henry thought with an odd pang, did he especially want to give Kate another horrible problem to figure out. The doctor was quite enough of a problem by himself.

"We'll put your friend in the kitchen," Kate said, raising her voice to be heard over the hiss of the wind and the rattling of the black branches all around them. "There hasn't been any new straw on the roof since Papa died. Peter said the bedrooms are leaking."

Discussing the roof was undeniably *not* discussing dead bodies and where they might have come from, and Henry seized the topic hopefully. He ignored the mention of Peter, his least-favorite brother, and instead focused on the important issue of thatch. "Where will John Mary have the wheatstraw in from, do you think? Do you think it might be cheaper to have it done in reeds?"

Kate didn't respond immediately, and Henry craned his neck to look at her face. He was not especially good at reading facial expressions, but he did know Kate very well, and he thought the way her face looked now meant something between *regret* and *heartbreak*. He wondered why asking about John Mary made her sadder than talking about her dead husband. He wondered whether John Mary was all right, and whether Kate would tell him if he weren't.

Henry had not thought about what coming home from the army would be like, but he had not suspected it would be quite so unpleasant as all this.

# CHAPTER THREE

It took Kate another two days to corner John Mary in the barn.

The barn was much older than the house, a little stone building hunched against the back of the hill. Papa had believed it to be the original Gravenor hall, constructed by the Saxons in the time of King Aethelstan, but Edward Gravenor had been given to elaborate flights of fancy. If it had been a house once, Kate thought it very tight quarters; only six of John Mary's eight cattle could be stabled along its length, and John Mary had to stand between the cross-beams to avoid knocking himself on the head. At the far end of the barn, a few boards had been nailed to the beams to make a small loft. This was where John Mary had been sleeping. He claimed it was to keep an eye on the animals; Kate suspected it was because the barn with six cows in it was considerably warmer than the house.

"What have you been *doing?*" Kate demanded without preamble. "There's barely enough roof on the house to keep the bedrooms dry. There's nothing in the pantry and I think the mice are building a city in Papa and Maman's bed. Twice when I've gone to get water, one of the cows has met me at the door. Henry's been chopping wood for two days straight to keep his doctor from freezing, because there's no dry fuel at hand."

She took a breath, decided she had made her point, and glared. She had last made it home two years ago, before the last, worst pregnancy, and the farm hadn't been in such awful shape then; at least, she didn't think it had been.

John Mary looked up at the rafters, rubbed his chin, and said nothing. Like Anne and Henry, he had inherited Maman's height, standing somewhere north of six feet. This made it very hard for Kate to stare him down, especially when he wouldn't meet her eye. Instead, he fixed his gaze on a hole in the thatch near the ridgeline, through which a cabochon of gray sky glared. In the cool, damp shadows of the barn, his auburn hair looked almost black, and his narrow, Gallic face impressively somber and poetic.

Kate rubbed her snub nose and sighed. She took after Edward Gravenor in every way, from his short stature to his homely features, but she had not inherited his sanguine confidence that all things would work themselves out in his favor.

If she were honest with herself, Kate found her oldest brother the most difficult of all her siblings to manage. If there was one skill John Mary had mastered, it was *disappearing.*

Kate could bully—*lovingly*—Anne into cleaning the manure off her boots before coming inside and not calling Gilbert Johnson's wandering pig or vicious wife rude names in public. Peter quite often let Kate read his sermons—or he had, before Will had found them and made her stop—and sometimes even listened when she told him which bits she thought would result in letters to the bishop. Even Jake had written her twice since going to the merchant marines, which was more than he had written anyone else. Henry, of course, had always taken her instructions to write her each month with deadly seriousness, which both soothed her soul and made her terribly anxious, when she thought about the amount of responsibility she bore for her twin.

Kate wondered in a secret corner of her mind if she would have trouble managing Dr. Holyoke, once his fever went down and he was lucid for more than a few minutes a day. Henry's letters had painted him as a sensible, knowledgeable man, so surely she would not.

John Mary looked at her now, one eye narrowed, a half-smile creasing one cheek. It was the same gently sardonic expression Maman had worn when she listened to English farmers condescend to her, English tradesmen try to cheat her, and English clergy justify themselves to her.

John Mary's long, mobile face, so much like Maman's, filled Kate with guilt. When she had married after Papa's death, she had been seventeen years old and filled with desperate purpose, to remove the burden of her upkeep from her family's shoulders. She had told herself that she would visit home every Saturday, to help Maman make the cheeses and John Mary care for the cows and chickens and Anne learn her lessons. But then Maman had disappeared, so there had been no cheeses, and soon, as the last of the money dried up, no chickens. And there had been so much to do on the Easting farm—what with the old house and his sick grandmother and the untrustworthy hired men, and Will had been so nasty whenever she was gone for longer than an hour or two—that the weekly visit had become a monthly visit. And then she had been pregnant, and had her first miscarriage, and too much walking had made her bleed. She had been so tired. The monthly visit slipped to every two months, then every three. Will had not liked Peter visiting after he became the vicar, because how a man treated his wife was his own affair and not her brother's, and technically the Easting farm was in Banfield parish, not Copstone, so Peter didn't have any right …

It had carried on like that for seven years, and so Kate had not been back to the farm or talked to John Mary since Easter of the previous year. She had thought she had known how things were for him, because Anne worked on the nearby Telford farm four days a week, and Will hadn't minded Anne stopping by on her way home occasionally.

In fact, Will had not minded so much that it had made Kate queasy, but she wouldn't think about that now. Will was dead, for better or worse.

The undeniable fact was that the Gravenor farm was in a terrible state, and Kate hadn't realized how very bad things had gotten.

I have been otherwise occupied, Kate told herself. It isn't my fault. I can't be everywhere at once.

Her chest felt hollow. John Mary looked very thin, and the shadows under his eyes very pronounced. He was her only sibling who did not possess Papa's wide, somewhat startled blue eyes. John Mary's were the dark brown of an unknown Frenchman, who Maman had never spoken of or referred to even once in all Kate's memory.

"J'ai peur que je ne pas avois compris," John Mary murmured.

"You understand me perfectly well," Kate said, her voice a little thick. She cleared her throat. "What do you mean, letting everything go like this?"

Nonnette took this moment to put her head over the stall and yell. Kate put up a hand and scratched the white blaze on the old cow's forehead. The animal looked vastly pregnant, and Kate grimly expected her to drop a calf in a hedgerow within the week. She wondered which neighbor's bull was responsible for this offspring.

"Bah, c'est quoi, ça?" John Mary said, rolling his shoulders.

Kate ground her teeth. John Mary always became impenetrably French when he didn't care to answer questions, as though he had not lived in England for twenty-six of his twenty-nine years. It made Kate feel very lonely. They all understood the language, because Maman had not seen any reason to bother with English when speaking with her children, but John Mary could speak fluently, and Kate could not.

"The house is a shambles," she said, articulating crisply. "None of the rights-of-way are clear. The cows are running amok. You've clearly no schedule for breeding them, and you weren't ready for Antoinette's little bullock. Henry is being uncharacteristically diplomatic about how the ditches look, which means they are all very bad. The hedges are rotting, and I don't think you've enough seed to plant the fields."

"Quand même," John Mary said, looking bemused.

"In any case, I know I ought to have been back to help before this," Kate said. If John Mary would not respond to normal tactics, she would deploy brutal ones. She adopted a brisk tone. "It's been very difficult since I lost the last baby to make the trip. I know it's only the four miles, and I could have made it on a Saturday, but I—I—" She caught herself on a gasp that only just missed being a sob. Kate closed her eyes. She had imagined that nearly a year on, she would be able to talk about the child who had not quite made it into the world with practical detachment, but it seemed she had overestimated her own fortitude.

"*Cat*," John Mary said, and abruptly he crushed Kate in a hug against his chest. For a long minute she could not speak or move.

"'m fine," she muttered, horribly aware that she was leaking tears and snot on his waistcoat. "'m just trying—to—explain—"

But John Mary was rocking her back and forth and stroking her hair, and Kate found herself slumping against him.

"Not about me," she muttered.

Nonnette lowed, a deep sound that reverberated through Kate's feet.

Will had not kept his cows well, she thought, nonsensically. More than once, Kate had found early mastitis in one of his herd, only for Will to refuse to believe her until it was so advanced that the cow lost that quarter of her udder. Once the cow had stopped milking altogether, and Will had sent her to slaughter.

"I know Henry will do what he can, now that he's

home," Kate said finally, turning her head so her face was no longer buried in John Mary's waistcoat. "But why haven't you hired anyone? Peter would give you some money, if you need it so badly. I could write to Jake—"

"Je vais pas demander de l'argent à mes petits frères," John Mary interrupted sourly.

Kate soldiered on. "You could have kept Anne home, so she could help."

"You could go back to the house and have a rest," John Mary suggested. Kate noticed that now that he was being helpfully obtuse instead of stubbornly disobliging, he switched to English.

"No you don't," Kate said. "I won't let you distract me. Why have things gotten so bad?"

"No money," he said succinctly. He sounded almost angry, but he did not push her away. "Bad harvest."

"But what about the milk? Surely you've been selling the milk?"

John Mary hesitated. "There was no milk last year."

Kate finally pulled away from her brother to frown up at him. "What? What do you mean?"

Her brother was looking up at the rafters again. "Mais bon, chai pas …"

"No," Kate said angrily. "You and Peter and Anne have been keeping things from me, and I won't let you do it anymore. Why wasn't there any milk last year? Do you mean you couldn't get a good price for it in town?"

John Mary gave her a last squeeze before letting go entirely. He tugged thoughtfully at his neckcloth, and

Kate could tell he was going to say something implacably French.

"I can make Anne tell me," she said. "She's only good at leaving things out, not lying."

John Mary sighed. "I couldn't hire a bull for love or money."

Kate wondered what else he was worried Anne might tell her, if he answered that question so easily. "But Ned Bell has a bull. And the Halvertons too, though he's not got good lines, I don't think. And you could have asked Will."

"I could *not* have asked Will," John Mary said grimly.

"But why not?" Kate asked, bewildered.

John Mary was silent for a long moment, during which Paulette poked her pink nose through the barn door and lowed at Nonnette, who responded with a fervent, exasperated moo.

"John Mary," Kate said warningly. "If I talk to Anne—"

"I may have said some disagreeable things to Daniel Lately," John Mary said. "He came round to call at the farm the summer before last." He ran an irritable hand through his hair.

Kate frowned. Daniel Lately owned the largest farm for ten miles on all sides of Copstone, and though his house was nothing like so grand as the old squire's, he was certainly the richest man in all the neighboring parishes. He was an unpleasant old skinflint who had made his living as a solicitor in Birmingham, before a distant cousin of his had died and left him the land in Shropshire. She thought there had been some bad blood between him and the cousin, or perhaps the cousin's children, but she couldn't remember what.

"What on earth could you have to say to Daniel Lately?"

"I told him that if he thought he was going to buy the Gravenor farm, he could eat his money and die shitting," John Mary snapped, temper coloring his cheeks.

"Oh, no," Kate said. Daniel Lately had spent the last twenty years buying up any parcel of his neighbors' land he could get his hands on. Of course he would have approached John Mary.

John Mary deflated just quickly as he had blown up. "You know Lord Houghton owes him money."

"I do now," Kate said. "But—"

"I told Lately off, and then suddenly there was no bull for me to hire and no fodder to buy," John Mary said heavily. "I had to go to Southbridge for everything, and I couldn't get a good price for any of it. We hadn't had a good harvest the year before, either."

Kate suddenly thought that there probably hadn't been a good harvest since the year Papa died and Maman disappeared. "I'm so sorry," she said. "I should have known."

"T'as été occupée," John Mary said, shrugging.

"Not that busy, now," Kate said, tears burning at the corners of her eyes. She shook her head and took a deep, shaking breath.

"You've that doctor to look after," John Mary said.

Kate thought of the thin, fretful form in the bed in the kitchen, skin hot to the touch, sometimes muttering and shouting things she did not understand. She thought, too, of Henry's large, worried face peering down at the older man as he stood at the head of the bed.

Dr. Holyoke had, somehow, brought Henry home to her. She thought again of coming down the path that ran behind Halverton's farm, her lantern slowly illuminating a peculiar shadowy form, until it caught the flicker of flaxen hair and a well-loved face. Kate had not let herself hope to see her twin again. She could not remember the last time something she had hoped for had come to pass, instead of being brutally stripped away.

Kate had been grateful to help Henry carry the doctor, because it had let her disguise her leaking eyes.

"Yes," Kate said. "I will do my best for him."

She had swaddled the doctor in as many quilts and coverlets as she could find left in the house; moths had reduced much of the linens to rags. Even with Henry's best efforts at chopping wood, the kitchen was too drafty to keep very warm. Kate had tucked a bed warmer full of coals at the foot of the mattress, but when the doctor had become restless, she had taken it out again rather than risk him spilling the coals and causing a fire.

John Mary was watching her with an odd, knowing gaze.

Kate shook her head, then tried again for brisk practicality. "Well, you've got Antoinette milking, and Nonnette will be soon. That's a little bit of money."

"And Alouette," her brother said. "She's in the lean-to."

"They all three got out?" Kate asked, in disbelief. "John Mary, you *must* be more careful."

He met her eyes with an expression so guileless that Kate was immediately suspicious.

"I suppose you were being *very* careful, weren't you?" she asked. "You didn't, for example, put all the cows in the paddock with the gate that Antoinette knows how to open."

"Mais voilà, bien sûr," murmured John Mary.

Kate considered Nonnette, who was now chewing thoughtfully on the back of John Mary's coat. "If you have to take the milk to Southbridge, that's nearly three hours' walk every morning," she said, thinking out loud. "You haven't time, and Henry can't do it."

John Mary did not contest this. The one time Maman had asked Henry to watch her cheese table at market, he had accepted a bouquet of daisies and a tin teapot with a hole in the bottom as payment for a pound of cheese.

"I don't—" Kate hesitated. She thought that if she walked that far that often, she would start bleeding again, but she didn't want John Mary to worry, or to tell their other siblings. "What about cheeses?" she asked briskly. "I know you haven't the time, but I do, and Maman taught me as well as you."

Kate hadn't been able to practice making Maman's special white-rinded cheeses for years, because Will hadn't trusted that she wouldn't ruin the milk and waste his money and her time. And there had been all the space the molds took up in the cellar, which he had said would be better spent on storing apples or beer.

The cheese really didn't take up that much space,

Kate thought defensively. And it wasn't as if John Mary had anything else in his pantry. Maman's molds were still probably somewhere in the house.

"Why not?" her brother said. "Things cannot be worse than they are."

# CHAPTER FOUR

Thomas glared over the edge of his coverlet.

He had pulled the blanket up to his eyes sometime in the night. A vicious chill uncurled from the flagstone floor, insinuating itself around his every bone. More cold air seeped down from the blackened rafters overhead. His sickbed was tucked in a sheltered corner of the big kitchen, wedged behind the chimney, where he might receive the benefit of the warm bricks. But the wind hissed around the splintering window frames and under the massive, mossy door. Dark timbers gridded the interior walls, but the plaster between them was damp and cold to the touch.

*That woman* balanced on her tiptoes as she leaned out the window on the opposite wall. A soft crackle came to his ear; she must have stoked up the fire while the room was still dark. She had clearly just pushed open the shutter, letting in the thin blade of winter light which had awakened him. Fifteen years of military service had left Thomas able to sleep through nearly any amount of clatter, but the first hint of sun brought him immediately to his senses.

The small woman wore a man's coat—Henry's? it

was far too large for her—over her shawl and bedgown. Humming softly, she turned away from the window and took down a crock of butter and half a loaf from a shelf.

Thomas willed himself to close his eyes, before the gut-wrenching thing which had happened the morning before happened again.

He did not close his eyes.

The small, horrible woman, the woman Henry had not had the decency to mention haunted this small, horrible house where a half-dozen generations of Gravenors had been born and died, laid the bread and the crock on the big table in the center of the room. The table looked positively antediluvian, a square, age-darkened hunk of wood that Saxon churls had probably butchered wolves upon.

The flint of cold light angling through the window sparked first off the heavy, untidy braid falling down her back, calling up licks of deep red and gleaming gold fire. But as Henry's sister turned and the winter sun sliced deeper into the room, the flames caught and raced upward over her head. She reached for a knife to cut the bread. In a moment her hair was a mass of orange and peach and gold, so much gold, shifting, glowing, seething in the sunlight.

Thomas thought the angel Gabriel must have appeared to Mary thus, or the burning bush to Moses. When he had been copying out Bible verses on his slate as a child, he had imagined that he would face such a sign of divine interest with equanimity. But now, staring bitterly at the radiant form in the center of this very cold kitchen, Thomas could think only that what little remained of his life was about to be burned to ash by this woman and her incendiary knowledge.

The hard cold light set the triumphal halo of curls about Kate Gravenor's homely, gentle face ablaze, and Thomas felt his stomach drop somewhere into the region of hell.

The doctor was staring at Kate again from his bed in the corner of the kitchen. Only his tousled black hair and half-shut eyes were visible over the bedclothes.

When Dr. Holyoke had awakened the day before, finally free of the raging fever, clear-headed and able to speak in complete sentences, Kate had been relieved and delighted. Her days of sponging his forehead, spooning broth into his slack mouth, changing the bandages on his leg, and sponging other, less dignified parts of his person, had borne healing fruit. He had been a good patient, though she supposed that was due more to how sick he had been than any manners on his part.

But when Kate had greeted him warmly and asked how he took his tea, he had responded with a sound like a snarl and receded beneath the blankets, not to appear again for several hours. He had snappishly refused her offer of a cool rag. She did not know how he had relieved himself, but it had not been with her help.

Dr. Holyoke had still not said a full sentence to her, though she had heard a gravelly voice address Henry when he descended the stairs. Perhaps her brother had helped the doctor perform all the necessary ablutions. Kate didn't smell anything awful coming from that corner of the kitchen, in any case.

Kate took down the wooden box where the tea was kept, lifted the lid, and swallowed a sigh. She had reused the last pinch of leaves again and again, until the tea they drank was only marginally darker than the water she drew from the well. Even with a sewing needle, she did not think she could get any more tea dust out of the cracks.

She closed the box and put it back on the shelf, hopefully surveying the rest of their larder. They had no sugar, of course. Kate doubted there had been sugar in the house since Papa had died. John Mary and Anne had been alone in this house for seven years, and neither was much of a housekeeper.

John Mary vanishing all the time to he-will-not-say-where *might* be part of the farm's problem, Kate thought, and immediately felt disloyal. But the house hardly feels like anyone's been living here.

There were some dried lemon slices on a string, left over from a Christmas basket Peter had received at the vicarage, and the very dregs of a jar of raspberry jelly from the same source. The lemons looked sadly the worse for wear, as brown and shriveled as a bit of old rennet. She considered. Could hot lemon water be considered a restorative tonic? They'd drunk hot water for breakfast often enough as children—Edward Gravenor had been absent-minded to the point of accidental starvation, and Maman did not consider tea a drink fit for human consumption—but Kate would rather not, even if she'd already hung the kettle over the coals this morning.

Kate shot a glance over her shoulder at the doctor,

and he snapped his eyes shut, apparently still committed to the fiction that he was not watching her.

The sigh was getting much harder to contain. Kate put a slice of bread on a toasting fork and pulled a stool closer to the fire. They could have toast with butter and a bit of jelly for breakfast, and then she would have to corner her oldest brother and ask if he had any little money she could take into the market.

Kate had only toasted the first side of the first slice when the gravelly voice she had heard yesterday emanated from the bed in the corner. "Good day, madam."

She almost dropped the piece of toast, only saving it by lurching forward. She turned toward her patient. Dr. Holyoke had pushed down the coverlet and raised himself on one elbow.

Kate considered him for a long moment. She had had plenty of time to examine his form in the last week, but during most of that time he had been half-conscious or asleep, his eyes closed and his jaw slack. Now he stared at her with eyes almost as black as his hair, eyes that burned with intelligence and not a little anger. In his current state, terribly thin and rather unclean, he could not be called handsome, but those eyes were magnetic.

It's different looking at a half-naked man when he's awake, Kate thought, feeling the first stirrings of alarm.

Dr. Holyoke had a nose a Roman centurion would have been proud of, long and arched, with a bump at the bridge. Kate absently fingered her own snub nose. In another face, the doctor's nose would have been overpowering. In his case, it was balanced by heavy black brows and a sharp jaw. Kate had not had the nerve to shave him while he was unconscious, and a fine dark mustache grew on his upper lip. The mustache suited him. Kate thought briefly of John Mary trying to paint boot blacking on the hairs on his upper lip as a young man; he doubtless would have appreciated the ancestry which had gifted the doctor with facial hair.

Dr. Holyoke's face was still very brown, which Kate supposed was from being sent all over after the war had ended. Even Henry was now a darker shade of pink.

Part of her wanted to respond to that dramatic profile, as well as the long, square fingers which gripped the coverlet.

Another part of her thought of Will, and how very charming and handsome she had thought him before she'd married him. Her stomach twisted itself into a tight little knot.

"Good day," she said, realizing the doctor was waiting for her response. "I'm pleased to meet you, sir," she added, after a moment.

The doctor's dark brows drew together. He did not look like he was pleased to meet Kate. "I presume your brother washed me while I was ill," he said, without preamble.

"No," Kate said, puzzled. A hint of char caught her nose, and she hastily pulled the piece of toast away from the coals and dropped it onto the waiting plate. "That is, Henry helped me turn you over, but John Mary needed him about the farm, so it's mostly been just me. I'm a good nurse," she clarified. "I nursed William's grandmother in her last months." The thought of the old woman, who had liked Kate significantly more than William had at the end, made her flinch. She put another piece of bread on the fork.

"I see," Dr. Holyoke said, his voice tight. "I would not normally reference such a topic before a lady—"

"Lady?" Kate said, half-laughing.

The doctor went on as if she hadn't spoken. "But I note that my smallclothes have been removed." He stopped and stared hard at her.

Kate felt her face pinken. It was the curse of having her complexion, she thought, that she looked guilty at the slightest provocation. "Yes," she said. "I'm sorry, but I couldn't clean your wound without undressing you."

She rotated the toasting fork. The doctor did not say anything.

The silence pressed down, and Kate found herself speaking very quickly. "The place where the horse's hoof hit you—Henry explained how it was, that the gelding kicked back and sideways just as you were passing—it broke the bone, obviously, but it made a mash of your thigh as well, and there was a terrible boil under the splint. I cleaned it," she said, swallowing hard at the memory of the quantity of white, bloody pus that had oozed from the doctor's leg. "But it's started healing properly in the past week," she ended, making her voice cheerful. "Really, you're lucky they didn't take your leg."

"The state of my luck remains to be seen," Dr. Holyoke said flatly. "If you cleaned my wound—"

"Yes, and I think I did a reasonable job of it," Kate said. "The swelling had gone down last night."

"Then where is my—" the doctor started, then cut himself off. Nothing about his facial expression changed, but his cheeks darkened a shade.

"*Oh,*" Kate said, suddenly understanding what he was asking about. Her own face went from pink to very red, and she dropped the toast fork. She snatched the piece of toast off the fire, singeing her fingers. She stuck them in her mouth and wracked her brain for a response.

Sewn inside the front flap of Dr. Holyoke's smallclothes had been a pouch, right over where another man's cock would have been. In the doctor's case, the cock had been detachable and carved from a piece of light wood—oak, Kate thought—with careful attention to detail. She thought of the wrinkle of the foreskin over the tip of the wooden organ and blushed even more hotly. She did not think she'd seen William's privates in the clear daylight once in the seven years they'd been married, only felt them press against her in the middle of the night.

She withdrew her fingers from her mouth and rubbed them against her skirt.

How to explain? Kate wondered. How to explain why she knew some men did not have a prick, at least not one they'd been born with? She'd die before she gave away John Mary, and in this flustered moment, she couldn't think how else she could have learned such a delicate piece of information. But she didn't *know* Thomas Holyoke, and even if he had his own secrets, she couldn't be sure he could be trusted with her brother's.

Kate looked at Dr. Holyoke, and he stared back at her with his burning black eyes. She had expected to see apprehension or worry in his face, but he only looked tired and resigned.

Her eyes went to the shape of his splinted leg under the blankets. Such a break should have killed him; it was purest negligence that it had not been amputated before it poisoned his blood with gangrene. But through the will of providence, that failure meant he might keep both his legs and his life. Most soldiers were not so lucky.

And that gave her an idea, born of a particularly horrible letter Henry had sent when he had first been pressed into the doctor's service.

"I know," she said primly, hoping he would mistake the shaking of her voice for embarrassment, "that many gentlemen have been—have been grievously injured in the line of battle—there being— there being the guns and artillery and all. I—well, I'm very sorry for what's happened to you. I've put your—I mean—I washed—there was some—some—well, in any case, I washed—" Now she was stammering, as mortification had truly overtaken her. How did one politely tell a man that one had wrapped his prick in an old stocking and put it in an empty jar for safekeeping? "Well, it's in the basket with your clean clothes."

# CHAPTER FIVE

She thinks the French blew my prick off, Thomas thought. Well, damn.

Kate Gravenor's face had gone nearly as fiery as her hair. This, at least, she had in common with her enormous brother. Henry turned the purplish red of freshly-sliced beets whenever he was embarrassed.

Thomas supposed he ought to think of her as Kate Easting, to remind himself that she was a respectable widow.

He opened his mouth, realized he was about to tell her that soldiers virtually never survived that sort of injury, given that a blast that ripped off the genitals would necessarily hit the femoral artery, then closed his mouth again.

Kate looked away from him, pulling another piece of toast off her fork. There was something odd in her face, something that made Thomas wonder if she wasn't being entirely forthright with him, but at that moment a piercing *moo* echoed through the still morning air, and the front door slammed open.

"Morning, Kate," Henry gasped. "Glad you're up. Have you got the fire going? Very good. Antoinette was in the copse—in Nathan Wheeler's copse."

"There's toast," Kate said, gesturing at the plate.

Henry was clutching something inside his coat, and his face was red with cold and exertion under his white-blonde hair. "I don't think Antoinette should have toast," he said earnestly.

Thomas squinted at the thing Henry was holding. It was covered in damp black fur. "That's a calf."

"I don't think the calf should have toast, either," Henry said.

The big man kicked the door shut behind himself. The *moo* came again, much closer, and this time it sounded like a battle cry.

"I don't know why Antoinette always has to calve somewhere she's not supposed to be," Kate muttered. She vanished into the sitting room on the other side of the great chimney, then reappeared holding a stack of ragged quilts. "There's a perfectly good yard right next to the barn."

A great pounding came at the door, as though a large animal were kicking it repeatedly with her front hooves.

"Antoinette is a cow?" Thomas asked.

"Madame Veto avait promis," Kate sang, half under her breath.

"Antoinette fait resolu," Henry sang back, in full tenor voice.

"*What?*" Thomas demanded, wondering if he were still feverish.

Kate put the stack of quilts on the edge of the hearth. "Quand Antoinette vit la tour," she muttered. "I've already got some water heating, thank goodness.

Bring it here, Henry."

"Antoinette is a *cow*," Thomas repeated, pushing himself up on his elbows. His leg spasmed, and he flinched.

"Well, she obviously wasn't *this* cow," Kate said, pouring steaming water into a basin and unfolding a quilt. The pounding on the door redoubled, accompanied by a moo that was almost a scream. Thomas craned his neck to see how the door was holding up, but the chimney blocked his view. "Our Antoinette would have had Robespierre roasted on a spit. Henry, dearest, bar the door, or she'll break the latch."

Henry unbuttoned his coat and tumbled a tiny, leggy creature into Kate's lap. She dipped a corner of one of the quilts in the hot water and scrubbed vigorously at the still little body. "Not the best of mothers, is our Antoinette," she said, in philosophical tones. "This poor little man's as cold as ice."

An enormous purple nose appeared in the open kitchen window, followed by a black muzzle and a rolling, rageful brown eye. Antoinette the cow *screamed*. Thomas jumped, and the motion sent another shock of pain through his splinted leg. He only kept from snarling a curse by grinding his teeth together.

Another voice, this one cheerfully masculine, echoed through the house from somewhere outside. "Good morning, siblings mine! It's a fine day—"

The shout cut itself off with a squawk. Antoinette's enormous head disappeared from the window, and a moment later she trumpeted another war cry.

"*Peter!* Go around to the back door!" Kate shouted.

"I'm *trying!* Blast!" the new voice shouted in return.

"Who's Peter?" Thomas asked, alarmed. He had not wanted Henry to bring him back to England at all, but he had not imagined that the family home of which his assistant had spoken so longingly would be quite this chaotic.

"Henry, go save him, please," Kate said in a calmer voice, still massaging the calf's chest and sides.

"He's already saved," Henry said, scowling.

"The Church of England isn't proof against trampling," Kate returned.

"Are you nonconformists?" Thomas asked, trying to keep his voice even. He had not suspected Henry of being a Quaker, but perhaps the Gravenors belonged to one of the more esoteric sects.

"Antoinette wouldn't *trample* anyone," Henry said. "Gore him, more likely."

More pounding came from the back of the house. Thomas levered himself into a sitting position, trying to see more of what was happening.

"*Henry,*" Kate said. "The *door.*"

"God ought to provide," Henry muttered and disappeared into the other room.

"Let me in!" yelled the strange male voice from the back door, sounding more panicked. "*Ow!*"

"I'm trying!" yelled Henry. "It's jammed!"

There was the sound of running footsteps from outside, then a loud smack, and then a new voice. "*Antoinette!* Stop that at once!"

This time, Thomas thought, the voice was a young

woman. His head hurt. Henry had mentioned a great number of siblings, but Thomas had assumed most of them would be married or employed or dead.

"Oh, Anne," Kate sighed. She looked up from the calf and met Thomas' gaze. Her eyes were huge and very blue. His stomach seized again, and he briefly forgot why he had planned to avoid England for the rest of his natural days. "I *am* sorry," she said quietly. "I really wouldn't have forced them all on you at once, but —"

There was the sound of a door screeching on its hinges, and then another fervent *moo*.

"Well, now you've let her in!" said the young woman's voice. She sounded very much like Kate.

"She's eaten my collar!" said the other man.

"She hasn't," said the voice of the younger woman —Anne? "You're being dramatic, Peter."

A thunderous moo shook the house, and hooves cracked against the flagstones. Now that he was sitting up, Thomas could see through the slot behind the massive central chimney into the parlor. A huge black form briefly blocked the light from the other room. When he turned his head, Antoinette the cow was appearing around the other edge of the chimney into the kitchen. Her short pale horns, black at the wickedly sharp tips, preceded her.

Thomas looked around wildly, trying to find something—anything—he could use to defend the small woman sitting on the hearth—a stick or a knife or a chamber pot or—or—he had seen hundreds of dead men, had been staring into the eyes of dozens while they breathed their last under his own hands, but the thought of seeing this bright human crushed in her own home—and why wasn't she fleeing up the stairs in the corner of the room? Surely it would buy her some time—

"Oh, *Antoinette*," Kate said, in tones of grave disappointment. "I'm sure you weren't meant to get in with the Wrights' bull."

"She *wasn't!*" That was the voice of the young woman, who Thomas supposed must be Anne. A moment later, Anne herself lurched around the corner and seized the cow by her left horn. "She's a wicked lustful thing. John Mary had to pay Ben Wright five shillings, because he wouldn't believe that we hadn't set her loose in his field on purpose."

"How interesting," Kate said.

Antoinette, shockingly, stopped her charge, turning to the young woman and sticking a tongue in the pocket of the enormous coat she wore.

Did all the women in this family dress in Henry's hand-me-downs? Thomas wondered.

"Pig," Anne said to the cow, running an affectionate hand down her spine. Thomas blinked at her. She was very tall, ridiculously tall for a woman, and where Kate's head was fiery gold, hers was dark red.

Anne blinked back at him, then turned to Kate. "He's not dead!"

"We haven't been introduced," Thomas said stiffly, very aware that he was only wearing a shirt and several blankets.

Anne and Thomas exchanged frowns. "Are you the doctor then? The one Henry brought home?" Without pausing for him to answer, Anne went on, "Can you doctor cows?"

"Well," Thomas started cautiously. He had never doctored cows in the past, and didn't particularly want to start.

"Henriette has the ague," Anne said.

"Henriette is a cow," Thomas said, trying to sound as though he understood what was being discussed.

"I don't think cows get the ague, beloved," Kate said.

"Well, she's been sniffling," Anne started. While she spoke, Antoinette pulled two apples out of her coat pocket with her long purple tongue, chewed them, and then swung her big head toward Kate. She snuffled the little dark creature on Kate's lap, who lifted his head and let out another pitiful yell. Thomas, in spite of himself, heaved a sigh of relief. Nothing he had seen in the last two days in this decrepit farmhouse made him think that the Gravenors could afford to lose even one puny calf.

The sounds of two men arguing in the parlor suddenly became loud enough that Thomas' attention was torn from the woman kneeling on the hearth.

"Oh, for pity's sake," Henry said, exasperated. "Couldn't you have latched the door? Now you've let in Georgette."

"I did not let in Georgette!" said the other voice, sounding put-upon. "She let herself in!"

A low, inquisitive moo came from the parlor.

"No," said Kate. "Absolutely not." She got to her feet, clutching the calf to her chest. "Henry, start a fire, please," she called. She leaned hard on Antoinette, but the cow did not move.

Anne produced another apple from a different coat pocket, and the cow spun to follow her hand. "Nice and slowly now, Madame La Vache," Anne informed the cow, backing around the chimney. Kate followed with the calf.

"Oh *Lord,* don't bring her back in here," yelped the voice that Thomas could only assume belonged to the much-maligned Peter.

"It's your own fault if the cows don't like you," Henry said, his voice echoing around the old house. Thomas winced. This, from Henry, was harsh criticism.

The new man came around the chimney into the kitchen, talking over his shoulder in an affected accent.

"I do think it's too bad of you, Henry. I only meant to check on Kate and bring a basket from the vicarage. As Paul says in his letter to the Corinthians —"

"Don't misquote Paul," Anne interrupted loudly. "Georgette, there's no food for you in here. No, you can't steal Antoinette's calf. She'll murder you, and then where will we be?"

"I translate rather freely, but I *never* misquote," Peter yelled back. "Hello, who's this?"

He stopped and stared hard at Thomas, who stared hard back at him.

Peter looked like an older and less absurd version of Henry, tall but not gigantic, his hair light brown instead of white-blonde, his expression genial but not maniacally earnest. He did not introduce himself, as Henry had seven years ago, by asking if Thomas ever thought about what sort of soil Plato's cave was dug into, and why the prisoners in the cave bothered about the shadows of things that weren't in the cave, when they could be inspecting the perfectly good dirt all around them.

Henry and Peter were not much alike, Thomas thought, studying Henry's brother carefully. He found at once that he didn't much like Peter. Unlike Kate and Henry, who both wore old clothes which were only a few mends from the rag bag, Peter's black breeches and coat were new, of good quality wool, and cut quite fashionably. His stockings were very white. He wore a priest's white bands at his throat, trimmed with a frippery bit of lace that made Thomas curl his lip.

Something about the way multiple expressions flitted around Peter's mobile face in rapid succession made Thomas think he was a very good liar.

"My name is Thomas Holyoke," Thomas said. He almost went on to give his rank, remembered he no longer had a rank, and found he couldn't breathe for a moment.

"The doctor, yes," Peter said. "Henry's letters have informed us of your long and storied career. How long has it been since you last set foot on good green English earth?"

"I served in His Majesty's Army as a medical officer for fifteen years," Thomas said tightly.

"Goodness me, you must be ever so old," Peter said, his light tone somewhat undercut by the way his eyes bore into Thomas' face like nails. "I'm Peter Gravenor, the second brother. I've the vicarage at Copstone. I see you've met Kate and Henry; they're the next after me. I wouldn't expect to meet Jake; it will be eight months before his ship returns. And of course

Anne is the youngest." Thomas noticed that Peter's voice grew more distinctly threatening with every sibling he listed, and he did not mention the absent John Mary, the owner of the farm, at all.

"I do appreciate that you kept my brother in one piece for seven years," Peter went on, regaining his cultivated accent. "I'm sure it wasn't an easy task." His intent gaze narrowed as he studied Thomas.

"No more difficult than any other aspect of war," Thomas returned oppressively. The name of Copstone made his stomach clench. He had known, of course, that Henry hailed from his own county; Henry had far too much to say about the management of cattle on Shropshire loam for anyone to have missed his origin. But he had rarely mentioned a village or a parish; the whole world, as far as Henry was concerned, centered on the ten acres belonging to the Gravenors. But Thomas had inquired no further, because he had foolishly assumed that his past could safely be left in the past.

Copstone was close, disastrously close. Thomas' family had gone to church in Copstone. Cousin Daniel, the miserable old bastard, had made sure their family pew was as grand as the squire's.

Cold panic loomed in Thomas' mind and gut. People might *remember* him in Copstone.

"You look rather familiar," Peter said. "Local man, are you?" An odd expression twisted his face, one that made him look much less like Henry. He walked closer to the bed, as though he might be able to place Thomas in one of his parish families by examining his face closely enough.

Thomas stiffened. There was no way Peter could know him. Thomas had left eighteen years ago; this insolent young fop would have barely started grammar school then.

There was no way, and yet the way the younger man looked at him made his blood run cold. Thomas was used to half-truths; there was no way of being the kind of man he was in the world as it was without accustoming oneself to misdirection. But he had not realized how close to peril he lay when he had awakened in this house the day before, and he had not prepared any pastiche of the truth.

So he looked Peter the vicar in the eye and lied. "No. I'm from Cheshire. My family is all dead."

## CHAPTER SIX

The next morning, Kate found some of the round cheese molds left on the top shelves in the pantry. Maman had made each one by rolling a thin sheet of birch bark into a hoop and lacing the edges together with twine, but most had shriveled and warped in the intervening years. The reed mats Maman had painstakingly sewn together to drain the curd had rotted as well.

Kate would have to ask Henry to go to Mobley Pond to collect more reeds and find her some birch logs. To keep her hands busy, she took what remained of the mats into the kitchen and pulled the most intact of the reeds from each. She could unravel a thread from her hem to start sewing them together again, and ask Anne to bring her some new thread next week.

The bed in the corner of the kitchen shifted.

"What are you doing?" Dr. Holyoke asked, in the tones of someone who wondered why whatever it was couldn't be done somewhere else.

It is because of this man that Henry has come home, Kate reminded herself.

"I would like to make cheese soon," she said.

"You make cheeses," Dr. Holyoke repeated, sounding suspicious. "To … sell?"

"That's the idea," Kate said mildly.

This was met by a silence so stony that Kate turned around to look at the doctor to make sure he hadn't had a sudden apoplexy and died. He had not, but he was glaring at her so fiercely that she was surprised her bedcoat hadn't caught fire.

This is my home, where you, sir doctor, are a *guest*, Kate thought, and then: I have cleaned out your chamber pot, and then: I have met pigs who were more grateful.

There is no point in yelling at this man who cannot even go outside to get away from me, she told herself, taking a deep breath through her nose. She cast about for some new conversational gambit. Henry had written about Dr. Holyoke often in his missives home. Henry was not the greatest of letter-writers, and so she had not been able to form much of a notion of what the doctor looked like or sounded like; how he dressed or what he liked to do; who his family were or where they had come from. She did know that Dr. Holyoke was not at all interested in the properties of soil, had once saved a cat from being run over by a military wagon, and possessed a large box of medical instruments which Henry was often tasked with carrying.

"Did the army take back your doctor's tools when you were discharged?" Kate asked. "I see that you have no case."

The doctor released a short, hard bark of laughter, and his response was fast and angry. "The army issues almost nothing to surgeons, but for a few yards of bandages and a pittance of laudanum. I purchased my own tools, madam, starting when I was in medical school in Edinburgh. A shilling sixpence, that first set of forceps was."

"That's very dear," Kate said, thinking, Lord, I could buy two weeks of bread and vegetables for that amount.

"They were made in Germany and brought by ship to Scotland," Dr. Holyoke said briskly. "All the best tools are."

"How many tools did you have?" Kate said, unpicking a thread from the edge of her wrap.

Dr. Holyoke rattled off a list of scalpels, forceps, catheters, and several other words Kate did not know. She could only picture a tenaculum because Henry had included a sketch in a letter he had written her four or five years ago.

"That's all very interesting," Kate said, turning to look at the doctor. "Where have you put them? Is a friend keeping them for you?"

Dr. Holyoke, who had a moment before been all flashing eyes and aggravated competence, deflated. He rubbed a thumb between his thick eyebrows, turning his gaze to the bricks of the chimney.

"Henry was not supposed to—that is—I asked Henry to—" The doctor shifted in his bed uncomfortably. "I asked Henry to sell my tools to pay for his passage back to England."

"And your own passage?" Kate prompted.

Dr. Holyoke would not meet her eyes. "There was very little likelihood that I would survive such a bad break. It seemed a poor use of two pounds ten to transport a corpse."

"Then how did you—" Kate started to ask, then stopped, her throat tight. The doctor had ended up on a ship bound for England because Henry had picked him up and carried him onto the ship.

Her heart twisted with a surge of love for her brother. "I suppose that Henry bought a passage for you both with the money."

"Yes, though I did not realize I was on a clipper and not dying of fever in the fort barracks until we were halfway to England." Dr. Holyoke now studied his hands, bending his fingers one at a time. He grimaced. "I expect you would have rather had the money than a crippled guest to look after, so I am sorry for that."

"I trust Henry," Kate said, without thinking, and the doctor looked at her sharply, suddenly.

It was not that she had not met Dr. Holyoke's eyes before this moment, but until this moment, Kate would have sworn that the man had not actually seen her. She was such a small nothing of a person; she was well-accustomed to other people, especially men, looking over or around or through her. She expected it would only grow worse over time.

But the expression on his face now was both strange and strangely familiar: eyes narrowed, one side of his mouth quirked up. It took Kate a moment to place it as the same face that John Mary made when listening to Henry explain his reasoning for bringing a puny calf to sleep in his bed upstairs, or emptying out his drawer of the dresser so he could arrange the different samples of dirt he had found around the farm in neat lines.

"Henry has been my assistant for seven years," Dr. Holyoke said, his voice very dry. "I would not call his judgment infallible."

More infallible than yours, taunting the woman who brings your bread and tends your wounds, Kate almost said, before swallowing down the words. She still wasn't being fair. Dr. Holyoke had looked after Henry for seven years, and she knew, from the seventeen years she had looked after Henry before that, that it was no mean task. Perhaps he did not understand the depths of Henry's character as she did, but he had been kind to her brother, and so few were kind.

"I am grateful," she said, then stopped, staring at the reeds she had laid out on the table. Perhaps she ought not say what she was about to say, but she could not let this lie. She took a deep breath and pushed onward. "I am grateful that you were able to see—to make use of Henry's good qualities as your assistant. He is so very careful in everything he undertakes." There, that was pleasant-sounding enough. She would try again to draw the doctor into agreeable conversation. "How did you come to find him, among all the soldiers?"

"Ah," Dr. Holyoke said.

"The army is so very large, with so many thousands of men. I should wonder that it is possible to find the proper man to do anything."

"Erm," Dr. Holyoke said.

"Was he recommended to you by another officer?" Kate asked. "Or did he recommend himself? It wouldn't be very like Henry to do so, but I suppose he might have thought assisting a surgeon would be like doctoring the cows. He's always been very good with the cows."

"Well," Thomas said.

He had felt himself slide from irritation to resentment to panic within minutes of Kate entering the kitchen.

Thomas had certainly not ranked highly enough to claim an assistant at will from the ranks of enlisted soldiers seven years ago, when he had sighted a terrified, terrifically tall young man being towed along in the wake of one of the regiments bound for Burgos.

Thomas remembered thinking two things upon seeing Henry: first, *That boy is simple*, and second, *With that white hair, the first Frenchman who sees him is going to blow his head off.*

Thomas had noted the regiment's standard in passing, experiencing his usual quiver of revulsion at the reminder of Shropshire and home. That knowledge had given him the slightest edge of authority when he had impulsively strode out of the church they had commandeered to use as a surgery and barked, "You! The tall Shropshire boy with the pale hair! Yes, you! You're to be a surgeon's assistant! Come along, I don't have time to waste." He had caught Henry by the sleeve and yanked him inside.

Henry had disappeared into the church sanctuary with him before the officers dragging the Shropshire regiment forward quite knew what had happened. The organization of military surgeons under the Army

Medical Department was less chaotic than it had been under the self-serving, powerless Army Medical Board, but it was not so precise that a determined doctor couldn't convincingly claim a set of orders that an angry sergeant bound for a losing battle could neither countermand nor investigate thoroughly.

The relevant sergeant and his lieutenant had been killed at Burgos, and no one else cared enough about Henry to come fetch him back. The other surgeons were only too happy to have another set of functioning hands to help.

Thomas didn't think he could say any of this to Henry's sister. He didn't know whether she would be offended that Thomas had assumed her brother was an idiot, or whether she herself understood her brother's full capacity. Henry was such a peculiar case; he was so awkward and easily confused, and yet he grasped complicated biological and philosophical concepts readily, with the barest modicum of explanation. He bumbled into other people when walking, but Thomas had never had anyone assist him in surgery with surer hands or a better knowledge of his instruments and methods.

There was so little a single doctor could do to stave the burgeoning flow of misery in a slow-moving war. Thomas had jumped at the chance to pull one boy out of the lines, but there had been hundreds of other children playing at soldiers who he could not and did not do anything to save.

Thomas realized he had not spoken for several minutes. Kate was now weaving a thread around each of her reeds, making a flexible sheet.

"Henry did better once there was no one yelling at him," Thomas said, because that was true.

"Yes!" Kate burst out, whirling to face Thomas. To his horror, love for her brother did the same sorts of things to her face that sunlight did to her hair, changing her visage from a rather average set of features to one that would not be out of place on a carving of the Annunciation. "Our schoolmaster never understood that. Henry is *very* intelligent. He can learn nearly anything, but you must speak in a moderate tone to him, or he panics. I am so glad that you understand."

"Perhaps," Thomas said stiffly. His heart was doing something awful, transfixed by Kate's blue eyes and her confidence in Henry. Foolishly, stupidly, he had felt his body relax, his shoulders dropping an inch when Kate had pronounced her brother's intelligence. She understood; he would not have to fight for Henry's continued existence in this house.

But when Kate's fierce, achingly blue eyes were on Thomas, he couldn't form a coherent thought, and what came out of his mouth was, "I have become well-acquainted with managing Henry's idiosyncrasies, in any case."

Kate went very pink and said quietly, "Henry wasn't meant to be a soldier." She turned away, her shoulders hunched.

"No, by God, he wasn't," Thomas said, relieved to be freed of that penetrating gaze. He considered pulling the coverlet over his face, then decided that would be cowardly. But how could a man be expected to withstand such an assault?

Abruptly the last several minutes of conversation

rearranged themselves in Thomas' head, and he breathed out a sigh. Yes. He and Kate understood each other, at least a little. "Henry Gravenor is a good man," he said abruptly. "As resolutely good a man as I have ever met. I am glad he will get the chance to be—to be in his dirt again. To farm the soil, I mean."

"Yes," Kate said, turning those heart-stopping eyes and smile on him once more.

## CHAPTER SEVEN

Three days later, Anne hurried along the path past Ned Bell's farm, worrying about cheese.

This was not in fact the fastest way to get to the Telford farm, which would have been a problem if Anne still worked on the Telford farm. But in fact she had not worked for Isaac and Penelope Telford for nineteen months, since Daniel Lately, that spiteful old bastard, had cornered Isaac in the Rolling Pig and hinted broadly that if he knew what was good for him, he wouldn't have anything to do with any of John Mary Gravenor's relations. Isaac Telford, who had always suspected Anne of being a secret papist on account of her French mother, was only too happy to turn her out on her ear. Anne took comfort in the fact that her former employer had surely not eaten an unburned meal since that day. Penelope Telford was not a bad cook, but she hated Daniel Lately and she liked Anne. More importantly, Anne had been her right hand in the dairy for the past four years.

Anne had not told John Mary his outburst had lost her the job she'd had since she turned thirteen, because she hadn't wanted to make him feel bad, and she hadn't told him when she got a new job, because she had thought he might object.

She should have known Peter would suspect; as vicar, he heard all the gossip from all parts of the parish. The Telford farm was near the hamlet of Rudge, and it was only a matter of time until someone noticed that Anne no longer walked in that direction when she left the Gravenor farm on Sunday evening and brought it to Peter's attention.

Even so, Anne had been surprised when Peter had cornered her with his new knowledge three days ago, during the general hullabaloo surrounding the doctor's waking and Antoinette's new calf.

Anne had just stepped inside the back door after putting Georgette back outside when Peter had seized her elbow and dragged her into the pantry.

"What on *earth* are you doing every week at Bassenthwaite House?" he'd hissed.

The calf had finally found his feet and was determinedly chasing Henry around the kitchen, and the noise of his pursuit was enough to cover the sounds of a muttered conversation.

"Maybe I've got a job as a kitchen maid," Anne hissed back at Peter.

"If Lord Houghton were employing you, you'd only have a half-day free each week, and you wouldn't be lying to John Mary about it," Peter whispered. "What mischief are you up to?"

"You don't know it's not respectable," Anne said under her breath.

"I do," Peter said, and Anne's blood ran cold.

But at that moment Kate had come to look for

Anne, to ask her to reunite the calf with Antoinette, and Peter had put on a great show of asking how the Telfords were, and wasn't the new baby just the sweetest child.

Anne, who had not known Penelope was pregnant, nodded furiously and tried very hard to look like she was only thinking about adorable infant girls and not about strangling her older brother.

Anne had avoided Peter until he left that evening to get back to the vicarage for his dinner, and then had avoided Kate all of today, in case she had overheard any little bit of their conversation, until it was time for Anne to, theoretically, head back to the Telford farm, at which point she had kissed Kate and rushed out the door before she could ask any questions.

That was the problem with Peter, Anne thought broodily, snapping off a hawthorn twig as she jogged past on the path. He knew the most about the goings-on in the parish of any of her siblings, but he was also the best liar. There was a chance he knew about the odd new job she'd gotten, but it was just as likely he was trying to bluff so she'd tell him herself.

She couldn't do anything about Peter now, Anne thought, and in any case she was more worried about Kate. Up until he'd spoken, Anne had been stewing over Kate's dairy plans. The trouble was, of the cows John Mary had managed to sneak up the road to the Wright bull, only Antoinette was a good milker. After John Mary, Kate, Henry, and Doctor Holyoke had had their fill to eat and drink, would there even be enough milk to make cheeses?

And just how long was the doctor going to be a

guest in the house? The way he looked at Kate when he thought no one was watching him made Anne very uneasy. Henry trusted him; but then, John Mary had trusted Will Easting, and look how poorly that had turned out for Kate. Sometimes men who did right by other men couldn't be bothered to extend the same courtesy to women.

Anne came to the place where the path split, one right-of-way sliding behind the Halverton farm and the other crossing the stream, and stopped.

Fred Halverton and Wendell Driver were dredging a large, muddy object out of the stream.

Anne froze, her mind full of cheese and doctors and secrets. If she were going to the Telford farm, as she ought to be on a Sunday afternoon, she would continue straight on, fording the stream. If Anne were going where she actually meant to go, she'd turn left onto the right-of-way that crossed behind the Halverton farm, which Fred would certainly notice.

Wendell looked up at the sound of her footsteps. He was the same age as Henry and Kate, only instead of going away to the army he had apprenticed to a doctor in Wolverhampton, before returning the year before to hang up his shingle in front of a narrow storefront in Copstone. He was a slight, delicate-looking young man, and right now his round face looked quite green.

His eyes found Anne's, and his mouth formed a horrified little *o*.

This was enough to catch Fred's attention, and his head snapped up. He also looked rather sick.

"Stay back, girl," he barked. "This is a bad

business. You stay back."

"What do you mean?" Anne demanded, but now her eyes were focusing on the dark, horrible thing the two men held between them. It was shaped, she thought, rather like a human body, but only if that human body had no head. She stepped forward, squinting to see better. The low sun and the profusion of alders and willows growing right up to the bank of the stream cast dark shadows, making it hard to see any detail.

"Oh, please, don't come any closer," Wendell said, sounding as though he might retch. "It's really not a fit sight for—for—"

"For anyone," Fred snapped. "Pull yourself together, man. I told you it wasn't good."

"You said he was dead," Wendell retorted, his face becoming, if possible, even paler. "You didn't say he'd been dead for so *long*. And you didn't say—"

The shape suddenly resolved itself in Anne's eyes, and she realized it *was* a body, a body dressed in a sopping wet dark coat and trousers, a body that now bent and swayed in a fashion that no living man would.

And the body had no head. Anne put her hand to her mouth, tasting bile, before she tore her eyes away from that horrible, darkened stump of a neck, sagging between the rag of a neckcloth and collar.

"What happened?" she squeaked. "Who is he?"

"We've no more idea than you," Fred said. Beneath his tan, he was also very pale. "I crossed this way to ask Ned the loan of some tools, and noticed it—him— sticking out from under these bushes. It was face-down —God—it was front-down in the mud, with the water running over it. I sent my oldest boy running to fetch the doctor before I'd realized—before I knew—" He shuddered.

"This isn't really my area of expertise," Wendell said, in a thin voice that was almost a moan.

"Whose is it, if not yours?" snapped Fred. "There's few enough people in this parish who would know what to do about a murder—or—or—or whatever this is." He heaved the body up the bank, toward Anne. She saw they had laid out a piece of tarpaulin to the side of the path to receive the remains. She took a hasty step backwards. Fred shot her an angry glance. "Not that this is a murder, mind. Don't you go spreading that about, Anne Gravenor."

"Hard to imagine a man losing his head by accident," Anne said, her mind whirring like a covey of partridge scared up from a hedge. Who was the dead man? Where was his head? Was he someone she knew? She ran through a list of her acquaintances and when she'd last seen them, but the shadowy, mud-covered *thing* in front of her made it very hard to concentrate.

"I suppose we'd better have the constable look at him," Wendell said.

"Right, and Joe will say that this fellow's head has been knocked off," Fred said disagreeably.

There was a reason this man, whoever he was, was killed, Anne thought, and why his body was left just here. It's so close to home, far closer than it has any business being. I want to know why.

*I need to know why.*

Anne felt very cold, even colder than the chill February afternoon merited. John Mary had been acting very odd, distant and reserved, for several months now. She had put it down to his worries about money, but did he know something he shouldn't know?

Had he *done* something he shouldn't have done?

Of all her siblings, John Mary took the most after Maman in manner and sensibilities. Anne had not thought that this extended to Maman's callous disregard for English law, but perhaps it did. If he had met someone on the path who he thought posed a threat to his siblings—but *who?* and what threat?—he might well have dealt with it alone, rather than asking for help.

"My brother Henry's back from the army," Anne announced suddenly.

"Good for him," Fred said, shifting the body. One of the arms came loose from the shoulder socket with an audible *crack*. Wendell let out a little sob.

"He was an assistant to an army doctor for seven years," Anne went on.

"You don't mean to say that Henry knows about doctoring now," Fred returned, his eyebrows furrowed in disbelief.

Anne fought a scowl. People did insist on talking about Henry like he was thick in the head. "What I mean is that both he and the doctor were given papers at the same time, after Henry did his seven years and the doctor was bad hurt. We've been hosting Dr. Holyoke for three weeks now, as he gets his strength back up. *He's* seen a fair bit of violence, men shot and bayoneted and so on. He'd probably be able to say what happened to this fellow."

Dr. Holyoke didn't know about Maman, or John

Mary, or Daniel Lately, Anne thought. He might draw conclusions, but he almost certainly didn't have enough information to draw the right ones.

Anne jerked her head toward the terrible figure, which flopped between the two men like a broken doll. "And anyway, our farm's close."

Fred gave her a wary glance, then nodded. "God knows I don't want to bring this home to the missus," he muttered. "Wendell, don't just stand there, *help*. This bug—this fellow is heavy."

"I'll just run back and tell them you're coming," Anne said, turning on her heel.

She ran through the wood as though the dead man were chasing her.

# CHAPTER EIGHT

"You found him in the stream," Thomas said.

"The stream by Ned Bell's farm?" Kate clarified from behind his shoulder.

Thomas ground his teeth. He wanted Kate to go upstairs or go outside to mess about with the cows or go into the pantry to do something with cheese molds or do *anything* but stand here, asking questions about a body she should never have to see.

"That's right," said the farmer. The younger doctor went pale and held his kerchief to his mouth.

The night before, Kate had slit Thomas' long underpants up the right side and sewn buttons on, so that he could put them on over his broken leg without overly taxing himself. The kindness made him so angry he could barely speak to or look at her.

When Anne had burst into the kitchen an hour ago, looking very pale under her freckles and stammering about a dead body that the local doctor didn't know what to do with, Kate had, without so much as a by-your-leave, whipped Thomas' trousers out from the basket under the bed and sliced open the side seam.

"You can't talk to another doctor in your underthings," she said briskly. "I'll pin it closed around your splint. No one will ever see the difference."

She had in fact done a fine job of pinning the trouser leg, and now Thomas sat on a stool by the ancient kitchen table, his broken leg propped stiffly on a chair next to him.

He wanted very much to throw Kate out of the kitchen. Every time he looked at her, he felt her small, deft fingers gathering the fabric down the outside of his thigh and calf, and saw her head, covered in her fire-of-angels hair, bowed over him in the bed. He thought of how his stomach had seized at her fervent defense of Henry. He had clutched the bedsheets to keep from reaching out to touch her hair, reaching out to touch *her,* and Kate had of course thought he was in pain and asked if she could bring him some willow bark to chew on.

It was too much, Thomas thought. He felt like he was on fire. His life was ruined, the vocation he had spent two decades working toward ripped from his hands, and now this horrible little woman was caring for him in ways he could not possibly reciprocate.

Around the cloud of his anger, Thomas knew he also didn't want Kate to see the foul thing lying on the tarpaulin-protected table right now. It was not the nastiest death he had seen, not by a long shot, but he didn't relish any civilian being forced to confront the knowledge of how cruelly a human body could be abused before it rendered its spirit up to God.

Kate had, of course, made sure to protect the rest of her family, sending her younger sister upstairs to make her bed, as she wouldn't make it back to the Telford farm tonight. When Henry had tried to come into the house, she had sent him out immediately to fetch water and more firewood.

"Henry has assisted in countless amputations," Thomas had said.

"I can help instead," Kate had said.

"He must have been in the water a good long while," Kate observed now, from behind Thomas' ear.

He shot her a furious glance. "Mrs. Easting," he said, only just remembering to use her proper name. "If you could occupy yourself otherwise, it would be appreciated."

"What if you need something?" Kate asked.

Thomas hoped the other two men couldn't hear him grinding his teeth. "Mrs. Easting," he said, as evenly as he could. "This matter is rather delicate."

He looked at the two guests for help. Thomas didn't think much of the local doctor, who had propped himself up next to the wall and was clearly close to fainting. Thomas reckoned that he had already been cauterizing artillery-smashed limbs at that age. The farmer, a square man in his mid-fifties, was more stoic, but he also could not look at the body for very long. His jaw muscles moved constantly, as though he were chewing on his fear.

"Kate, would you take Wendell somewhere else," the iron-haired farmer said suddenly. "He's going to collapse and knock his head on something if he doesn't sit down."

"Of course," Kate said, and then she was enveloping the young man in a flurry of efficiency and solicitousness, offering him lemon tonic and toast as she gently led him into the parlor.

Immediately, Thomas felt a ripe seam of hatred for Wendell Driver open in his chest.

"Thank you," he said, keeping his voice low and nodding to the other man. Halverton, Kate had said his name was. Fred Halverton.

"She's always been like that," the farmer muttered, sighing. "Run herself into the ground if you let her."

"Ah," Thomas said, surprised more by the source of this revelation than the revelation itself.

"Their father was … well, Edward Gravenor was a good man, but he'd not the sense of a day-old lamb. His children learned to look after themselves." Halverton stared into the huge fireplace, only just lit by a small heap of coals, tight lines bracketing his mouth.

This was clearly a subject about which Thomas should inquire no further, a subject in which he should not be interested at all. He had no business inquiring into the childhood of his former assistant or his assistant's sister. "I see," he said. "But … he produced Kate?"

"Without a doubt," Halverton said grimly. "She's his spitting image. But he thought himself a poet. His wife did what she could, but she was French."

Thomas raised an eyebrow. "I beg your pardon?"

"The French can't be trusted with a poet," the farmer said. "Can't keep their heads about poetry." He glanced down at the decapitated corpse and flinched.

"I don't think poetry did for this fellow," Thomas said, wishing Halverton could have stayed on the subject of Kate's parents a little longer.

"No, I don't expect so," Halverton said. Then, so reluctantly that Thomas could tell he didn't believe it even as he was saying it, he went on, "I don't suppose there's any way all this could have happened naturally, like."

Thomas looked at him, then back down at the body. He tried to imagine a natural way in which a man could lose his head, but not his hands or his feet. "There are always dogs," he said doubtfully. "The wild ones can do a lot of damage, but seeing as you've plenty of livestock hereabouts, I imagine you'd know if there were a pack nearby." He drummed his fingers on his leg. "If I had my tools—"

He let himself think longingly of his medical kit, with its assortment of finely-made steel forceps, picks, scalpels, and a very excellent bone saw. There had been an instrument maker near the medical college who also imported more costly tools from abroad. Thomas had pinched and saved to put together a decent set of tools by the time he graduated, and he had judiciously added to the collection over the years that followed.

*A man is no better than his tools,* Thomas thought, *and I don't especially relish the thought of doing an autopsy with a fork and cleaver.*

When that goddamned horse had broken Thomas' femur, he had assumed he would die. He couldn't be seen to by another doctor without discovery and humiliation, and he certainly couldn't amputate his own leg. Most men did not recover from the infection that followed such a terrible injury, in any case. Thomas had told Henry that the medical kit ought to fetch at least ten pounds and to book the first passage he could find leaving Gibraltar for England. He had thought Henry's papers were in order; he had prayed they were in order.

Thomas' plans for himself had been entirely contained in the bottle of laudanum he kept for his surgical patients.

But the laudanum had not been mixed to specifications—or perhaps someone had diluted it— for Thomas had awakened in a berth on a schooner, with Henry's large, pink face hovering over him. Guilt scratched at Thomas still. Henry had wasted two pounds his family desperately needed on a slim chance that his officer would wake from his fever.

The front door creaked open. "I've got the water," Henry announced loudly.

Kate's voice came from the parlor, on the other side of the fireplace. "Thank you, Henry. Now, if you would just—"

"I need Henry's help in here," Thomas said, a little more loudly than was necessary.

"Are you sure?" Kate asked.

"You do?" Halverton asked, frowning. "But Henry's—"

"I do," Thomas repeated, cutting him off. "I was not joking about the amputations."

Halverton blanched.

Henry stomped in, holding a bucket of water in each hand and trailing mud behind him. "Yes, sir?" His white-blonde curls stuck up all around his head, making him look bizarrely cherubic, and his ears were brick-red with cold.

He stopped short before the body on the table, looking at it, then at Thomas, then back at the body.

Henry's brow knit. "Sir," he said, then, "Sir?"

"This body was found nearby," Thomas said. "I have volunteered to do an autopsy."

Henry's eyes fell to the body's stump of a neck, his forehead folding itself into a map of worried wrinkles. Well, Thomas supposed, it was one thing to deal with corpses on the battle field; it was quite another for them to show up in one's childhood home.

Thomas glanced at the darkening windows, and the nasty thought presented itself that they would likely have this mutilated body in the house overnight.

I've seen worse, he thought, and this house has likely held worse.

"Sir," Henry said tentatively. "I think—"

"I need a sharp knife and some pins, and a lantern, if you've the oil to spare," Thomas said. "Can you find me those, please?"

Halverton shot Thomas another disbelieving look, as though he'd asked a donkey to do sums. Thomas gritted his teeth.

"Yes, sir," Henry said. He set down the buckets on the hearth and went to the narrow staircase in the corner of the kitchen.

"Wipe your feet before going upstairs!" Kate yelled from the other room.

"Oh, right," Henry said, and went up the stairs, not wiping his feet.

Halverton shook his head, and Thomas swallowed the urge to snarl at him. Instead, he unbuttoned his cuffs and rolled up his sleeves.

A thundering of footsteps, rattling, banging of doors and trunks, and two loud voices emanated from upstairs.

"Well, I haven't seen it," came Anne's muffled voice. "Have you looked—"

There was more muffled discussion, and then Henry clomped back down the stairs. In one hand he held a candlestick with a tin reflector; in the other was a large bundle of rags.

Through seven years of practice, Thomas repressed a sigh. For all his many fine qualities, Henry took direction in non-emergency situations about as well as a large squirrel. "Did you get some pins, Henry?"

"No," Henry said, setting the candle on the table.

Halverton snorted loudly.

Then Henry untied the bundle, revealing a delicate forest of glinting steel pieces.

It took Thomas a long moment to understand what he was seeing: his own array of forceps, tweezers, scalpels, and clamps, all sewn to the inside of a ragged flannel shirt. "Henry," he said, very carefully, wishing there wasn't a stranger in the room to witness this conversation, "didn't I ask you to sell these, for your— that is, didn't I ask you sell my medicine case?"

Henry's brow knit. "I did sell the case, just like you said. And your bone saw and the big knife," he said, after a minute. "I couldn't carry those, anyway. But the tools hardly took up any space at all."

There was no way the case and the bone saw had fetched the price of two berths on a ship bound for England. Thomas stared at the neat rows of glimmering steel, a very strange feeling in his chest. His eyes found his long bullet forceps, then the much shorter pair he used to pick surface shrapnel out of a wound. Henry had even saved the silver catheters, always deeply unpleasant to use, cushioning them with extra layers of flannel.

I had thought I would be dead by now, Thomas thought, skimming a hand over the spring-loaded forceps he had used to prise away shattered bits of skull from the brain of a soldier who had been clubbed in the head. He hoped he looked like he was pondering the correct tool to begin this procedure, and not like the reality of his own survival was crashing down on him, crushing him under its weight.

Thomas cleared his suddenly-tight throat. "Thank you, Henry," he said, his voice blaring in his own ears. "Having my tools will make this autopsy much easier. If you would aim the candle's light on the neck wound and pass me a scalpel."

Henry did as he was told, lighting the candle and angling the reflector so the faint beam fell on the severed neck.

Halverton was suddenly overcome by a fit of coughing and stepped back.

The body had been in the stream for quite some time, and while the cold weather and water had done something to preserve the flesh, all the limbs were swollen and distended. The neck wound itself had blackened, and it was almost impossible to distinguish muscle from ligament now. Some small animals—and some not-so-small animals—had been at this body, and it would be impossible to say what had happened to it when.

But Thomas thought he could still find out what

he wanted to know. The flesh of the neck might be too damaged by time and weather to leave any indication of what had taken the man's head off, but his bones would still bear the impressions of what had happened. If a dog had chewed through the neck—something Thomas thought was vanishingly unlikely, given that the corpse's hands were still attached—there would be marks from the teeth.

If the head had been taken off with a blade, there would also be marks.

He supposed a man trained in taking apart pig and cattle carcasses could cut between the vertebrae without damaging the bones on either side, but it would take a very sharp knife and a lot of skill. If he found no marks at all, he would make inquiries about the homicidal tendencies of the local butchers.

Thomas sliced away the tatters of the indigo cloth tied around the man's neck. It was the same sort of neckerchief he had seen worn by hundreds of working men from Shropshire to Edinburgh and London. The fabric of the corpse's coat was coarse, as were his shirt and trousers.

Thomas indulged a brief moment of despair—if the man were an itinerant laborer, they might never know who he had been or who had put him in the stream—before he delicately cut away the mash of flesh around the cervical vertebrae. The windpipe had been crushed, but there was no way of knowing whether that had happened when the man died or after.

Thomas privately thought that the body being dumped in the stream exculpated every neighboring farmer of the man's killing, because what farmer would foul a perfectly good source of water? Unless two different people had been responsible for the killing and where the body had ended up.

Thomas bared the first vertebra. The bone looked faintly purple and slimy. He heard Halverton retch.

Then, a very unwelcome voice spoke from close at hand.

"What are you doing?" Kate whispered. She must walk as quietly as a ghost, curse her.

"If you faint, I can't help you," Thomas snapped, aware that he was being very ungracious. Kate had shown no sign of fainting so far, and she had certainly gotten an eyeful while the corpse was being laid out on the kitchen table. "Henry, two of the small clamps, please."

Henry passed Thomas the clamps, and he pinned the flesh back so that he could see more clearly what the scalpel had revealed. The first vertebra had been smashed, as though someone had clubbed the fellow right in the back of the neck. Or had he been shot? No, Thomas didn't think so. He'd tended to plenty of bones shattered by lead during the war, and this was still of a piece, with no shards embedded in the muscle around the spine.

"That doesn't look like something a dog would do," Kate said very quietly.

"No," Thomas said, wishing she would move away from him. He should not be thinking about her small warm body while he was wrist-deep in a murder victim's neck.

"While you're here, you can hold the candle, so Henry can turn the body over for me," Thomas added.

At least then she can't move without me noticing, he thought.

The siblings complied with his request, Kate moving to the head of the table while Henry used the tarpaulin to lift the body onto its side. Thomas wished that his subject had been left anywhere else but a fast-running stream; any evidence of how the body had fallen—patches of mud, damage to the clothing, protected bits of fabric—had been washed away. In corpses that lay on the battlefield for a long while before they were collected, blood and other fluids pooled in the lower side of the torso and limbs, but the water had distended this one all over. He did not see any large holes in the body's dress which could have admitted a bullet or a knife. He supposed the fellow could have had a heart attack and fallen down dead on the path, before a maniac had come along and chopped the head off for fun.

He doubted it, though.

The third cervical vertebra Thomas uncovered was conclusive. There was a slice across it, as though someone had slammed a very sharp, very heavy blade into it.

"There," Thomas said. He looked to Halverton to deliver his verdict, but the man had a hand over his mouth and looked like he might vomit. Thomas addressed himself to Henry instead. "I'd swear to a magistrate that this man's head was cut off on purpose, with a blade. No wild animal did that, nor the natural action of decay. He could have been dead when he was decapitated; the blood that would tell one way or another has washed away. But there's something very foul afoot here."

Kate sucked in a deep breath, and the light of the candle wavered. But when Thomas looked at her sharply, her face was only anxious, not nauseous.

"How will we find out who he is?" she asked, her voice subdued. "His family ought to know what happened to him."

"Have you gone through his pockets?" Henry asked.

Halverton nodded, not taking his hand from his mouth. "All gone to mush," he said.

Thomas considered the body grimly. "Then we'd best undress him and look for identifying marks."

The parish constable, Joseph Fine, arrived during this procedure. He took one look at the body, blanched, and backed into the parlor with the timid Dr. Driver.

"What are you up to, Dr. Holyoke?" Constable Fine called from around the fireplace.

"Same as I would do on a battlefield with an unknown soldier," Thomas said crisply. "I imagine you'll want to find out who this fellow was and then lay him to rest as soon as possible."

"Of course, of course," the constable said. "What have you discovered about the body, then?"

"The corpse is that of a man, not old," Thomas responded. "Between thirty and forty is my guess. No obvious signs of arthritis in the joints or other past serious injury. A few scars on his knees and back, but none very unique." He turned over the pale, bloated hand closest to him. "Palms are callused. The fingers have seen some damage, which might have been wild animals. A few are half gone."

The light from the candlestick jerked once more, and Thomas shot a sharp look at Kate. But Kate was frowning into the air behind him.

"That could be anyone," Halverton grumbled.

"He might not be from around here at all," Constable Fine said, sounding hopeful. "Mayhap he's some sort of vagrant."

"Maybe," Thomas said.

Even people in the smallest villages have secrets they'd kill to hide, he thought.

## CHAPTER NINE

Thomas did not sleep well. There had been no question of the headless body staying in the house during the night, but there had been some little discussion about where to store it. Dr. Driver had suggested that it might be put in the barn, but the Gravenor siblings agreed that Antoinette the cow would certainly eat the corpse, and so it was shut up in the woodshed. Constable Fine took a message to Peter asking whether the body might be buried in the churchyard, and the constable himself promised to ask around to see if anyone knew of any strange doings in the past two weeks. Thomas assumed this meant that the constable would get roaringly drunk at his pub of choice and tell the story of the headless corpse to a horrified crowd. Everyone would relate their own tale of a horror which had happened in the next county, and no one would have heard or seen anything locally.

No part of it should have troubled Thomas so, but still he could not sleep. It was not as though murder were unheard of in His Majesty's Army; Thomas had heard of any number of officers poisoned by their batmen and men shot by comrades in the heat of battle. And why should a singular murder bother him any more than murder on a grand scale, murder that was approved by king and country, murder that targeted the young and the poor?

Thomas' leg ached from the bone out and the skin down, ached so that every time he shifted unconsciously, the pain burnt across his nerves like a branding iron, and he had to grit his teeth to keep from cursing aloud. When in the dark, cold hours of morning he did finally dip below the edge of consciousness, his dreams were of men torn to pieces by artillery, their bodies distended and warped as cannonballs slammed through them.

Henry woke him when it was still dark, as he had every morning in this mossy, decrepit building, with a thunder of footsteps down the stairs at the back of the kitchen. Henry then burst out of the house, banging the front door open and closed. Thomas sighed deeply and relaxed into a proper sleep.

An hour or so later he was awakened again by much quieter footsteps on the stairs, then murmuring at the front door, then a series of creakings and scratchings from somewhere in the vicinity of the great kitchen table.

"Whatever you're doing, is there a reason it can't be done somewhere else?" Thomas snapped.

There was a pause, and then Kate's measured voice came back to him. Of course it was Kate. "I am making new cheese molds."

Thomas forced an eye open. Kate sat at the table, her hands bending a long, narrow bit of something into a hoop. Thomas squinted and discerned that it was a piece of bark, likely originating from the short fat log sitting at her feet.

"That doesn't answer my question. Can't you work in the parlor or something?" Am I really trying to throw this woman out of her own kitchen? he thought, but his head hurt and his leg hurt and his mind was full of terrible fragments of memory.

Kate gestured at the window. "The light is very good just here. Would you like a cup of tea?"

"I would not. Would the light not be the same in the parlor?"

Kate set the piece of bark she was working with down on the table and went to the hearth to get the kettle. "I do not care to work in the parlor."

Thomas watched Kate as she set the kettle on the table, pulled down a wooden box from the shelf, and added a pinch of dark leaves to a homely teapot. "Why not? Does it leak?"

This startled a laugh out of Kate, which was exactly what Thomas did not want. Kate laughing was not something a human heart, or at least not his human heart, could resist. She poured a stream of hot water into the teapot, for all the world as though he had not just refused her offer of tea.

"If you must know," Kate said, resuming her seat on the stool, "it makes me sad to look at my father's books. None of us are much for poetry except for Jake, and he's gone at sea. I think Papa's copy of Milton is growing mushrooms."

Halverton thought their father was a layabout, Thomas recalled, startled. Thomas himself had not been in the habit of thinking of poetry as a corrupting influence. "Did Henry—er—" He stopped, unsure how to ask if Henry had been exposed to a disastrous amount of poetry at a young age.

"Henry takes after Grandad," Kate said serenely. "Grandad had a collection of agronomy pamphlets which he was very proud of, but he didn't read otherwise. Papa and Grandad never really understood each other. Papa—well, Papa found Song of Songs in the grammar school Bible when he was eight, and he was never quite right after."

"Thy lips are like a thread of scarlet, and thy speech is comely," Thomas quoted, before he could stop himself.

Kate turned toward him, her eyes warm and her mouth ready to smile, but her face stilled and became thoughtful when she saw his expression.

Thomas flushed. "I'm sure every boy looks it over at some point," he muttered. "All that talk of … comeliness." He swallowed uncomfortably. He had also been about eight when he had found that book in the family Bible, and he had understood immediately that he was the Lover, not the Beloved.

Kate set a mug on the table and tipped the teapot over it. "Well, it led Papa straight on into Donne, and then there was nothing else that suited him but poetry."

"That had better not be for me," Thomas said suspiciously, as Kate added a healthy glug of milk to the mug from a small pitcher. "What's wrong with Donne?"

"There's nothing wrong with Donne," Kate said, holding the mug before her in both hands as she came toward the bed. "Papa was susceptible to notions, that's all."

"I don't want any tea," Thomas snapped, aware that he sounded childish, but Kate only stood in front of him, holding out the mug, her face calm.

"Did you read Donne?" she asked, as though this were a social call, and they both sat in the parlor together, stiff and starched, rather than her in a shabby housecoat and him in a state of half-undress. "How did you find him?"

"I read every book in the house," Thomas grumbled, reaching out to take the tea, unable to bear his own rudeness any longer. Kate, thankfully, did not stand over him while he drank it, but turned quickly away, crossing the kitchen again and picking up a new strip of bark and a long needle.

"Your parents were lovers of poetry?" Kate asked, punching holes in the edge of the strip.

Thomas hesitated, wondering how much he ought to say. He didn't think any of the Gravenors had ever moved in the same social circles in his parents, even when they had all been alive and living within ten miles of each other. "Not as such. My mother had notions that I ought to have a good education." Had he said too much? "I suppose your mother was the same."

"Maman," Kate said thoughtfully, "taught us dirty songs in French."

Thomas snorted a mouthful of tea.

"I am sorry. Do you need a handkerchief?"

"I do not. Why—why—"

"Papa thought it would be very nice if she could teach us French poetry—the French having a profound connection to the natural state of sensibility, you understand—er—only—Maman was not really the *feeling* sort of French person, more the *bah, fais ton travail* sort of French person, you see?"

Thomas, who had seen any number of front lines populated by any number of French farmers' sons, thought he did see. "Perhaps she would have gotten on with my mother. She was—" He searched for a word that neither revealed too much nor dug too deep. "— very practical."

"Maman taught me how to balance an account book," Kate said, briefly clutching the birch bark close to her chest.

She briefly looked so very young and so very lost, her blue eyes seeing someone who was very far away from her, that Thomas' mouth volunteered for him, "My mother taught me to ride."

That was too much, and Thomas regretted saying it immediately. It was not a skill he used very often, and he would be better off pretending he'd never acquired it. A yeoman farmer would not own a riding horse, and a normal boy would not learn to ride from his mother, unless she had been, for example, the daughter of a successful horse trader who had herself learned to ride as a toddler. There were only so many wealthy farmers in any county; there were certainly very few married to the daughters of notable dealers in horseflesh. Thomas was quite sure his had been the only such family in Copstone parish when he had been born. If Peter had not believed Thomas' lie about being from Cheshire, which the vicar surely had not, it would be the matter of a few minutes to figure out who Thomas was, who Thomas *must* be, if he knew this small tidbit about

Thomas' childhood.

And Thomas looked like his mother. He did not think any of the Gravenors were old enough to have been acquainted with her, but they certainly had local acquaintances who could recognize her profile in his face.

He had now been silent for several minutes, and Kate tried to break that silence. "Was she—"

"I'm very tired," Thomas said flatly. "Please leave me alone." And then, as though that was not rude enough, he pulled the coverlet over his head.

## CHAPTER TEN

Kate made her first cheese the next morning. Nonnette and Alouette hadn't yet calved, but she had milked Antoinette the last two days and saved the milk in a crock in the pantry. The pantry was so cold that she wasn't sure the milk was even sour enough to start the cheese, but she hauled the crock to the kitchen anyway.

She ought to have asked John Mary to kill Antoinette's little bullock, so they could have the meat and she could pull out the fourth stomach for rennet to set her curd. Calf stomach worked best. Maman had spoken vaguely of different plants used in France to make cheese—thistles, fig sap—but Kate had never tried any of these, and she didn't want to risk any milk when she had so little.

But Kate also wanted to keep the calf, as the first thing which had gone right this year. When John Mary had presented her with a fresh-killed lamb the day before, she hadn't asked where he had gotten it. It looked like a hawk had struck the poor thing, but the closest field with sheep in it belonged to Daniel Lately.

Now the lamb's fourth stomach was sitting in a jar

of salt water on a high shelf in the pantry, and she had made stew with the rest of it.

Dr. Holyoke had even eaten a bowl. She had thought he might refuse her cooking outright, after their strange conversation and his sudden angry reticence. She wondered whether it was especially difficult for him to talk about his mother, or if he resented Kate's prying into his personal history. His confidences had been stilted, reluctant, as if every sentence were a sharp piece of bone she drew out of his heart, liable to cut him as it emerged.

But he had produced that piece of Solomon's poetry like it lived in his lungs, his eyes burning, if possible, more intensely than they usually did. It was hard not to wonder—well, there was no use wondering. Kate was not the sort of woman who inspired men to poetry. She was a *fais ton travail* sort of woman. If she resented Papa for anything, it was infecting her mind, even a little bit, with the desire for poetry that she would never have.

Kate raked some coals to the front of the kitchen hearth and set a tripod over them, then ceremoniously set Maman's great cheese pot over the fire. She poured in the milk and spooned in some of the filtered liquid from the lamb's stomach. If all went well, the curd would be set in two hours, aided by the slow heat of the coals.

Kate set a lid over the milk and turned to ask the doctor if he would care for a cup of tea, but he was not in his bed. The coverlet and sheets were smooth, the pillow neatly lined up at the top of the mattress.

The front door swung open, admitting a blast of

cold air and her large, red-faced brother.

"Morning, Kate," Henry said.

"Good morning Henry," Kate said, a little breathlessly. "Henry, Dr. Holyoke isn't—"

But as she spoke, a dark-haired figure crutched after her brother, his splinted leg held stiffly above the ground.

"You're not wearing a hat," Kate gasped. It was not the right thing to say, but it was the first thing which came out of her suddenly numb lips.

Dr. Holyoke scowled at her.

"You'll catch cold!" Kate went on, feeling scared and not a little angry. He'd been so close to death when he'd arrived, limp and burning with fever, and she had been so relieved when he'd finally awakened. But if he opened his wound again, or, God forbid, fractured his still-fragile bone by putting too much weight on it—

"*I'm* not wearing a hat," Henry pointed out.

"You'll catch cold too," Kate said, twisting her hands in her apron. "Where *is* your hat, Henry?"

"He's not a child," snapped Dr. Holyoke. "Treat him with some respect."

"But your leg—"

Henry vanished into the parlor and reappeared with a chair, which he inserted beneath the doctor.

"My leg is fine," Dr. Holyoke said through tight lips. "I wanted to look at the body again."

"It isn't Christian to lie," Kate said reprovingly, swinging the iron arm with the half-full kettle over the coals at the back of the fireplace. The doctor couldn't have been more obviously in pain if he'd written it on his forehead. Kate hoped desperately he had not made his injuries worse.

"I thought you were nonconformists," Dr. Holyoke said, massaging the bridge of his nose with one hand. Henry appeared again with the little footstool that Papa had liked and put it under the doctor's splinted leg.

"I think nonconformists believe in Christ also," Kate said.

"Don't you *know* what nonconformists believe in?"

"Papa mostly believed in Shakespeare." Dr. Holyoke turned an outraged glance on her and she added hastily, "He liked George Herbert too."

Kate took down the tea box and put a tiny pinch into the pot. She had not rationed the precious leaves from the paper twist Peter had included in his last basket as carefully as she might have.

"Thank you, Henry," the doctor said behind her back. It was not the exasperated tone he used with Kate.

"You're welcome, sir," Henry said. "Why did you cut open the body's chest, sir?"

Kate drew in a sharp breath, her head flying up to interject, but Dr. Holyoke was already responding. "I wanted to see if there was anything wrong with his organs that might cause a man to die suddenly. As far as I could tell, there was no plaque in the arteries around the heart, and the liver was in fine condition."

"I see, sir," Henry said. "So not apoplexy, then?"

"It still could have been a brain storm," the doctor said. "Without the head there's no way of knowing. And the lungs are so full of water that I couldn't make anything out. There could have been a problem there, and I'd never know." He rubbed his chin thoughtfully.

"So," Henry said, sounding nervous. "It *could* have been an accident."

Kate frowned at him. Her brother was rarely nervous about anything.

"The head coming off was never an accident," Dr. Holyoke said dryly, but not unkindly. "About the man's death, though, I still couldn't say."

Kate watched Henry watch the doctor, and her heart gave a painful little twist. Henry *trusted* Dr. Holyoke, and what was more, she had seen nothing in the doctor's behavior so far to indicate he oughtn't. He had treated her brother as the intelligent, careful man Kate had always known him to be.

Kate knew that after nursing him for a week, she felt a certain tenderness toward Dr. Holyoke, but that was the same pity she might feel toward a sickly calf or a dog with a broken leg. The curious warmth in her chest now did not feel like pity.

The doctor stared into the fire, rubbing the thigh of his good leg, his eyebrows drawn low. "I wonder why the body only turned up now," he muttered. "It was clearly in that stream for a good while."

Henry flinched visibly.

That flinch brought Kate back to herself with a snap. During the autopsy, she had been looking at Henry when the doctor had mentioned the corpse's missing fingers. Her brother's eyes had grown very round, and his mouth had opened, as if he'd suddenly remembered something important. It might have nothing to do with the body. She certainly hoped it was nothing to do with the body, and indeed Henry often associated things that no one else would. Kate had meant to question him more closely, but had lost track in the hubbub of taking care of poor flustered Wendell, and then offering hospitality to Constable Fine, who was the sort of man to expect biscuits and tea in any house he stepped foot in, no matter how poor.

And then yesterday she had been so delighted with the birch logs and reeds that Henry had brought her that she had wanted to start making new molds and mats right away, and then she had had that strange, flustering conversation with Dr. Holyoke, and she had forgotten again to question her brother.

"Henry," Kate said carefully. "Did you notice anything about the body yourself?"

Henry started. "What? What do you mean?"

Kate's heart sank. Henry had absolutely noticed something he thought was important; he wouldn't equivocate if he hadn't. Now the question was whether he would tell Kate.

Dr. Holyoke looked between the siblings, but he didn't say anything.

"Well, you sat up a bit when Dr. Holyoke mentioned the body was missing some fingers," Kate said gently.

"Anybody might be missing some fingers," Henry said.

"Ye-es," Kate said. "I suppose that's true. Did that make you think of someone else who was missing some fingers?"

"And anyone might *forget* about some missing fingers," Henry said, "if one was very busy with other work, what with the ditches and all."

"Of course," Kate said soothingly, while her heart stuttered into a gallop. Where had Henry encountered disembodied digits? "The ditches are very important, Henry. I know that."

"And if a body has already lost his fingers, there's nothing I could do about it," Henry said, as though he were reassuring himself.

"Henry," Dr. Holyoke said in a soft voice, "who had already lost his fingers?"

Don't rush him, Kate thought very hard at the doctor. He won't be able to think clearly if he's upset.

"Well," Henry said. "Well." He ran his hands through his dandelion fluff hair, making it stand up on end. "I suppose—I suppose—I don't know *who*—"

Kate shot Dr. Holyoke a warning look, but Dr. Holyoke was watching her brother's face and did not see it.

"I suppose," Henry said. "Kate. Do you remember—on the night we both came back to the farm?"

"Yes," Kate allowed, "I do remember that night." Am I supposed to remember something in particular about it? she wondered. Because I was too sad and tired to notice anything beyond it being wet and cold and dark.

"I was carrying Dr. Holyoke," Henry said. "I *was* carrying Dr. Holyoke. I couldn't put him down, you understand?" His voice took on an extra urgency in those last few words.

"I understand," Kate said, meeting her brother's eyes.

"I've been very busy with the ditches," Henry

reminded her.

"No one blames you for the ditches, Henry," Dr. Holyoke said, quietly and firmly.

That interjection, rather than oversetting Henry as Kate had feared it might do, seemed to steady him. He nodded to Dr. Holyoke, then turned back to his sister. "Well, I met you just after I'd gone through the stream, carrying the—sir, *you*, sir, because you weren't fit to walk any farther."

"Yes," Kate said, relieved that she could help Henry with this part. "You said you'd walked from Wolverhampton. You were wet to the knee and muddy. I thought you'd just come up the bank. I was so worried you'd catch cold."

Now Dr. Holyoke was glowering at her, as though he thought mentioning the possibility of colds would silence her brother. Kate did not have a face made for glowering, but she wrinkled her nose at him.

"I thought I saw something in the stream," Henry said.

Kate swallowed hard and glanced at Dr. Holyoke. Lines of strain appeared around the man's mouth. She cleared her throat.

"It was dark, and I wasn't sure," Henry said.

"What do you think you saw?" Dr. Holyoke asked.

Henry stared past both of them, flexing and curling his fingers once, twice, three times. Finally, he said, "I thought I saw a hand. I thought—there was a hand in the stream, sticking on from underneath the alders into the crossing, and I tripped. It was dark and I couldn't stop. The hand—there might have been a body, but I couldn't *see* a body, and I couldn't stop. The hand was definitely dead."

Kate wasn't sure she could breathe. Fred Halverton and Wendell Driver had pulled the body from beneath those same alders a scant two days prior.

"I didn't stop to look at it, because the doctor—sir—was in such a bad way, and I thought, well, Dr. Holyoke—sir—isn't dead yet, and whoever this hand belongs to is. And then I came up the bank, and there *you* were, Kate, and I didn't have time to think about it any more."

Dr. Holyoke looked like he wanted to say something that would make Henry clam up. "Of course," Kate said wildly. "I—well—yes—I'm sure that was very distracting and all. Did you—did you think of telling me, or John Mary, perhaps? About the hand?"

What if someone found out Henry had seen the body and said nothing for weeks? she thought. What if they decided Henry was hiding something?

"I forgot," Henry said, his face going as red as a brick. "There's been the ditches and the cows and all. And I couldn't stop," he added, a note of pleading in his voice. "I was carrying the doctor, and I couldn't stop."

"Of course you couldn't, dearest," Kate said. She breathed in deeply through her nose and willed her stomach to stop roiling. No one who knew Henry would think him capable of deception, she reminded herself. But not everyone knew Henry.

"I'm sure I shouldn't try to make things more complicated," Dr. Holyoke said. "And I would not like to think there are so many unclaimed corpses rolling around in rural Shropshire. But Henry, are you *sure* the hand you saw in the stream belongs to the body in the woodshed?"

"Yes," Henry said. "Well, I think so." He stretched out his hands in front of himself and stared at them intently for minute, folding one thumb down and then the other. "Yes," he said again, this time more confidently. "This one." He held up his right hand. "The hand was missing half the thumb on this hand, when I saw it. And *you* said, sir, during the autopsy, that the body was missing some fingers, and when I looked close I saw it was the same thumb that was gone."

"That's some small comfort, I suppose," the doctor muttered.

Kate thought he was missing the point. "So whoever it was—is—he already didn't have his right thumb, two weeks ago," she said.

"So the dogs got it to early," Dr. Holyoke said, lifting one shoulder in a slight shrug.

"But—"

Dr. Holyoke cut her off. "If it's the same body, then it all comes to the same. I'd rather not have people questioning why Henry didn't say anything before now. I'd rather not have anyone questioning Henry at all, to be frank."

He had a point, and Kate bit her lip. But Henry wasn't done talking.

"I don't think," Henry started. His face had gone even redder. "I don't think the thumb had been bitten off, like. It wasn't bloody. It was dark, but I think I would have noticed that. It jabbed me in the ankle," he added. "Real stiff, that hand was. That's why I noticed it."

Dr. Holyoke went very still. "Henry, you've carried bodies out of my surgery after they died," he said. "Do you think the hand was that sort of stiff? Was it in rigor mortis?"

Henry stared at the wall. "It might have been," he said.

"What's rigor mortis?" Anne's voice asked from the stairs, in tones of great interest.

Kate spun toward her, horrified. "*Anne!* You were supposed to have left already! You were supposed to have left *yesterday*. What will the Telfords think?"

"I sent a note," Anne said, but there was something shifty in her face. "You were saying about rigor mortis?" She jumped down the last two steps into the kitchen, stuffing her braid under her one and only bonnet.

"Rigor mortis is the stiffening of the muscles in a corpse, usually starting within four hours of death," Dr. Holyoke said calmly, as though Anne had been there the whole time. *Had* Anne been there the whole time? "Two days following death, the rigidity ceases."

"Please don't tell her these things," Kate pleaded.

"Even when the body has been in water?" Anne said, a terrifyingly thoughtful look on her face.

"More or less," Dr. Holyoke said.

"No more! I'm sure she doesn't need to know any more," Kate said.

"So he—whoever he was—had just been killed when Henry tripped on him," Anne said, her eyes glinting.

"*Anne,*" Kate said, foreboding curdling in her stomach. She put her hands on her hips and gave Anne her most authoritative glare. "I don't want you to go about asking questions. This isn't a game."

"I don't think it's a game," Anne said. "Aren't you worried about there being a murder this close to the farm?"

"*Anne.* You don't know it was a murder," Kate hissed.

"It was probably a murder," Dr. Holyoke said.

"You're *not helping*," Kate said, spreading the glare in his direction. "Whatever happened, Anne, you mustn't give anyone the excuse to come digging around the farm. I don't want any stories going around about John Mary, or Henry. Do you understand?"

Anne was already moving toward the door. "I won't tell anyone anything they shouldn't know."

"Anne! Don't put this about." Kate grabbed for Anne's arm, but her sister ducked away from her.

"I know what I'm doing."

"*Promise me!*"

"Don't worry!" Anne dodged her hand again, spun around Henry, and yanked open the front door.

"Anne—"

But Anne was out the door and running

"I'm sorry! I'm late!" she yelled over her shoulder.

"But breakfast!" Kate yelled back. Anne had already disappeared around the big elm at the edge of the farmyard.

Kate set about making toast. Henry fled upstairs, apparently overwhelmed by his interrogation, however brief.

Thomas slumped back in the chair, thinking. The

man whose corpse was now in the woodshed had died two weeks ago, probably the very day he himself had arrived in this strange house, and that man had lost half his right thumb long enough before dying that it had healed over. That gave them an identifying feature to ask about and a time period to pay attention to, should they continue to involve themselves in this line of questioning.

He was not at all sure that either the Gravenors or he had any business mucking about with this affair. The thought that someone had chopped the head off a body that was already dead with a very sharp blade was an unpleasant thought; the thought that someone had killed a living, breathing man by slicing his head off was a terrifying one. It was mid-morning, perhaps the most cheerful hour of the day, and Thomas still had half a mind to tell Henry to go fetch his younger sister back to the farmhouse and bar the door. How much strength did it take to decapitate a human? Most of the examples Thomas had seen during the war had been in the path of heavy artillery. He'd seen a few poor sods hacked to death by a cavalry saber, but generally their heads stayed attached.

Did the lack of other injuries on this body mean something? Had the headless man been surprised?

Was he obsessing over the murdered man because it was less painful than thinking about what his future might be, now that it had spun out of his control?

"Toast," Kate said, and she was standing so close that her skirt brushed his thigh. "I haven't had time to make more butter, but there was honey in Peter's last basket."

Thomas jerked out of his reverie, the motion sending another painful jolt through his broken leg. "Jesus, woman. Don't you make any sound when you walk?"

The words hung in the air, unfathomably rude, ruder yet than any of the rude things he had said to Kate so far, particularly when directed at a woman who had probably saved his life, who was the sister of a man who had most definitely saved his life multiple times in the past three months.

"I'm wearing boots," Kate said, nonplussed. "Would you like milk in your tea?"

"You keep creeping up on me," Thomas said shortly. It was an unreasonable thing to say, and he knew it was, knew somewhere very deep down that his rage was not at this small, perfect woman but at the world that had dragged him before her in this broken and helpless state. He wanted Kate far away, as far away from his humiliation as she could get.

He could *smell* her.

"I'll try to make more noise," Kate said, a little laugh in her voice.

"Stop it," Thomas heard himself say angrily. She was refusing to understand, and it infuriated him. "I've been a terrible guest, and no friend to you. You've no call to be kind."

Kate stared at him, the laughter visibly draining out of her countenance. A divot appeared between her enormous blue eyes. She was so short that even sitting, his eyes were nearly on a level with hers.

Thomas' mouth went dry. Her face was very close.

"I am grateful to your brother for saving my life,"

he lied. He was grateful to Henry for many things, but not that. "But his action does not obligate you to me."

After a moment she reached down, took his hand —oh lord, he was going to feel her touch for hours, maybe days—and wrapped his fingers around the edge of the small plate she was holding.

"Eat your toast," she said.

"I do not want your kindness," Thomas said, and it did not sound like a lie even to his own ears.

"There's the honey," Kate said, gesturing.

"Are you listening to me?" he demanded.

"Dr. Holyoke." Kate breathed in deeply and then let it out.

Her eyes caught him and held him, and for a moment there was nothing in the world except endless blue.

"Dr. Holyoke, I have no husband, no children, no money, and no parents. I am too short and too plain to have dignity, too practical to have principles, and too tired to have much hope. All I have is kindness." She let go of his hand, and he almost dropped the plate of toast. "I understand that it is not what you want, but you are not in a position to choose."

She turned away from him and went back to the fire to tend her cheese.

That night, Kate lay in bed, staring up at the piece of canvas John Mary had tacked to the underside of the leaking roof. Henry slept on the other side of the room, snoring quietly.

The curd had set up well, she thought. She'd had enough to fill three of her new molds, which were now draining into a pan on the kitchen table, covered by a tent of dishcloths. Hopefully there was still some of the proper white mold lying dormant on the old reeds she had salvaged from Maman's mats. In the morning, she'd flip each round of cheese again and salt each one. Then she would collect the whey from the pan and use it in her next batch of bread.

If she didn't close her eyes, she wouldn't see Dr. Holyoke's dark gaze boring into her.

There was still a crock of salt in the pantry, left over from Maman. There was barely enough to finish off this batch, but John Mary had promised to buy Kate more next time he went to Southbridge.

If she filled her mind with the details of her cheese, the exact amount of salt she would measure out into her mortar and crush to a fine grit, she would not think of the snarl in Dr. Holyoke's voice, and the foolish thing she had said in response. Seven years of being married to Will ought to have taught her that there was no point in trying to have the last word, no point in trying to disagree at all. She might have had a point, but that had never mattered to a man who wasn't one of her brothers.

Kate rolled to her side, trying to find a comfortable position. There was a lump in the mattress where Maman had darned it long ago, and the seam kept digging at her hip.

It wasn't as if she wanted the doctor to be grateful for her nursing, only—only—

Kate rolled to her other side. She should have kept her mouth shut. She knew how hellish being in close quarters with a man who despised her could be, and yet she had still not been able to swallow down that retort.

The worst part was that she hadn't been exaggerating in the slightest. She was a twenty-four-year-old widow who had suffered three miscarriages and one stillbirth. Even before it was clear that she was barren, Will had often commented that she was lucky he had married her. He had said it to win arguments, but Kate knew he was basically correct. Her nose was too short, her upper lip too long, and her chin too weak. Her father had squandered whatever respect the Gravenor name had once had on his poetry and his French wife.

The future stretched out in front of Kate as a dim, gray cloud of nothingness. She could have respect, love, kindness inside these walls, from her own siblings, but what would happen to her when they married and left her? What if John Mary lost the house, or its ancient timbers finally gave up and fell in on themselves? What Kate had left to offer the world was her usefulness and her good nature. If the world did not want those things, she would have nothing at all.

Dr. Holyoke is not the world, she reminded herself. He does not want what the world wants.

That should have been a cold, hard thought, a miserable thought, that the doctor did not want what little service she could do for him. And yet she could not shake the feeling that he *did* want Kate, wanted something from her that had very little to do with fetching cups of tea and bandaging his leg.

# CHAPTER ELEVEN

"What are you doing?" Thomas asked.

He sat across the kitchen table from Kate. He could feel yesterday's foray out to the woodshed in every pulse of blood through his damaged leg. The pain had woken him up; every unused muscle ached mightily, especially those he had used to hold his splint clear of the ground. He had hurt too much to refuse when Kate had brought him willow bark tea. He had silently watched her roll up a blanket and wrap it around the hot kettle, and he had continued to not comment as she lay the hot cloth over his leg.

Kate had kept plying him with willow bark and reheating the quilt until lunchtime, when she disappeared outside with a loaf of bread and a covered bowl of soup for her brothers. Thomas wondered, in a vague sort of way, why he had still not seen nor heard the fabled John Mary.

Thomas had felt well enough by then to struggle out of bed and crutch himself over to the table, where Kate had left another bowl and half-loaf for him. Eating slowly, he stared at the three pale moons of new cheese lined up along the far side of the table. The upper surface of each bore the crisp impression of the reed drainage mats they lay upon.

When Kate had returned to the kitchen and taken down a mortar and pestle, Thomas found his eyes creeping toward her as she worked. He had hoped she would be angry with him; her patience was deflating. He had snarled at Kate, and to what end? He would have liked to say he was protecting her from himself, keeping her from developing any silly notions or tenderness toward him, but he was flattering himself that hers were the feelings which needed protecting. Kate, for all that she was more than ten—he grimaced —years younger than him, had lived in the world. She was not kind because she was naive, but because she was defiant.

He felt ashamed of his own cowardice.

"I am crushing the salt," Kate said finally, giving the pestle another twist. Thomas' eyes shot to her hands. "It soaks into the cheese better if it's finely ground."

"What's wrong with a sweet cheese?" Thomas asked.

"If they're not salty enough, they'll spoil while aging," Kate said.

She did not look at him, and Thomas found he did not care for that. He wanted—no, he had no business wanting anything. The sky was overcast today, so he was spared the sight of the sunlight striking her magnificent hair alight. But the day was also mild, so she had eschewed Henry's giant, form-obscuring coat for a shawl she had wrapped snugly over her bust. Kate tended toward plumpness, and she had quite a lot of bust to be wrapped. Thomas forced his eyes back to the cheeses.

Kate took a pinch of salt and rolled it between her fingers, humming softly. Apparently satisfied, she sprinkled the tops of the cheeses, then pressed grains of salt against the vertical sides with quick, sure movements. Thomas' eyes were caught again, and he watched her fingers work steadily, pinching, pressing.

He cast about for something else to say.

"The first day I woke properly from the fever," he said, as she moved surely from cheese to cheese, "what was the song you and Henry sang to each other?"

"Song?"

"It was about Antoinette," Thomas said.

"*Oh*," Kate said, and she laughed. "It's the Carmagnole. It's a song the sans-culottes sang in Paris when—when—well, you know. When they were ridding themselves of Their Majesties. Maman taught it to us when we were small." She flipped the cheeses neatly, one, two, three.

Thomas remembered Kate's sadness when talking about her mother, and he spoke cautiously. "Your mother was a revolutionary? A Republican?"

"No," Kate said, shaking her head. "No. She—oh, I don't know. I shouldn't say. She didn't talk about France, except about cheese. I know her mother taught her to make this cheese I'm making now, and her father took care of the cattle. The two lead cows were named —erm—Mouse and Rabbit."

"She taught you to look after the cows," Thomas guessed.

Kate began sprinkling salt again. The pleasant

                    *J. Winifred Butterworth*

sour-sweet aroma of the cheese wafted up to Thomas' nose. "Yes and no. Papa wasn't good at moving the livestock, but the cows liked him, because they could eat the books and apples out of his pockets, and he wouldn't make them go anywhere they didn't want to go. They never dared such impertinence with Maman. Your mother was good with horses?"

Kate had three freckles on the back of her right hand. Thomas wondered what it would be like to press his lips to each one, with the same firmness Kate used to press the salt into the sides of the cheese. "What? Yes. I suppose she was."

I shouldn't say any more, he thought.

I'm already damned, he thought.

"My father had a good eye for horseflesh, but my mother was the one who broke the yearlings to saddle," Thomas said stiffly. It was not a memory he had thought of in a very long time: his mother, very tall and lean for a woman, standing in the middle of a paddock, spinning slowly as a young chestnut mare trotted in circles around her. She had not been a demonstrative woman, but he remembered her gentleness with the yearlings. And she had been very good at training; those horses had fetched high prices from gentlemen in all the surrounding counties.

"To side-saddle? I wouldn't have thought there were so many ladies in this part of Shropshire."

"She rode astride," Thomas said. "She was … eccentric." He supposed that eccentricity was why his mother had not been overly bothered that her only child insisted on wearing trousers. Perhaps if she had lived longer, she would have understood that Thomas' reasons for doing so were quite different than her own, but she had not.

Except, Thomas thought, his heart doing a peculiar little cartwheel, I don't actually know what her reasons were.

"I suppose," Kate said slowly, "that Maman was also … eccentric." She finished salting the cheeses and covered each one with a large bowl. "She did not especially prefer *institutions*. Not king, country, revolution, God——" Here she glanced at Thomas, apparently checking his face for shock. He only raised his eyebrows. "She did not trust many people."

Thomas could appreciate that, and yet somehow the thought of Kate being raised by an isolated foreigner in this decrepit building made his chest tighten. "Is that what she taught you?"

"I haven't lived through massacres and been forced to flee my country," Kate said mildly, turning the question aside. She turned away from him, wiping her hands on her apron.

Between one thought and the next, Thomas leaned forward and took Kate's wrist. Her skin was smooth and warm there. She turned and met his eyes.

We weren't done speaking, Thomas' brain finally suggested, as a reason for his completely unreasonable behavior.

I'm a rude bastard, he counter-suggested to his brain.

But Kate did not pull away from him. She only studied his face, with the air of someone looking at a map of a strange country for the first time. Thomas found himself rendered speechless by that study.

Was she staring at his mouth? It felt like she was staring at his mouth.

Kate's lips parted.

"Daniel Lately's curricle is coming down the road!" Anne's voice floated through the parlor window from somewhere outside.

The horrible combination of those horrible words hooked into Thomas' brain and dragged him back into the present moment.

"*What?*" Thomas shouted. He dropped Kate's wrist. "*What?*"

"Anne, aren't you supposed to be at work?" Kate yelled.

How did Cousin Daniel find out that I am here? Thomas thought, his stomach churning. None of the siblings talk to anyone, except Peter. Did Peter mention me in church? It must have been Peter. I'm going to kill him, but if Cousin Daniel finds me first—

"*Damn,*" Kate said fervently. Thomas blinked at her; it had not occurred to him that Kate could curse. "Maybe he's going to see the Halvertons?" she called toward the window.

"Eleanor's with him," Anne said, her voice moving around to the side of the kitchen.

"So he's pretending it's a social call," Kate said. "Drat and blast."

"*He can't be allowed to see me,*" Thomas said.

"He'll expect tea and cakes and probably whipped cream, for all the privilege of his esteemed company," Kate went on, uncharacteristically sarcastic.

"*Kate,*" Thomas hissed, and the sound of her given name on his lips made her pause and look at him again.

How could he explain? There was so much, and if Kate hadn't understood immediately when she washed him— "I know Daniel Lately," he said between clenched teeth. "And he knows me. He cannot see me, or know that I am alive, or all the kindnesses you have shown me in the past two weeks will have been for nothing."

Kate stared at him for a moment longer, before she shook her head and straightened her shoulders. "Anne, come and help me take Dr. Holyoke upstairs."

"Won't he ask to see your guest?" Thomas asked, his mind spinning.

"You've had a turn for the worse today after over-exerting yourself yesterday," Kate said promptly. "Will he recognize your name?"

"Not if he doesn't see me," Thomas said, after a moment. "I—used a different name, when he knew me."

The front door flew open. "I'll hit him with a stick if he tries to go upstairs," Anne said, looking very eager to carry out this threat. "Or send Antoinette after him."

"Less talking, more helping," Kate ordered. "And *why* aren't you at your job?"

"Mrs. Telford sent me home," Anne said, looking over Kate's head. "Are we carrying him?"

"*No,*" Thomas snarled.

The stairs up to the second floor were very narrow, so Anne went before and Kate followed close behind while Thomas painfully levered himself up a step at a time with his makeshift crutches. He jarred his splinted leg twice, almost falling the second time, but Kate put her shoulder against the back of his good thigh and stood steady until he regained his balance. It was humiliating, and only the thought of Cousin Daniel bearing inexorably down on the house kept Thomas from snarling in rage and pain. He felt sick.

At the top of the stairs, Anne gestured to a large bed partly obscured by moth-eaten draperies. The house was apparently too old to have hallways; the stair led directly into the main bedroom. "You can sit here."

Kate looked at her younger sister, and Anne blushed. "Well, it's not as if anyone is using it," Anne said, sounding defensive.

"Through here," Kate said, pointing to a low door behind the fireplace. "There are fewer leaks in the back bedrooms."

Thomas allowed himself to be herded by the sisters into a smaller room, this one with two beds along the wall and a piece of canvas pinned to the underside of the thatch overhead. Another door at the back of this room presumably led into the last bedroom, all in a row like three siblings shoulder to shoulder. His mind spun.

"Why is Cou—why is Daniel Lately here?" he asked. Kate had not seemed surprised to hear about his visit; was there some other reason, besides hunting Thomas, that he might come to the Gravenor house?

"He wants to buy the farm, and he thinks he can bully Kate into bullying John Mary into saying yes to him," Anne said.

"Really?" Kate said, sounding surprised.

"That's what Eleanor thinks, anyway," Anne said.

"Who is Eleanor?" Thomas asked.

"When did you last talk to Eleanor?" Kate asked, a

note of suspicion entering her voice.

"Oh, ah. Well, that's what I heard she thinks," Anne said. "But we'd better tidy up the parlor right away," Anne said over her shoulder, already disappearing into the larger bedroom. The sound of her thick-soled boots clomping down the stairs echoed through the house.

"*Anne!*" Kate yelped, picking up her skirts and running after her sister.

Thomas put his head in his hands.

Daniel Lately was a tall, distinguished-looking gentleman, his thick white hair combed back from a high forehead. He wore an old-fashioned black suit and carried a gold-headed cane. His overall manner was that of a seagull waiting to rip a sweet out of a child's unsuspecting hand.

Kate and Anne had only just finished sweeping the parlor and scraping the worst of the dust off the settee when the sound of hooves had come from the yard. Kate had darted into the kitchen to make tea and hack what remained of the bread into presentable slices, while Anne shepherded Mr. Lately and his ward, Eleanor, into the musty parlor and bade them make themselves comfortable.

Kate supposed they were lucky that it had taken this long for the old monster to decide to call under some pretext or another. He had been an irregular visitor at the Easting house, during which occasions Will had plied Mr. Lately with Kate's baking in a futile attempt to curry favor, while Kate herself had been told in no uncertain terms to take herself out of the way of such important manly conversations. Her husband had always treated Daniel Lately with a deference bordering on obsequiousness, and Kate knew her late husband's behavior had made her hate that gentleman more than was his due.

"Sit up straight, Eleanor," Mr. Lately snarled. "Even if your surroundings do not require it, you at least ought to do our family credit."

And Daniel Lately was due quite a lot, Kate thought. "Miss Lately, will you take some bread and butter?"

"Yes, please," Eleanor said.

Eleanor was nearly as tall and thin as her guardian, though her hair and eyes were both black and shiny. There couldn't be more than a dozen men in the parish who were as tall as Eleanor, and probably no more than a half-dozen who were taller. She was a year older than Anne, at eighteen, but she had very little of Anne's self-assurance. Kate had never been quite sure of Eleanor's relationship to the old man, but there were rumors that she was the child of some unfortunate cousin who had come to a bad end.

"You don't need any bread and butter," Mr. Lately snapped. "You'll grow fat." He looked significantly at Kate, who was much shorter and rounder than anyone of the Lately lineage.

Eleanor watched Mr. Lately out of the corner of her eye, her shoulders hunched and her hands tight around her teacup. They sat side by side on the ancient settee, which Kate was quite sure had at least one live mouse presently in its cushions. Anne had lit the fire, but the chimney didn't draw well from this side. The room had become rather smoky.

Mr. Lately stared at the plate of bread and butter Kate had put on the table with barely-concealed contempt. She half-wished the last basket from Peter had contained more of those lovely lemon biscuits Mrs. Plunkett made, except Daniel Lately did not deserve lemon biscuits.

"Is there no sugar for the tea?" he asked.

"There is not. And to what do we owe the pleasure of your company, Mr. Lately?" Kate asked.

Out of the corner of her eye, she saw Eleanor mouth something to Anne, who sat on a chair just behind Kate. She could not see if Anne mouthed anything back.

That was another thing for Kate to worry about, once she had gotten through this unwelcome visit. Why hadn't Anne been at her job at the Telford farm? Anne and Eleanor had always been friendly, or at least as friendly as anyone could be with Eleanor when she was rarely allowed to leave the house, but Anne had clearly gotten word of this visit from someone, and that someone had to be Eleanor. Try as she might, Kate could construct no route to the Telford farm which went past the Lately house.

"—understand you have a guest," Mr. Lately said. Kate shook herself and tried to focus on the conversation.

"Yes," she said, staring at one of his winged eyebrows. "Dr. Holyoke has been here for two weeks as he recovers his health." She held her breath, but no obvious flash of recognition crossed Daniel Lately's face when he heard the name.

"I had hoped to meet the esteemed doctor," Mr. Lately said.

"I fear our guest is resting. He returned to England after a serious injury, and it troubles him." She hesitated, then decided that the situation called for brutal conversational tactics. "No doubt you have heard of the body discovered in our stream three days ago."

Mr. Lately did not rise to this bait. "I'm sure that isn't an appropriate subject to bring up in front of two young girls," he snapped.

Kate was certain that Anne had already snuck into the woodshed to get a good look at the corpse, and based on the horrified, inquisitive look on Eleanor's face, she would have very much liked to discuss the dead man as well. When the girl saw that Kate was looking at her, she went pink and bowed her head.

Kate gave a little cough. "Of course. But you will understand that we are still all in disarray."

"Constable Fine said your doctor was well enough to do an autopsy," Mr. Lately said, his eyes very cold.

"Yes. I'm afraid that Dr. Holyoke overextended himself, which is why he is not well enough to receive visitors. Will you have more tea?" She took a sip of her own cup and winced. This was the third steeping from these leaves, and it was very watery.

Mr. Lately bared his teeth in an expression that was certainly not a smile. "Do you suppose the doctor will make a full recovery?"

"I don't think he's that tired," Kate said, taken aback.

"I *meant,* will he recover from his broken leg," Mr. Lately said. "I am given to understand it was a very serious injury."

"Erm," Kate said. She wasn't sure what the point of this line of inquiry was, but she was sure she would not like it.

"I see that you do not wear mourning for your husband," Mr. Lately added.

"I haven't left the farm for three weeks," Kate said. She thought about adding that she owned no black clothing and could not afford to buy new fabric or dye, but why should she reveal herself to be so pathetic before this awful man?

"I hope you do not imagine that you will right your family's finances by an advantageous marriage," Mr. Lately said. He had not yet taken a sip of his tea, but now he set down the cup with a *crack*. "A man with any prospects at all would only unite his future with yours were he terribly deceived about your character and ability to bear him children, and a Christian neighbor must be moved to correct that deception."

Eleanor looked faintly green, and Kate heard a smothered gasp from Anne.

Ah, Kate thought. And this is why he is here. "I have no reason to suppose Dr. Holyoke intends such a thing." She also had no reason to suppose that the doctor had any money at his disposal, but perhaps Mr. Lately imagined there would be a military pension.

"You would do better by all your relations to encourage your irresponsible brother to sell to me, rather than try to ensnare an innocent man," Mr. Lately went on. "I of course cannot offer the price for the land I was willing to give the summer before last, but you are hardly in a situation to turn down any money."

He looked pointedly around the room, his eyes lingering on the crumbling plaster and cracked window panes.

"You cannot imagine that I could tell my brother what to do with his property," Kate said, in as mild a voice as she could muster. She took another sip of weak tea.

"This house is ready to collapse in on itself," Mr. Lately said, staring at her with his seagull eyes. "Where would your family be then?"

Kate very much did not like the tone of his voice, threat heavy in every word. But before she could think of a suitably noncommittal response, Anne shot to her feet.

"Oh, Mr. Lately. I think El—er—Miss Lately is unwell."

"Nonsense," he said. "Eleanor is fine. Don't interrupt me, girl."

"It's very smoky in here," Anne went on in her loudest voice. "I'm sure Eleanor is going to faint. Eleanor, why don't you come outside with me. You need fresh air."

"Oh, thank you," Eleanor said, springing up from the settee with enough alacrity to belie any claim of illness. "Sir, I'll be back in just a moment."

"No, you will *not*," Daniel Lately hissed. He would have grabbed her wrist, but Kate, unsure of what her sister was doing but sure that Anne was putting this show on for a reason, shoved the plate of bread into his hands.

"*Do* eat some bread, and *do* come look at my cheeses," Kate said brightly. "I've decided to start making them again, just as my mother used to do. Do you recall her white cheeses? She won a prize at Copstone Fair …"

Eleanor was just able to twist away from her guardian and follow Anne out the front door.

Kate was then obligated to spend an unpleasantly long period of time showing Daniel Lately her three cheeses. He made several nasty comments and stuck a finger in one. Kate thought about the body in the woodshed, about the strength it would take to cut a man's head off so cleanly. She did not let herself pursue that line of thought, but instead imagined shutting Mr. Lately up with the body and leaving him there, as she prattled on about salt and milk, until Anne appeared again in the door with Eleanor behind her, her face very white and her eyes very wide.

"Sir, I feel ill," Eleanor said to Daniel Lately, clutching herself with her skinny arms. "I fear I have caught the head-cold which the cook had two days ago. Might we go home?"

Mr. Lately spat out several things about ungrateful young chits, who demanded to be taken on visits and then whined the whole way, and snatched up his hat and his stick with poor grace.

"I trust you will bring my *generous* offer to your brother's attention," he said to Kate. "I bid you good day." He turned and strode out the door before she could respond.

"Good day," Kate said, smiling through clenched teeth. John Mary must have offered to break his nose for him, she thought. Otherwise I can't see why he'd bother with bullying me. She thought of the cheeses and gritted her teeth even harder. She could probably scoop out the dent he had left in her cheese with a spoon and fill it in with new curd. Once the bloomy mold grew up over it, no one would know that his dirty old fingers had touched it.

"Good day," Eleanor whispered, shooting her a panicked look she could not interpret. "Kate—Mrs. Easting—"

"Let us *go*, Eleanor," shouted Mr. Lately from the yard.

It was not until the sound of the curricle's wheels rolling down the drive came through the kitchen window that Anne whirled to face Kate and grab both her hands.

"*Kate*," she yelped.

"Anne," Kate said wearily. "What—"

"Eleanor knows who the dead man is," Anne said. "And we must get him buried right away, before anyone else finds out."

## CHAPTER TWELVE

Thomas watched the tall, black-haired girl climb into the curricle next to Cousin Daniel from the tiny window in the back bedroom. All his limbs felt like they were made from lead. There was no question of who she must be; she was the right age, had the right coloring, and, when she turned her head to one side, the right profile. The Holyoke nose, and the Holyoke chin. His mother's profile.

Eleanor, Kate had said. They had named the child Eleanor, after his mother. It was fitting, he supposed.

He crutched back to the small bed and lowered himself painfully down onto the mattress.

Your own blood will destroy you, he thought, but then: I left that child there, in that house. I did not know, but I did it.

With Cousin Daniel.

He stared at a knot in the floorboards, his mind numb and blank. He had gone to the window finally in desperation to get away from the smell of Kate that permeated her bedsheets. It was far too easy to imagine how warm and soft she would be under her clothes when he sat upon her bed, and now, for his sins, he could not even think of that.

"Dr. Holyoke?"

His head jerked up. Kate stood at the door, twisting her hands in her apron. Her eyes were enormous and very blue in her pale face. She took a hesitant step into the bedroom.

"Could you overhear anything we said?" Kate asked him.

"Eleanor is my daughter," Thomas said.

Kate opened her mouth and closed it. She turned to look behind her, then kept turning until she made a full circle and was facing him again.

I think I've just jumped off a cliff, Thomas thought, and the nothing I am feeling right now is the air rushing past me before I hit the ground.

Kate abruptly dropped onto the bed next to him. The weight of her small body made the mattress dip, and the thigh of his good leg pressed tight against her thigh. She was, indeed, very soft.

"The man whose body was found was one of Daniel Lately's hired hands, Rob Baker. Eleanor recognized him from his missing thumb. She overheard Mr. Lately send him to *talk* to John Mary about selling the farm three weeks ago. He hasn't been seen since then."

Silence filled the bedroom for what felt like a very long time.

"Why are you telling me this?" Thomas said finally, staring at a bit of crumbled plaster on the opposite wall.

"Well," Kate said, then stopped. She twisted her hands in her apron, her brow furrowed in thought.

Then, very carefully, she asked, "Who is Eleanor's ... other ... other ... other parent?"

Thomas found he could not look away from the shadow the broken plaster had left.

Kate was quiet, and he hoped for a moment that maybe she had not understood, that she was rearranging her understanding to accommodate the apparently well-known fact that one needed an operational cock to go about life in trousers, but then she went on, warily. "Who is Eleanor's ... other ... father?"

She knows, he thought, his stomach freezing into a solid block of ice. And then, he realized: She's known all along. His whole body tensed, as though he could flee with his half-healed leg and no money, as if there were any place safe for a battered man such as himself. He needed to correct Kate's assumption before it sank in, to lie convincingly enough that she would be embarrassed of her mistake. He turned, the better to press her back into the version of reality he could tolerate, the better to cow her with the force of his personality.

But when he opened his mouth, the words which came out were not denial.

"Daniel Lately is the father of the child I left in my parents' house eighteen years ago," he said.

Kate sucked in her breath sharply.

Thomas' mouth continued on without him. "I thought she was already dead. It was not—it was a horrible birth. My—the cook took her away. I thought she was dead."

"I'm sorry," Kate said, and her voice shook on the

second word. He did not want to see the emotions in her face, whether they were pity or sorrow. Henry had not intentionally told him about Kate's miscarriages or her stillbirth, but he had asked for medical advice for a woman who bled sporadically after losing a child, and then, years later, advice for a woman who could not carry a child to term. Henry had meticulously copied all of Thomas' words and folded them into a letter, and Henry only wrote letters to his sister.

"Thomas, I'm sorry." Kate's voice.

He could not look at her. His own name felt like a blow to the gut and a caress on his face all at once. "Yes."

"I—you—"

Don't try to comfort me, Thomas thought, *don't*, though if anyone had the right, maybe it was this woman, for whom childbearing had brought only sorrow.

But Kate's fingers slid down her thigh and toward his, and before Thomas had recognized what was happening she had seized one of his hands in her two smaller ones. He nearly yanked his hand away—*Do not comfort me, do not think who I was in that horrible house has anything to do with who I am now*—but Kate clutched his hand as though she were drowning. He felt warmth radiating up his arm from where her fingers wrapped around his.

"My brother," she said, then stopped.

It was not the response Thomas had expected. His shoulders relaxed a breath.

"I'm worried that John Mary killed Rob Baker," Kate said in a rush.

It took another long minute for Thomas to understand what she had said, and connect it with what she had said earlier.

Well, he thought, that shows me, thinking that I have the worst problems in this house.

Thomas turned to Kate and stared into her huge, worried eyes for a minute. Then that was too much, so he squeezed his eyes shut and rubbed the bridge of his nose with his free hand.

She has a sword at my throat, and instead of pressing her advantage, she has given me a sword to hold at hers, Thomas thought. Altogether I would prefer a situation less filled with blades.

"Lord Almighty," he said finally. "Any man might kill given the right circumstances, but to behead someone—"

"Well," Kate said. Her voice did not sound like the voice of a woman who was shocked by the notion that one of her siblings might be a murderer. "You must admit it looks very strange, all the same, that Daniel Lately has been harassing a farmer, and then one of Lately's men shows up dead at that man's farm."

"But do *you* think your brother did this?" Thomas asked. "I've not met the man, after all, for all he's supposed to live here."

"He's been out in the field," Kate said vaguely. "I wouldn't have thought him capable of it, but—but— people will believe the worst."

"Daniel Lately is given to harassing dozens of people at a time," Thomas ground out. "Your brother is not the only one with reason to hate him."

Kate's fingers squeezed around his, but then she

burst into speech. "Wait a minute. I've just thought—Daniel Lately has always said that Eleanor is his ward. He's said that for *years*. And Anne says that he tells Eleanor all the time she ought to be grateful that he took her in at all. How *dare* he, when she's his natural daughter? She's a right to be in his house!"

Thomas looked at her.

"Why would he *do* that?"

Thomas rubbed his forehead. "So he wouldn't have to acknowledge the marriage, I expect."

He heard Kate swallow. "Oh, no," she said, in a very small voice.

"I don't know if it was even legal," Thomas said. "But I was sixteen and I didn't think I had any choice, and the vicar—well. Cousin Daniel gave very generously to the parish church."

"I suppose that would have been George Beauford," she said. She gripped Thomas' hand so tightly that he could not feel his fingers. "Peter said—well, he said—well."

"Has Cousin Daniel tried to marry again?" Thomas asked grimly.

"A few times," Kate said weakly. "He tried to court Miss James—that is, Lord Houghton's youngest daughter—but she ran away with a cavalry officer instead. I think Lord Houghton was relieved. He couldn't have turned down an offer, because the family has no money and everyone knows it, but no one would want to be related to Daniel Lately." She realized what she had just said and turned a white face toward Thomas. "I'm sorry. I shouldn't have—"

"You're right," Thomas said. He could taste bile in

his mouth. "I'd rather be related to a sack of maggots."

"It's all a horrible mess. I can't—I don't—" Kate whispered, her shoulders slumping. "And Anne's not been going to her job. I don't know what to do."

Thomas wondered what that had to do with anything. He wondered what Kate thought she ought to do about her brother possibly being a murderer, the sort of murderer who beheaded people with very sharp knives. He wondered what Kate thought she needed to do about the man sitting next to her and his unmanly history.

"Kate," he said, because if she was going to use his given name he was certainly going to use hers, "when did you know that I am—that I am not—" He wasn't sure how to finish that sentence, but Kate had gone from white to pink.

"I—I—I—well," she said. "As soon as I washed you."

Thomas narrowed his eyes at her. "You let me think that *you* thought I'd—ah—lost the relevant anatomy during the war."

"Men can be very touchy about their—their relevant anatomy," Kate said, turning even pinker. She stared down at their clasped hands.

Thomas thought he should reclaim his hand, but now that her grip had loosened, it was not entirely unpleasant to let her press her palms to his. He wanted to ask more questions. Something about the way she had phrased that last made her think she wasn't just talking about cocks and balls. Did she know other men like him, who had made their own manhoods? How on earth had she met such men in this backwards little corner of Shropshire? Could he talk to them? Also, did she want to examine his relevant anatomy a bit more closely, and possibly while he simultaneously examined hers?

It doesn't matter, he reminded himself. None of this matters. This house, this family, this woman do not belong to you. You knew you could never come back to England, and yet here you are. Nothing will save you now.

"I have to tell Peter," Kate said.

"You will *not* tell Peter," Thomas snarled, surprised and stung. He pulled his hand free and seized her forearms. He pulled Kate toward him until their noses almost touched. "Look at me. You will not tell *anyone* what I have told you just now."

A sound escaped Kate's mouth like a very small squeak. He loosened his grip, but did not let go.

"I meant about Rob Baker and John Mary," she said. "He can ask the deacons to bury the body as soon as possible."

"Ah," Thomas said, embarrassed. "I'm sorry." But then her words registered, and he demanded, "You would ask the *vicar* to help you cover up a murder?"

"It isn't the worst thing Peter has lied about," Kate said. "*Oh*. Pretend I didn't say that."

He did not let go of her arms. They were almost embracing. He ought to—no, fuck that. He'd left *ought* behind at the beginning of this conversation, if not decades before that, and there was no point in pretending he could protect Kate with proper behavior.

And she had reached out to him first, took hold of him and kept hold of him like she needed him.

She's also asking *me* to cover up a murder, even if she hasn't said it out loud, Thomas thought. That's why she came up here.

"Kate?" That was Anne's voice; it sounded like she was standing on the stairs. Thomas started. How much had Anne heard?

Anne went on, "Kate, how are you going to fix this cheese? It's got a big hole in the middle."

"I should—" Kate looked at him anxiously, but she didn't pull away. "I should really—"

Thomas closed his eyes and, with a great effort of will, uncurled his fingers from around her arms.

It was lucky, Kate thought, that Nonnette had decided to calve this afternoon, because Kate needed to be as busy as possible right now. Anne had followed the bawling of the new creature to the middle of a clump of blackthorn.

The damage Mr. Lately had done to Kate's cheese was not enough of a problem to keep her mind from spinning into new and dangerous territory. She had scooped out the dents from his dirty fingers with a metal spoon, then sliced a thin piece from the edge of the cheese and formed the soft curd into the empty spots. Once the white mold grew over the entire surface, it would mat over the broken bits; once the cheese started to ripen, the inside would become one smooth mass. There was a chance that a different mold would grow in the crack, perhaps something blue, but Kate thought she'd rather risk that than whatever filth had been under Mr. Lately's fingernails.

Then Anne had come rushing in to tell her about

the calf, and they both went out to battle through the hedge to remove the tiny new heifer from the thorns. The calf's fur was shiny, glistening black, with a white blaze down her forehead and one white sock. Nonnette waddled after them, complaining, but allowed herself to be coaxed into the pen by the lean-to. There was not enough hay, so they foraged an assortment of weeds for her to eat from the closest hedgerows.

Soon, Kate thought, there would be enough milk to make four cheeses a week. She ought to be able to sell a pound of cheese for at least twice as much as the gallon of milk it took to make it, and the cheese had a much better chance of surviving the trip to Southbridge market.

Kate needed to send a message to Peter, and she needed help getting the corpse out of the woodshed and off the farm. The body must be buried, and it must be buried in an unobjectionable way as soon as possible. She needed to talk to John Mary, or she needed *not* to talk to John Mary, and she hadn't quite figured out which yet. His recent evasiveness and misdirections made a great deal more sense, if this is what he had been hiding. The beheading was truly peculiar, and she wouldn't have thought John Mary could have done it. But he had been under a great deal of stress for many years now. Being threatened by Daniel Lately's man might have pushed him over the edge.

Or pushed someone else over the edge, who John Mary felt obligated to protect. Could Peter have possibly…? No, if Peter had been attacked by Daniel Lately, he would have poisoned the man, and no one would have ever been the wiser. Henry couldn't have done such a thing, and he hadn't been home anyway. Jake was at sea and would be for months longer. Anne? As devious as Anne could be, particularly when evading questions about her continued employment, Kate didn't think that meant her seventeen-year-old sister was capable of murder.

Who else would John Mary lie to protect? Me, Kate thought bleakly. If I had done a murder, snapped and pushed Will out of the barn myself, he would have lied to protect me. John Mary simply wouldn't go to such trouble for someone who wasn't family. One of his siblings; Papa; Maman. Papa had no more been capable of such violence than Henry would be. And Maman—

She drew in a deep breath. Maman was gone. It didn't matter whether Maman could have taken a man's head off, because Maman was gone.

As long as Kate kept busy—with the cheese and the calf and the man her brother had *maybe* murdered and poking around the kitchen garden to see if there were any parsnips left growing along the fence row— she could push away the memory of how Thomas' hand had felt clasped between hers, his large knuckles and long fingers; the sensation of those strong hands wrapped around her arms, holding her still. If she took even a moment to rest, she felt fingertips pressing into her skin—not hard enough to hurt, but hard enough that she knew Thomas was very, very serious about what he was saying. Perhaps he thought she didn't understand how very dangerous his secret was; well, Thomas didn't know about John Mary, nor the years

the Gravenor family had spent protecting her oldest
brother.

If Kate stopped moving for a moment, she saw
Thomas' face, his dark eyes burning, his mouth so close
to hers that she might have leaned forward and kissed
him with no effort at all. His mouth was very nicely
shaped, she thought, before she could stop herself. She
had thought he had thin lips, but he just had a habit of
pressing them together very tightly when he was in pain
or worried.

She had found Henry excavating a ditch and had
bundled him back to the house to help the doctor
downstairs, because she could not face the owner of
those eyes or those lips right now.

Instead, Kate stood in the dry, brown kitchen
garden and stared down at a clump of wild carrots,
wondering if she should pull them up for the evening's
soup. Of course John Mary had not kept up with the
kitchen garden. John Mary had been busy with
something else.

Papa and Timothy Easting, Will's father, had
loaned each other tools and horses now and again.
That had been how John Mary had met Will and
become friends; but then, John Mary had made friends
easily in those days. Will had been charming and good-
looking enough that when he had offered for Kate
after Papa had died, she had felt lucky. He had been
attracted to her—or at least, he had wanted to have sex
with her. Was there a difference? She had liked being
kissed, even forcefully; Will's forcefulness when taking
her to bed had seemed like evidence of his desire for
her. It had been proof that she was wanted, when she

had felt like there was no place in the world for her.

All the Gravenor men were, to some extent, vague and sidling people. It took a lot of effort to pin John Mary, Henry, Peter, or Jake down to an honest opinion about anything, and it had been simply impossible with Papa. Papa had not known what he thought about anything unless Maman had told him what to think. Kate had often felt a peculiar sort of loneliness when growing up in this house, the loneliness of only being sure of her own thoughts.

She had always known what Will wanted from her, even toward the end, when he had hated her for what she could not give him. At the beginning, she had thought his confidence in his own opinions a marvelous thing, and had even loved him a little for it. She had thought—and what an awful little fool she had been for thinking—that she had inspired some particular trust in this man, that he was so ready to share what he thought, what he desired, even, sometimes, what he feared.

It hurt to remember how badly she had misunderstood. Will was—Will *had been* the sort of man who shared everything he thought because he assumed all women were empty vessels, waiting to be filled up with the intentions and seed of the man nearest her. Kate could do nothing with his seed and, after the novelty of the marriage and its constant closeness had worn off, even less with his self-importance and quick temper. Her future had stretched before her into new frontiers of loneliness, bounded by despair on all edges.

She had assumed that this despair had inoculated

her against feeling deeply for a man, any man, ever again. How could it not? How could things be any different for her in the future? She was no one and nothing special, that a man who wasn't already tied to her by blood should treat her with care.

Kate ought not spend time thinking about Thomas' hands or his dark eyes or the line of his jaw. There was no reason to suspect that Thomas was interested in her on more than the superficial level that Will had been—*here is a creature who exists to serve my will.*

Thomas was a different sort of man, Kate thought; he had to be, given the place he had started and the things which had happened to him. She had assumed, without really thinking about it, that he and John Mary shared a history. Maman had hardly spoken of France, but once she had said, in an off-handed sort of way, that during all of the badness—*la méchanceté*—she had started telling people John Mary was her son. She and John Mary had been moving steadily cross-country, hiding in abandoned houses and barns, eating what food they could scavenge or steal, and it had seemed safer. Maman wanted nothing to do with anyone waving a gun and a sword around. People were not interested in dirty little boys in the same way as pretty little girls, she had said, and Kate had not known what she meant.

But when Maman and John Mary had finally escaped to England, and Maman had successfully wheedled herself a position as housekeeper for a daft-seeming country farmer named Edward Gravenor, John Mary had demanded breeches and raged until Maman cut his hair. He had been about three, and

Maman an exhausted nineteen.

At this point, as she often had, Maman had offered only a cryptic shrug and a, "Bah, voilà," which meant the story was over. John Mary was a man; John Mary was always going to be a man.

But that had not been Thomas' story. Someone had once thought him a girl. He had once had to act as a girl, subject to a man's whims. Not just any man; *Daniel Lately*. Kate shuddered. She would throw herself in the river before she'd marry a man like Daniel Lately, and Thomas, or the person he'd been before he was Thomas, had had no choice.

Kate tipped her head back and looked up at the white-gray sky, then back down at a clump of threadbare dill shuddering in the breeze. She sighed. She didn't think she was supposed to know any of these things. Maman had told her about John Mary when she was a little girl, because Kate had seen him undressing and wanted to know why his parts looked more like her parts than Peter's or Henry's.

These things happen, Maman had said; it's common enough, if you keep your eyes open. But people don't like thinking about how little they know about everyone around them. It is dangerous to frighten your neighbors so, and that is why we must never speak of this to anyone.

Kate could not stop thinking about what she knew of Thomas, and what more she wanted to know. She wanted to know what he had dreamed of as a young man, what he had felt when he had read Song of Songs and John Donne's exhortations to his lover. She wanted to know what Thomas' hands felt like on her hips, her waist, what his lips felt like on her neck.

Kate was sure she ought to be done with wanting things altogether, and yet here she was, standing in the garden, staring at her boots, imagining herself sitting tight against Thomas on the bed, his hands holding her arms, his face a breath from her face. He could have pressed her onto her back, and she would have let him, and she would have enjoyed the weight of him atop her. She could have—well, she would have to be very careful, because of his leg, but she could at least have kissed him. That wouldn't hurt his leg at all.

And he couldn't hurt me the way Will hurt me, Kate thought, by giving me four children I couldn't carry. Her eyes prickled with tears, but that might have been the wind.

Why was a living child given to—forced out of— Thomas Holyoke, who had been bereft by the violation, and not to Kate, who had wanted nothing more? Why had Eleanor Lately—Eleanor Holyoke, shouldn't she be?—been given to a terrible old man to raise, and not to her real father?

"I would have done a better job than that buzzard," Kate whispered to the garden. "For all that I'm only six years older than Eleanor. I practically raised Henry, didn't I?" She aimed this last, fierce question at a clump of garlic chives which had escaped the herb bed and were now spreading over the path.

But Thomas had escaped to save his own life. Kate could hardly blame him; hadn't she done the same, when she had refused to lie with Will after that last stillbirth? His escape had been more effective than hers —after he healed fully, he would have his skills as a doctor, a prestigious military career, and his solemn, handsome countenance to take with him wherever he decided to start anew. Kate would still be a widow with no money and little more to recommend her than a gift for dairying.

I could go with him, Kate thought, poking at another wild carrot with her boot. Even if he went to a proper city, Shrewsbury or even London, I could have goats in the yard and sell cheeses out of the kitchen.

For a moment the idea made her heart bloom with hope. She was so tired of being weighed down by grief, moving sluggishly under the weight of her own losses and other people's expectations of her as one who had lost. In a city, no one would *know* her, or think they knew her because they'd known her father and grandfather and great-grandfather, and had also seen a cartoon of a Frenchwoman once in a newspaper. She would still be small and drab, but she would be small and drab and *anonymous*.

Kate let herself be swept up on the fantasy of living in a small gray house, maybe one which had been built this century, cooking meals for Thomas and laundering his shirts. Maybe they would take turns reading out loud in the evenings. Then she shook herself.

I cannot go with him *anywhere*, she thought. I have responsibilities to my brothers and my sister and this farm. I have cheeses to make *here*. I am a fool for thinking I can try again.

## CHAPTER THIRTEEN

"How many letters do you have for us today?" Eleanor asked the elder Miss James.

"Five," said Lord Houghton's aunt, her wrinkled old face twisting into a death's-head grin. "I always look forward to you and Miss Gravenor's translations, my dear."

"Thank you, ma'am," Anne said. She always looked deeply uncomfortable in Miss James' little parlor, fitted out with Persian rugs and delicately-turned Queen Anne furniture. Anne wore her best dress, which Eleanor had patched at the elbows and hem, and a pair of plain slippers Eleanor had given her. She had never been pleased about her own large feet, until she had needed to provide footwear for Anne.

Miss James was the sort of person who enjoyed mockery like a sporting event, but Eleanor suspected she wanted Anne's help more than she wanted the entertainment of making her feel small. After all, there were not so many fluent French speakers in this part of Shropshire, and fewer still who would elicit no comment visiting the squire's house. Anne's family thought she still worked for the Telfords. Everyone else in the parish, who saw that Anne was certainly not walking to the Telford farm every week, thought she was now doing odd jobs for Lord Houghton's difficult old aunt; which, Eleanor supposed, she was.

Eleanor found Miss James unnerving, with her bulging eyes and that knowing way of tapping her lips she had, but it was a such a relief to spend time with anyone who was not Cousin Daniel. Eleanor eyed the packet in the elderly woman's claw-like fingers. "Are these ones from Correspondent G, or Correspondent M?"

"They are from Correspondent G, addressing Correspondent R," Miss James returned, her eyes sparkling maliciously. She gestured at the table, where a single sheet of foolscap lay, covered in spidery writing. "There is your lesson for the day; it is about the proper manner in which to decline an invitation from various members of society. I will ring for tea in two hours. You may begin your work."

Miss James offered Anne the packet of letters, and Eleanor the foolscap. They both curtsied deeply to her, before filing through a small door at the side of the room into the lady's private library.

Eleanor was quite sure Lord Houghton had no notion of the complicated information network that his maiden aunt maintained about the smuggling of luxury foodstuffs, particularly fine cheeses, throughout Britain and the continent, nor that maintaining said network involved the regular theft of letters belonging to certain Flemish and French merchants working in London. She was equally sure that when Cousin Daniel had started sending her twice weekly to Miss James to be taught proper manners two years ago, he had imagined that the old woman would batter Eleanor into a decent marriage prospect, not entice her into criminal conspiracy.

Miss James, however, resented mightily the imposition on her free time that the lessons had represented. She had been hounded into taking on Eleanor's tutelage by her brother, who owed rather a lot of money to Cousin Daniel, and it had pleased the old lady to spite both men. She had discovered Eleanor's facility for French in the third week of this arrangement and asked her if she wanted to make some pocket money. Then Eleanor had proved herself rather better at decoding this specific group of letters than Miss James herself, allowing the old woman to focus on other parts of her spy network.

When Eleanor had found out that Cousin Daniel had forced the Telfords to fire Anne, she had suggested that Miss James hire her too. She and Anne had been friends during the few years they had both attended the dame school in Copstone, before Cousin Daniel had decided Eleanor needed stricter supervision and Anne's parents had died.

Eleanor had thought this suggestion rather a gamble, as Anne's manners were none too polished, but Miss James had been oddly struck by the mention of Anne's name.

"Gravenor," she had repeated. "*Gravenor.* That would be Ophélie—that is, I suppose that is Edward Gravenor's child. The youngest? Goodness. I had no idea so much time had passed. And she speaks French? Of course she does, she would—well, I wonder what else she has had from her mother. I suppose I owe—well—I ought. Yes, bring her here, and we shall see what the two of you can do."

It had been a notably peculiar thing to say—what could the squire's sister owe to a displaced Frenchwoman?—but Eleanor had been so relieved that Miss James had agreed to hire Anne that she had not dared ask any more questions. Every time Cousin Daniel did another awful thing, Eleanor felt a weight of guilt pulling her heart downward. She could fix so few things, but she could help Anne in this.

"Right, then," Anne said now, passing her the packet of letters.

"Allons-y?" Eleanor said, unfolding the first letter in the stack.

Anne took down the notebook she used from the top shelf and laid it open on the table, then sharpened a quill. She looked expectantly at Eleanor. "On y va."

Eleanor cleared her throat and began to read. "Mes chers amis, je voudrais vous expliquer ma situation…"

This was how they always began; she read, and Anne translated, making note of any phrases that sounded odd to her ear. Anne spoke fluent and rather idiomatic French from her mother and older brother, but did not read as easily as Eleanor did. Eleanor, whose French had come entirely from a Lancashire-born governess, could not always pick up the deliberately strange wording of the letters. But, once Anne picked the peculiar bits out, Eleanor could usually see how they were connected. It wasn't a specific code, but rather a series of allusions and puns that added up to a private language. They'd compiled a dictionary of terms in the back of Anne's notebook, adding new terms that built on the old ones as they came up.

Not all the letters had secret messages, and indeed many of them spoke of domestic matters or local politics around Paris or Brussels. Miss James wanted to know all of this too, but she especially wanted to know when eight odd turns of phrase put together suggested a drop of a hundred pounds of the finest Gouda in a particular dyke at the edge of the Fens in Lincolnshire on the fourth of September just after midnight. Eleanor had once gotten up the courage to ask Miss James what she did with this information, but the old woman only smiled. "There are people who would like to know, dear." Miss James' pale blue eyes had skated over Anne, and her face stilled. "There are people who might know what to do with such information."

*Who*, Eleanor had wanted to ask, but Miss James had sharply detoured into a diatribe about the proper way to brew tea.

Eleanor would have liked to speculate with Anne about who the *people* Miss James spoke about were, but they very rarely had a moment alone after the lesson. Cousin Daniel brought Eleanor in his curricle at exactly one o'clock, and he was always waiting in his curricle outside the stables exactly three hours later. She had tried to suggest that she might walk, the distance from Lately House to Bassenthwaite House being less than four miles, but Cousin Daniel had been coldly unreceptive to the idea. Miss James seemed to know her scheme would be for nothing if one of the

Gravenors was discovered in the lesson room with Eleanor, and so every week she sent Anne away at a quarter to four with her shilling.

After Eleanor returned home from her lessons, she hid in the kitchen with Margaret, the elderly cook, and reviewed the lesson on deportment from Miss James. Aunt Margaret had looked after Eleanor since she was a tiny child—since before Cousin Daniel had found her and made her his ward, in fact. Eleanor thought the old woman suspected there was something untoward happening in Miss James' lessons, but she never asked questions.

It was all terribly interesting, certainly the most interesting thing which had ever happened in Eleanor's sheltered life, but today she couldn't focus on what the letter said. Anne, too, seemed unusually anxious. She kept glancing at Eleanor, her brow furrowed, and opening her mouth as though she would speak.

"Anne," Eleanor whispered, after two paragraphs about the looms in a wool mill in Leeds. "Have they buried the body yet?"

Anne shot a nervous look at the door. Miss James usually eavesdropped. "Kate sent me to talk to Peter yesterday after you visited," she said under her breath. "He said we should at least pretend to look for the head first. Erm."

Eleanor flinched. She had not liked Rob Baker at all—he had pinched her bottom when passing her in the yard in front of the house, and then told all the other hands that she was bony as an old chicken—but it was not pleasant to think of his head rolling by itself around the parish. It had been rather horrible to follow

Anne into the shadows of the woodshed, where the still, water-swollen body lay atop a bier of wood. The Gravenors had wrapped the horrible thing in a sheet, but a single hand protruded. Eleanor had spent enough time avoiding the fingers on that half-thumbed hand to recognize it immediately. But she had fled before Anne could flip back the sheet to show her the stump of the neck.

Last night, Eleanor had dreamed of that hand, dreamed of sitting in the woodshed watching, watching, watching, waiting for the slightest movement of those hated fingers.

Eleanor shuddered. "I hope they never find the head."

There was a little noise from the other side of the door, as if an elderly lady were moving her chair closer to hear. Eleanor hastily read another few lines from the letter, trying to empty her brain of pictures of swirling cold water and dead bodies.

She went on, "Do you think—erm—your brother knows any more?"

Anne jerked. "Hrm, well, he knows something," she said, carefully nonchalant. "Eleanor—"

"Oh, I see," Eleanor said. Miss James couldn't follow spoken French, but she was the devil for understanding tone. "It shouldn't be 'couper la laine,' then?"

"No, it's 'tondre' for wool," Anne said. She made a note on the page. "Eleanor, I think—"

There was a soft hollow *thwop* from the door, as thought Miss James had put a cup against it.

Eleanor pinched the end of her nose in

frustration. Her opportunities to speak to Anne were very few; Cousin Daniel hardly let Eleanor out of the house, but for these lessons. But she didn't trust what Miss James might do with the information she gathered eavesdropping. They might write notes, but Miss James would certainly notice if any of the paper she had given them disappeared.

Eleanor read the next paragraph, which seemed to be a long complaint about the quality of the fleeces received, and then added, in shakier French still, "Has your brother—erm—employed a new man?"

"I think that should be 'embaucher,'" said Anne, but her face had gone rather pale.

"I *saw* a new man, in fact. He's very big and—erm—has white hair and—ah—a red face, and he looked at us from the barn when we visited two days ago," Eleanor said. She felt rather winded by producing that much French all at once.

"Oh, do you mean *Henry?*" Anne asked, breaking into English. "Yes, he's been back for weeks now. But, Eleanor—"

"Oh, right, of course, I should have known," Eleanor babbled. Her face felt hot. The nature of the curiosity she had felt for the unknown young man felt very uncomfortable indeed to disclose to the young man's sister. "Oh yes, well," she said. "He's very tall."

The sound of an elderly lady clearing her throat came from the other side of the door. Eleanor coughed and began to read again. The fleeces, it seemed, were moldy. The mill workers were having trouble preparing them into bats which could be spun efficiently. Anne gave Eleanor an anguished look. There was clearly something she wanted to say which she felt she could not risk Miss James overhearing.

The two and a half hours passed. Anne pointed out six odd phrases in the letter about mill looms and fleece quality. Eleanor noticed that they all rhymed, and Anne remembered a song her mother used to sing with those words at the end of each line of one verse. She was trying to remember the chorus of the song when Miss James rang for tea. A moment later, the door of her parlor opened and the murmurs of the old woman , giving instructions to the maid began.

Impetuously, Eleanor seized Anne's hand. "Anne," she whispered. "Please tell me what you were going to tell me."

"I *can't*," Anne hissed. "Not here. There's another man staying at the farm, and he's—he's—oh, Eleanor, you have a right to know, but I can't—"

Eleanor heard the outer door close and Miss James' purposeful step turn toward the library.

"Lady Day is in two weeks," Eleanor hissed. "Cousin Daniel will be out collecting rents. I'll fake sick and meet you—meet you at the ford of the stream behind your farm."

Anne looked stricken, but the library door swung open, and Miss James was there, leaning forward on her polished walking stick, her eyes glinting.

"And what do you have for me today, girls?"

# CHAPTER FOURTEEN

"Sir," Henry said.

Thomas rubbed his bleary eyes and tried to focus them. He had not yet been out of bed, and mercifully Kate had let him rest, though he had heard her moving around the kitchen. He supposed he had frightened her when he had grabbed her yesterday, which he might have felt worse about if he didn't feel so awful already. Every muscle in his body throbbed. The pain wrapped around his limbs, crackling as though his veins themselves were on fire.

From being dragged up and down those cursed stairs yesterday, he thought.

From finding out that you have a living child, the chill air of the Gravenor house whispered back.

Thomas considered being sick.

"Sir," Henry repeated. "There's a problem, sir."

Thomas squinted up at the red face looming over him. Henry's large, open countenance had scrunched into a caricature of anxiety, making him look rather like an enormous blonde baby.

"Is someone hurt?" Thomas said. The words came out as a croak. He cleared his throat. "Are *you* hurt?"

"*Sir.*" The word scooped upward in a panicked crescendo.

"Henry. Take a deep breath. I'm not going to be angry. What's the matter?"

Thomas noticed then that Henry clutched something to his chest: an old hand-sickle, sharpened so often that its blade was as thin as a crescent moon, the wooden handle wrapped tight with twine to keep it from splitting.

Henry's nostrils flared, and his eyes went vague as he clearly thought very hard about breathing. His giant shoulders heaved up and down. Finally, he said, "I was just thinking I would cut the grass around the garden."

Thomas gritted his teeth and did not interrupt. Trying to encourage Henry to get to the point usually meant he lost his place and had to start over.

"I'd been using my pocket knife to do such work, and I thought to myself, that's not very sensible. You could cut yourself, and if you had the proper tool you could work faster. The proper tool is a sickle, sir, with a long curved blade. John Mary has one, but he can't loan it me, for he'll be using it all day. So I thought: well, where would I find an old sickle? I didn't think they'd be in the barn, for Antoinette eats metal."

I must never get on the wrong side of that cow, Thomas thought. "Go on."

"And I thought, well, Maman used to hide her own tools in the woodshed, because she thought Papa wasn't careful enough cleaning and sharpening them after he was done working. And for all it's been seven years, I thought, well, maybe she left something behind. John Mary probably had taken everything out, but he's been distracted, you see?"

"I see," Thomas said, not seeing. "Wouldn't you have noticed any tools left when we went to look at the body for heart defects? There's hardly space to hide anything in that shed."

"Well," Henry said. He took another huge, shuddering breath. "I went into the woodshed. I *did* go in the woodshed. I went … I went …"

"It seems you found a sickle in there," Thomas noted, keeping his voice as even as possible.

Henry, overcome, silently held out the tool to him. Thomas took it by the handle and rotated it, dread building in his chest. The sickle was well cared-for, but someone had recently used it to cut something large, heavy, and wet. There were bits of hair and other unmentionable materials caught on the blade, and the twine around the handle was damp with dark fluid. It smelled like death.

"It was at the base of the wood pile," Henry said. "Right at the base, where no one would miss it, as though it had just been set down. Did you see a sickle in the woodshed before?"

"No," Thomas said. "Henry, where is Rob Baker's body?"

"Gone," Henry said, swallowing hard. "It's gone. And the top layer of the wood, where it—where he— where that was lying was *wet*, sir. But … a sort of *thick* wet, you understand."

Thomas did understand. It wouldn't be blood, not this long after the man had been killed, but the body would keep decomposing, producing more and more unpleasant fluids. His brain jolted into a gallop. Cutting a body up, he supposed, would make it a great deal easier to carry away and dispose of, and once it was gone, there was only hearsay to say who it might have been. Was this to hide the murder from Cousin Daniel, or someone else? Where had those parts ended up? Had they been buried or cast away in a ditch somewhere? Were they headed to another town in the bottom of a cart? He looked down at the sickle again, his eyes tracing the glinting edge. Had this been the weapon which had been used to behead the poor fool Rob Baker? It looked sharp enough.

How many blade-wielding maniacs did Thomas think were roaming the Shropshire countryside? It had to be the same killer, returned to hide the crime. A shiver ran up his arms and down his back, and he rolled his shoulders to push the sensation away.

"I think I'd better have a look at the woodshed again," Thomas said. His leg spasmed in protest.

The walk to the shed was not as bad as he had feared, with Henry supporting his bad side, but Thomas still had to stop and retch with pain before they were halfway across the yard. Fortunately, he had not awakened for breakfast or lunch or tea, so there was nothing in his stomach. The sun was already dipping low against the horizon.

Henry helped Thomas to sit on an auxiliary pile of wood outside the shed and then threw the door open. The hinges screeched.

"How did whoever it was get in there without waking us all up?" Thomas asked, feeling very slow. The door had screeched like that before, too, when he had gone out to inspect the body's heart. "I was dead tired, but I wasn't so tired that I wouldn't hear *that*."

"Oh," Henry said. He frowned, shut the door, and then opened it again, this time lifting the bottom edge of the door with one foot and the handle. The wood creaked, but no more loudly than the branches of the trees swaying in the wind around the yard.

Thomas crutched after Henry into the shed, wishing he had the strength to try Henry's trick with the door himself. Was it easy to hit the right balance so the hinges didn't squawk, or did one have to practice the motion? He thought of Kate's conviction that John Mary had killed Rob Baker; here was some support for that idea.

Though, he supposed any one of the Gravenors could be the killer. Kate herself. Anne. Henry. Thomas let out a strangled laugh.

"Sir?" Henry said.

"I was thinking about what a bad murderer you would make," Thomas said.

Henry considered this carefully. "I would think it would depend upon the specific situation, sir," he said, after a long minute.

Thomas shuddered and turned to look at the wood pile, the last repose of Rob Baker. The killer had left nothing solid behind, but there were what Thomas could only describe as puddles of sludge slowly soaking into the logs, at the points where the body had been hacked up. From the spacing, he guessed cuts had been made at the knee, the hip, and the shoulder.

Henry hovered close to him, and when Thomas glanced back at him, he forced a small smile. "It's not as bad as an artillery blast," Henry said.

"It's not," Thomas agreed, thinking of the exploded legs and half-skulled men he had eventually run out of opium to help. He stared at the stained logs. There were a few blue threads caught on bits of bark at the end where the neck had been placed, presumably ripped from the man's kerchief.

"I suppose we should call the constable to look at this," Thomas said, though he heard the doubt in his own voice. He did not think Joseph Fine would have any brilliant conclusions upon examining this grisly scene, though he might come to the correct one.

"Erm," Henry said. "Well, Kate sent Anne to tell Peter to come fetch the body for burial. He's supposed to come by this afternoon with a wagon and one of the deacons."

As if summoned by mention of his name, there was the creaking of wheels on the drive and Peter's sonorous *halloo* in the yard.

"Hell," Thomas said, rubbing his forehead.

"Yes," Henry said meekly.

"How much do you think your brother's told his deacon?" Thomas said, struggling to stand upright again.

"Nothing," Henry said. "He doesn't tell anyone anything, if he can help it." He looped an arm around Thomas' ribcage.

"I suppose that's good," Thomas muttered, as they shuffled outside together. He hoped he wasn't about to collapse in front of his least favorite Gravenor sibling.

Peter wore another fine black suit and polished shoes, as well as a cape of dark green and a tall hat with a bright green ribbon. Kate stood in front of the door of the house, a strange smile stuck to her face as she stared at the visitors. A minute later Thomas understood why; Peter had his arm interlinked with Anne's, who was definitely supposed to be at her job today. Anne, for her part, looked both defiant and nervous, and Thomas surmised that Peter had a very good grip on her elbow.

"Look who I found strolling through the wood!" trumpeted Peter, giving Anne a smile with just a bit too many teeth. "Mr. Hines, wasn't I saying that this was the most agreeable piece of luck, to see so many of my brethren in one day?"

Mr. Hines, a dour man of fifty-odd with dark, sparse hair drawn into a queue, looked at Anne, then at Kate, then at Henry and Thomas approaching them from across the yard, and said nothing. Behind him, a gelding with almost his exact demeanor and coloring flared his nostrils and slumped in his traces.

"I see the good doctor is still here," Peter said, turning his blood-freezing smile on Thomas. Thomas swallowed hard and wondered why Kate didn't suspect this brother of the murder. "I hope you are appreciating my sister's exquisite hospitality."

"Peter," Kate said tightly, and then, "Anne. Aren't you—"

"I had the day off and decided to help Peter," Anne said, the lie so obvious that it might as well have come out of her mouth as a plume of smoke.

"How incredibly generous of you, dear sister," Peter said, patting her hand. Anne flinched.

"I hope you haven't come about the body," Thomas said brusquely, deciding that it was better to get through the worst of it immediately. "It's gone."

The face of Mr. Hines, which had until this moment remained completely immobile, contorted briefly to produce an expression which was not a smile, but which might have been a smile if it had been allowed to mature another few weeks. "You won't be needing my cart, then," he said.

"One moment, Mr. Hines," Peter said, the steel in his voice briefly overcoming the honey. He took a breath and turned back to Thomas, once again sweetness and light. "Where has—"

"I'm sure he doesn't know that," Kate burst out, her face very white. "I'm sure none of us—it must have been dogs. You know, there are dogs wandering everywhere in this day and age—"

"Dogs that could open the latch?" Henry asked, sounding puzzled.

"It's more likely Antoinette than dogs," Anne said, interested, leaning forward to look at Thomas. "She's terribly clever about opening doors, and I've never known a cow for eating carrion like her. Did you see any hoofprints in the dirt?"

"Ah, no," Thomas said, briefly stunned.

"I suppose it could have been dogs," Kate said, her words tumbling out as she came to stand between Peter and Thomas. "I couldn't know, none of us could know, but I suppose it *could have* been. Don't you think, Peter? Henry? But I'm sure you don't need to question Thom —him—I mean—Dr. Holyoke—"

"I don't know about any dogs or cows," Mr. Hines said, his face returned to stoicism. "But I'd rather not have a dead body in my cart if it's all the same, and seeing as how you've no dead body, I'll be heading home." He touched the brim of his hat in Kate's direction and shot Peter an uneasy look. "Reverend."

"Of course, of course," Peter said magnanimously. "You'll of course be around the rectory next Tuesday to help with that little matter I mentioned on the way here, yes? Yes, of course. Do give my regards to Mrs. Hines."

Mr. Hines, rather than turn his back on Peter, took a long step backwards toward his gelding and his dog-cart, then another, then another, until he could pull himself into the seat, all without taking his eyes off the vicar. He touched two fingers to his hat, picked up his reins, and clucked sharply at the horse, who put on a surprising turn of speed when turning out of the yard into the lane.

"Well," Peter said.

"Anne," Kate said. "You are going to tell me what's going on *now*. Isaac Telford never gave you a free day. He's as hard as flint."

"Aren't you a little more worried about the *missing corpse?*" Peter said sharply, giving Thomas an openly hostile stare. He did not drop Anne's arm, but moved forward, so he was standing between his youngest sister and Thomas.

"I could go look for it," Anne volunteered. "The body, I mean."

"You'd be looking for chunks of leg and arm, not a full body," Thomas said shortly, irritation and amusement warring in him at Peter's reaction. Did the man think Thomas could overcome Anne, who was a head taller than he was and accustomed to dragging cows about? And why wasn't Peter trying to protect Kate? "It looked like the fellow came back to get rid of the evidence and did a fair butchery. I don't think it's a good idea for you to go out looking for such a man."

Anne looked a little frightened but more intrigued by this information, which Thomas thought did not bode well for her following his instructions.

Kate, however, went quite pale, pressing a hand to her stomach. "*Oh.*"

Without thinking about it, Thomas put out an arm to steady her. His injured leg screamed, and he felt Henry shift behind him, ready to snatch up both his sister and his former superior. Thomas barely choked down a bitter laugh, but then Kate took hold of his hand, and he found he was not thinking of Henry anymore.

"And how do you know that?" Peter snarled. "Perhaps from your own experience cutting people apart."

"There were leavings in the woodshed," Henry said, when Thomas did not immediately reply.

Thomas felt something like pain stab through him at the stern loyalty in Henry's voice.

"I've a fair amount of experience cutting people apart, that's true," he said, leveling his gaze with Peter's. The man's eyes were unnerving; fury made them almost green. "But I can tell you I had not the strength nor the will to go outside yesterday, as Kate—as your sister will attest."

Peter looked at Kate and Thomas' joined hands, and something frightening passed across his face. "I would be interested to know if you have any evidence of that which does not depend upon importuning my sister," he said softly.

"Henry, do you mean leavings like guts?" Anne asked hopefully.

"*Anne*," Kate said, and she looked even queasier. She did not let go of Thomas' hand.

"Well, it's probably four parts of leg and two arms and the trunk that are out and about now," said Henry, and Thomas wished he could stuff a sock in his former assistant's mouth. Kate looked positively green.

"Like a side of pork," she muttered, swaying a little. "Cut up like a side of pork."

"Kate, get away from that man," Peter said. Thomas had no doubt that his parishioners obeyed that cold, authoritative voice without question, especially when it followed his affected joviality. "He's not who he says he is."

Thomas' stomach contorted brutally. Peter had put the slightest emphasis on the word *he*, the slightest doubt, the slightest insinuation.

But Kate shook her head as if to clear out the nausea, then gave her brother a look which held even more ice than his tone. "Peter, you'd better think very carefully about what you're about to say. You aren't going to surprise me, but you may well disappoint me."

"I just want to look after you, Kate," Peter said, and in spite of his affected manner, Thomas thought he might actually be sincere. He felt a certain unwilling empathy for any man who was trying to take care of Kate.

"You're about seven years too late for that," Kate said, and Peter actually flinched. "I don't care to talk about this in the yard. I'll make tea and you'll stay to dinner."

As soon as he had a cup of tea in his hand, Peter went on the attack. "I don't suppose the names of James and Eleanor Lately, *née* Holyoke, mean anything to you, dear sister."

Even if Thomas had not told her what he had, Kate could have guessed based on how rigid the doctor's shoulders became against the chair. It was odd how poorly he could hide his emotions, for a man whose entire life depended on hiding certain other parts of himself.

All of them except Henry sat around the kitchen table, on stools and chairs from the parlor. Henry squatted by the hearth, patiently stirring the soup Kate had dashed together.

"I would guess they are cousins to Daniel Lately," Kate said, taking a sip of tea that was mostly milk.

"Indeed they were," Peter said. "And I wonder if you know what happened to their child, born the fourteenth of April, seventeen eighty-three." He stared at her expectantly. This was how Peter liked to argue: drop an artillery shell of a statement into the conversation and then attack when his opponent scrambled away from it.

"I do," Kate said, glancing at Thomas' hand where it lay on the scarred surface of the kitchen table. She thought of how he had struggled across the yard to support her, when the understanding of what had happened to Rob Baker's body had struck her like a blow. He ought to have sent Henry to her, but he had not thought of that.

She had stayed silent too long for Peter, and he burst out. "Don't you think it is the smallest bit suspicious that a *man* with such a tight connection to Daniel Lately appeared back in the county just before Daniel Lately's hired man was killed?"

"No," Kate said.

"Kate, you are letting your feelings make you unreasonable."

"I am not being unreasonable," Kate said. "Dr. Holyoke took care of Henry for seven years, including two years of war." She thought of Henry's letters, full of descriptions of foreign cities and surgeries and above all, interesting rocks. It had been rare that a paragraph had not mentioned Thomas—Dr. Holyoke —and from the technical wording Henry had used to describe the medical procedures, she suspected that Thomas had helped him write parts of his correspondence. "I am grateful to Dr. Holyoke. *You* should be grateful to Dr. Holyoke, for taking care of our brother."

"And I took care of him," Henry added.

"You did," Thomas said.

Peter scoffed audibly, and Kate picked up the honey jar, contemplating throwing it at his head. She knew that the reason Peter and Henry would never get along was that Peter lived in terror of what the world might do to a man it assumed to be simple, and terror made him brittle and condescending. And Henry only recognized the condescension, and not the care, from his brother. Kate knew all this, and it did not make her patient.

"So your fair doctor might have asked our brother to do any number of things, and expected his cooperation," Peter went on.

"Do you think *I* told Henry to cut up the body?" Thomas barked.

"Why not?" Peter said, shrugging. "You can't deny you've a rather large secret to hide from Daniel Lately. It is all to your benefit that he not come visiting again."

"That doesn't explain who did the first killing, though," Anne commented. "Dr. Holyoke was too sick to even call for the chamber pot. I saw him."

Kate whirled on her sister, suddenly recalled to another subject of panic. "Anne, we need to talk about your job. You'll be fired if you keep on skiving off like this."

Anne had the temerity to look indignant, but Peter cut her off. "Anne hasn't worked for the Telfords for over a year. Stop changing the subject, Kate."

"How do you know that?" Anne said, sounding appalled.

"Yes, how do you know that?" Kate demanded, feeling as though the floor beneath her feet had suddenly vanished.

Peter gave his youngest sister a scathing glance. "Maybe because you don't ever go to the Telford farm anymore? Maybe because—"

"That's no one's business but mine," Anne yelled over him, turning very red.

"It's my business too! I'm your sister!" Kate said, strangely close to tears. "Anne, what have you been doing?"

What have you been doing, when I wasn't here to

look out for you? she thought, her thoughts bubbling hysterically. When I wasn't here to protect you?

"*None* of that is to the point," Thomas snarled, breaking into her thoughts. "Someone violently killed a man on your property, and then, as soon as he was identified, cut him up and dragged him away. How can you not take this seriously?"

But Kate's mind was already skipping ahead, and her throat closed up with fear and grief. It was one thing if John Mary had killed Rob Baker in a moment of angry self-defense, as she had first assumed; it was quite another if her brother had desecrated the man's body so horribly to hide his crime.

You weren't going to turn him in, her conscience hissed. So what's the difference? Maybe it's better that the body is gone.

He's my *brother*, Kate thought, but that was neither exoneration nor condemnation.

"I am of course delighted to return to the topic you would like to discuss, Dr. Holyoke," Peter said, his unctuous manner back in place. "But *do* consider that you might come under suspicion, given the nature of the man's demise."

At that, Henry stood up from the hearth and pointed a finger at Peter. "He isn't," he said, his voice laced with anger. "You're just saying that to be awful."

"If the fine doctor has made one of my siblings party to his perversions, I have even less reason to like him," Peter returned, his tone even more arch. He knew Henry hated when he put on his public school voice, so he made a point of doing it whenever he was near Henry.

Kate's annoyance at Peter and Henry was currently fighting a violent round of fisticuffs with her terror and sorrow for John Mary in her gut.

"*You* could have done it," Henry said levelly, his finger still aimed at Peter. "I know what you did to Elijah Baker, and Lionel Walker's dog."

Peter applied himself to stirring his already-stirred tea. "That was nearly twenty years ago, dear brother. I fail to see what relevance it has now."

Thomas gave Kate a bewildered look, and she bit her lip, wondering how much she could or should explain later. Peter had been the only bookish child among the Gravenors, to Papa's great delight. Edward Gravenor had exhausted what little liquid cash the family had possessed, as well as much they did not, to send Peter to a good school, the sort of school which educated sons of gentry. By all accounts her brother had done very well. Perhaps that was why her father had never tried to correct his son's strange and violent behavior.

"You put the dog's body in Lionel's bed," Henry said.

"That animal attacked Jake more than once, and he was lucky to get away the last time with only stitches," Peter said, slamming his mug down on the table. "That dog could have killed him."

"What about that boy? The one at your school?" Henry asked.

Kate sucked in a breath, and she heard Anne do the same. Peter never spoke about what happened to *that boy*. She wondered what Thomas thought they were talking about; but then, it probably wasn't as bad as the truth.

"I have no idea to what you refer," Peter said. "I have comported myself exactly as both our parents would have wished, protecting those to whom I am obligated. None of this has anything to do with the body of Rob Baker or *who killed him.*"

"Not Papa," Henry said, refusing to be dissuaded. He had tried to have this argument with Peter before, Kate remembered suddenly, before he had gone to the army. "Papa wouldn't have wished this for you."

Henry and Peter locked eyes for a long moment, and Kate wondered if they were thinking the same thing she was thinking. Papa had hoped Peter would be a gentle scholar, the sort of man who kept himself busy with gardening and reading, but Maman had never fooled herself about Peter's nature. She recognized herself in her son.

"Papa didn't mean to drown, either," Anne said abruptly. "He wanted to dodder about the hills reading poetry into his nineties. So I suppose what he wanted hardly matters now." She bounced to her feet, took a bowl from the shelves, and bent over the burbling pot on the hearth. She wrinkled her nose. "Lots of greens, I see."

"Whoever killed Rob Baker four weeks ago is still hanging around the farm and watching," Thomas said into the silence. He nodded to the sickle, which now lay in the center of the table on top of some cheesecloth. "I would bet a large sum of money that this was the tool used to behead him and then to cut up the body last night, before it was taken away. Whoever it was knew the trick with the woodshed door to open it quietly." He took a deep breath. "I rather think they were very close at hand indeed, because they waited until we knew who the body was to spirit it away."

"There were people in and out of the house all of yesterday," Kate said, her heart beating faster. It *has* to be John Mary, she thought. Oh, no.

Henry, however, looked with narrowed eyes at Peter. Peter narrowed his eyes right back.

Kate's heart sped up again. Either of them might have done it, if they thought they were protecting the rest of us, she thought. But no. Henry had been carrying Thomas home. And Peter—Peter—

"Well, we know Peter didn't do this because it was all a great mess," Kate said, as calmly as she could. Her heart felt like it might tear itself out of her chest.

This provoked a bark of uncomfortable laughter from Thomas, but Peter, Henry, and Anne exchanged a look.

Henry ladled a portion of soup into a bowl for Kate, for Thomas, for himself, and then pointedly sat down before doing the same for Peter. Kate let out a little growl and started to get to her feet.

"NO," said Thomas, Henry, Peter, and Anne, and "Sit down," said Thomas, and "I'll serve myself, dear sister," said Peter. Kate felt her face go very pink.

"I might have done the killing," Anne mused.

"Did you?" Thomas asked.

"No," Anne said. "Oughtn't you suspect everyone, though?"

"My goal is to keep you safe, not play games with you," Thomas said, but his eyes were on Kate when he said it. Her heart slowed slightly.

"Very well, since we've so generously acquitted everyone in the room, what next?" Peter said.

John Mary, Kate thought, and she felt her lips shape his name.

"I want to talk to John Mary," Thomas said, and his eyes were still keen on her face.

Henry cleared his throat, and everyone looked toward him.

"John Mary isn't here," he said uncomfortably. "He wasn't here last night, either, or if he was, not until very late and gone early. I looked in the barn for him, and in the two closest fields."

"How unexpectedly intelligent of him," Peter snapped. "Though I suppose it hardly matters. Fred Halverton said the head had been sliced clean off, and Henry's a lot stronger than John Mary. One of them will be accused of it, if Daniel Lately ever puts two and two together and realize the man he sent to intimidate the Gravenors is now dead."

"That leaves you with one choice, then," Thomas said. "You have to find out who *did* kill Rob Baker, before Cous—before he decides that one of you did."

# CHAPTER FIFTEEN

"They're … furry," Thomas said.

"They're supposed to be furry," Kate said, patting the nearest cheese. The surface was soft and velvety under her fingers. A sweet, sour, yeasty smell wafted through the pantry, and she breathed in deeply, happily.

Everything outside is frightening and filled with death and blood, she thought, but inside there are cheeses. The cheeses will always be here for me.

Thomas stood in the door of the pantry, several paces behind where she stood at the table, but he felt very close, too close. The thought that he could limp toward her and press against her back made her mind freeze and her fingers still for a moment.

It would make things foolishly complicated if he did any such thing.

Kate wished he would.

She had now made five cheeses, three from the first milkings from Antoinette and two from Antoinette and Nonnette. The first batch had already sprouted a patchy white carpet of mold.

"How do you know?" Thomas asked, crutching another step into the pantry to look more closely.

"How do I know…? Ah. This isn't the first time I've made these," Kate said, glancing at him out of the corner of her eye.

"Your mother taught you," Thomas said.

"Yes. As she taught John Mary and Anne. Or at least, she had started to teach Anne when she … when …" Kate let her voice trail off, and she stared disconsolately down at her cheeses. They had never found Ophélie's body. She hoped it had not been as poorly used as Rob Baker's corpse.

Kate and Anne had fought last night, after they had finished dinner and Peter had announced loudly that he was going home to sleep on a real mattress after all this excitement. The moment he had been out the door, Kate had seized her sister by the hand and demanded to be told the truth about how she was now making money. Kate had brought up safety, and honesty, and the risk to Anne's reputation, but Anne refused to tell her any more than Peter had.

"I gave you my shilling," Anne had said, her exasperation making her words shoot out of her mouth like pebbles. "And before that, I gave John Mary my shilling every week. Why do you care how I earn it? You can't do the work for me, so it ought to be my choice what kind of work I do."

"I should make Anne apprentice to me," Kate muttered darkly. "It would keep her out of trouble."

She caught Thomas' frown out of the corner of her eye.

Then he said slowly, "Not all trouble can be avoided."

Kate turned and looked at him then, looked at the

way the light from the narrow-paned window at the side of room picked out a handful of silver hairs at his temples, awoke blue lights in his black hair, and shaded in the crows' feet around his eyes and the faint lines around his mouth. She thought of Daniel Lately and then, because she hated thinking of Daniel Lately, she thought of what Thomas would have looked like when he was Anne's age. Probably even more hair, she thought. And even more defiance in his eyes.

"I just don't want her to go courting trouble," Kate said, and saw immediately in Thomas' face that it was the wrong thing to say.

"There are many good reasons why a young person might need more privacy than their family might think," he said stiffly.

Kate felt her cheeks go red. "Oh, of course, but —"

I don't think Anne is like you, she thought; I don't think she is a girl who is going to grow up to be a man. She's known John Mary all her life, so she knows what she could be, and that is not what she has chosen.

But without breaking John Mary's confidence, there was no way to say that to Thomas that didn't sound simply like Kate was pushing him away, wishing he was something he wasn't. Anne was tomboyish enough, and cared little enough for womanly pursuits, that maybe it was a natural conclusion from his perspective—

"What if she's selling her favors?" Kate blurted out. Her stomach did a slow, horrible flip, and she wished she hadn't eaten quite as much at breakfast. It didn't make sense—Anne would have to walk to

Southbridge to find someone who didn't know the family—but she hadn't realized until this moment that it was something she was afraid might happen to Anne.

"Her favors?" Thomas repeated, raising an eyebrow.

"You know," Kate hissed, looking around herself, in case Anne had crept back and was now eavesdropping. "What if she gets pregnant? Or sick?"

"What if she's a farm girl who knows how to be careful?" Thomas asked, his voice a study in neutrality. "Would you think less of her?"

Kate swallowed. She had not really thought of Anne being careful. "It's *dangerous.*"

What if Anne is like me? Kate thought. Or worse? What if a pregnancy would kill her?

She could not make her mouth form those words.

"It's dangerous to be alive," Thomas persisted, moving closer. "Would you love your sister less, if she decided it was worth it?" Though his face was still watchful, his eyes had gone intense once again. And then, in case Kate had misunderstood him, he said clearly, enunciating every word, "If Anne decided it was worth it to lie with a man she had no intention of marrying, for money."

"I—" Kate started, then stopped, feeling rather dizzy. She did not think she had had so frank a conversation with anyone since Maman had gone. "I don't want Anne to hurt herself for us," she said.

"She might not consider it a hurt, or not the greatest hurt," Thomas said, his voice very quiet. "There are other trades a woman might make." He rested his hand on the table next to her waist.

"Thomas—have you—do you—"

He did not drop his gaze, and though Kate's face flamed, she did not want to turn away from him either. She was not sure what she was trying to ask him. Had he ever sold his body? Had he ever purchased the favors of another? Did he know what Anne was doing to make money?

"The woman who taught me how to—how to lie with a woman, in *this* body—" the way he said *this* made it clear that he meant *this body which is not as I would have it be* "—in a way that I could tolerate—"

"In what way?" Kate asked, when Thomas paused.

"I suppose you would call it a transaction," Thomas said. "I met her in Lisbon in a—in a—in a brothel, though it was a pleasant enough version of what it was. I visited her for as long as I was posted in Portugal. She was able to rent her own flat two years into the arrangement." He took another step toward her, and Kate felt his gaze rake her face in intimate detail. Was he looking for signs of disgust? Horror? Was he trying to upset her?

"Why are you telling me this?" Kate asked. He was so close now that she had to tip her head back to look up at him.

Thomas did not speak. His brows drew tight together.

"What was her name?" Kate asked.

"Luisa Oliveiras," Thomas said, his voice very soft. "She was a widow, and her husband left her very little. I wondered often about what sort of man her husband was. She was very comfortable with me." Though he did not smile, his eyes crinkled slightly as though he might. "We had only about a hundred words of bad French in common between us. I suppose that is why she took up with a Portuguese officer as soon as she could. It is very trying to not be understood in one's bed."

Kate brought her hands up, wanting to touch Thomas, almost sure that he wanted her to touch him, but unsure of how and where. "Did you love her?" She wondered what they had done in bed together, and whether it had involved the wooden cock she had found sewn neatly into his smallclothes. The idea made her cheeks redden even more.

"I loved being with her," Thomas said. "I would not like to think that her family was ashamed of her. She did what she needed to do to survive, and she— she was very kind to me. Kinder than she ever needed to be."

"We all do what we need to do to survive," Kate said, and dropped her eyes.

"We do what we need to so that we might feel human," Thomas said, sounding angry. "Surviving is not enough. I knew—there are men who risked their lives to become lovers to other men, because they could not feel whole otherwise. The army was full of them. It is not *enough* to survive."

Kate felt an involuntary squeak escape her mouth. Of course Thomas did not know about Jake; Thomas had never met Jake, and it was not as though he had had time to roam the county, interrogating the neighbors about the wicked deeds the youngest Gravenor son had gotten up to before shipping off to become a merchant marine. Thomas had met Fred

Halverton, but Fred was hardly likely to disclose the compromising position he had found his son in with Jake. As far as Kate knew, poor young Roger had been married off to a wheelwright's daughter on the other side of Southbridge, and was now semi-diligently making wheels.

But Thomas heard the squeak, and then he took hold of her hand. "But you know that," he said softly. "Who do you know that from?"

"If Henry hasn't told you, I'm certainly not going to," Kate said, and then felt the blood leave her face all in a rush, because wasn't that as good an admission that one of her brothers was queer as saying it out loud? "But our mother was French," she went on defiantly. "You can hardly expect us to have perfect English morals."

"Henry once forged my signature on a medical release for a soldier who was being blackmailed by another man in his unit," Thomas said conversationally, drawing his index finger down the center of her palm. He had drawn infinitesimally closer, until her breasts almost brushed the front of his waistcoat. "The other fellow saw the soldier get buggered by a local man, and then demanded half his weekly wages for months after."

"Oh," Kate said.

"Did you know that?"

Of course Kate hadn't known that; Henry wouldn't have written such a thing in a letter. Henry might not even think she would be interested. "*If* Henry did such a thing, it was because he felt it was the morally correct thing to do," Kate said. Thomas' finger left a trail of gooseflesh in his wake, and she thought of what it would feel like if he kept stroking it up her wrist, to her forearm, to the tender skin inside her elbow.

"I see," Thomas said. "And you do not trust Anne to have the same judgment?"

Kate almost gasped at how neatly he had turned her words back on her. "I do not think you quite understand what it is like to be raised by a father who only thinks about poetry and a mother who respects no law made by man or god," she said finally. She was shaking slightly, from fear or desire or both. "And I don't think Henry forged your signature. His handwriting is very distinctive."

Thomas looked down at her, his eyelids lowered. "Indeed. He wrote the release on a letter I had scratched out."

"When did he do that?" Kate asked in a whisper.

"Six years ago."

Kate dropped her eyes to study the pattern of the gray neckcloth Thomas wore. "You know who we are," she said to the neckcloth. "You've known for quite some time now."

"I think you begin to know me as well," Thomas said softly, but he dropped her hand and stepped away.

## CHAPTER SIXTEEN

Thomas waited until Kate went out to do the afternoon milking of the three cows to escape the house. He had watched Henry rub a little lamp oil on the back door's hinges the night before through the crack at the back of the chimney. It creaked only a little as Thomas eased it open now.

He did not think he could or should face Kate again so soon after he had told her so many things about his most intimate person—so soon after he had almost kissed her, if he were going to continue being repulsively honest. If she came after him to question what he was doing, smelling of cheese and cow and laundry soap, he was not sure what he would do.

He could not think about Kate right now. He ought to be thinking about murders and disappearing bodies, Daniel Lately and potential discovery.

The Gravenor house sat just below the crest of a hill covered in trees, and an old, tangled hedge separated the kitchen garden and the farmyard from the patch of woodland behind it. Some of this was apparently Ned Bell's field, though it looked an unrelieved mass of trees. Thomas limped slowly along the hedge with his crutches. He thought in another few days he would ask Henry to help him change the heavy, plastered splint he had been wearing for a lighter one made of wood. The broken leg ached, and Thomas thought it ached as though it were healing.

In the back corner of the kitchen garden, there was a low gate, opening into a pathway cut through the trees. Thomas let himself out into the right-of-way.

Even with the branches of the trees mostly bare, save for a few coppery beech and oak leaves flickering in the wind, the path was close and dark. Thomas kept his eyes on the ground as he levered himself over the heavy roots which ribbed the earth.

If Thomas focused on the path, he would not think of all the things he had told Kate, things he had no business telling anyone, let alone her. If he were an unselfish man, maybe he could have recast his decade-ago liaison with Luisa into something sordid, something greasy, that would disgust Kate, push her away from the idea of a life with him. He could not let the two of them simply drift together. He needed to get out of Copstone if he were to have any hope of regaining his career as a doctor. He had no desire to end up like Charles Hamilton or James Howe, humiliated in front of a magistrate for the crime of wearing the name and clothing which belonged to him.

But then Thomas had been caught up in that memory of Luisa, and it was a *good* memory, and he had not been able to speak of it otherwise. He thought Luisa had been in her late thirties or earlier forties when he had first visited her in a narrow building in Lisbon, following her up flight after flight of rickety stairs, passing what felt like dozens of narrow doors, from behind each of which emanated whispers, moans, shouts. He had been so nervous, both wanting desperately to lie with a woman and unsteady at the thought. He had not had either the bravery or the money to go out bawdying with the other medical students in Edinburgh, but Lisbon was so far from home.

Thomas soon understood why this house, and this lady in particular, had been recommended to him by the sly staff sergeant, dropping one eyelid in a lazy wink as he muttered the name. Luisa had drawn out a case of dildos of various sizes and a leather harness which someone might wear about their hips; but instead of putting it on herself, she carefully guided Thomas' hands to the buckles and straps, loosening them to accommodate a body larger and more muscular than her own. He did not like others to touch those parts of him that felt wrong, unnatural on his own body, but Luisa had shown him how he might be. It had felt good and natural to lay between her thighs as she reclined on the bed, her legs wrapped around his hips as he thrust into her, kissing her neck and rubbing himself against her soft body.

Now, it was all too easy to imagine Kate as the soft form beneath him, the shining hair spread around them fire-brilliant. She had been surprised by his sudden irascible need to tell her unmentionable things, but she had listened, and she had asked the questions he had wanted, not the ones he had expected. *Did you love her.*

Thomas had very nearly told her about Albert Percival as well, who he had met when he and Henry had been sent to Cape Town to advise on the sanitation of the military hospital and barracks there. Percival had been a naval officer, a jovial and slight young fellow who had enjoyed a glass of port, a game of chess, and a thorough buggering. Percival's hair had been sun-gold, rather like Kate's, and Thomas had only just caught himself from saying his name. Thomas had only just caught himself, but he could not endanger Percival so, who he now understood to be married to a tyrant slip of a girl from some family in Sussex.

But Kate had not been shocked by the notion of men loving each other either—or she had been shocked, but because she thought he understood some secret about her family. He wondered which of her brothers was the queer one. The apparently murderous Peter? The absent Jake? The mysterious, unseen John Mary?

Thomas paused to rub at the top of his splint as he leaned against the smooth white trunk of a beech. Aside from the persistent throb of his bones knitting themselves together, his leg itched like mad.

Kate's many difficult brothers made the inside of his mind itch even more. Peter had accused him of cutting up the body and taking it away. The idea was patently ridiculous; where could Thomas have stowed a sack of body parts without anyone noticing? Why would Thomas do such a thing?

To protect Kate, his mind answered him. To protect Henry.

Thomas sighed. He would have protected Henry better if he had not told Kate what her brother had done for that young private. He had wanted—he wasn't sure what he had wanted her to know, when he had told her that.

*I, too, can keep secrets for the people I love.*

*I could keep your secrets.*

Thomas drew in a deep breath of icy air through his nose. He had touched Kate's hand, her tough but smooth palm. He had thought how that hand might feel as she touched him, drawing her fingers along his neck, his shoulder.

No. There were far more pressing things for him to worry about than the aching longing in his chest. He crutched onward.

The right-of-way went over the top of the hill and then curved down along its far side, a tunnel through the oaks where the icy ghost of the wind hissed. Thomas shuddered and tugged the collar of his jacket higher. It was already the first week of March, but it was still bitterly cold.

The path turned a little more, and suddenly Thomas was looking down into the stream, just visible through a narrow opening in the bowing alders. The water was not yet deep, but the steep banks on either side foretold a spring flood.

Henry had seen the body—no, not the body, the body's thumbless hand—while standing in the middle of the stream on a dark night, Thomas thought. So it couldn't have been more than a few feet from the crossing.

Thomas inched down the bank with his crutches and stepped into the frigid water. He clenched his jaw at the shock of the cold and the pull of the current. Standing in the center of the stream, turning slowly from side to side, he saw that it widened in one direction and narrowed in the other. From Kate and Henry's descriptions, he knew that downstream the water passed the Halverton farm; upstream went west for a bit, then curled north, toward Daniel Lately.

Thomas, without thinking, bared his teeth at the water.

The alders grew more thickly in that direction, almost meeting over the water. They would have obscured most of a body lying beneath them. Thomas considered, and then took a few slow, painful steps upstream.

A half-hour later, he was soaked to the knee, deathly cold, and had found nothing for his troubles beneath the low-hanging alders except an irate water vole. Unsurprisingly, the water had borne away any traces the body had left on the streambed, and he found nothing caught on an alder branch or lodged among their roots.

Thomas dragged himself out of the stream on the other side, his teeth chattering and his mind whirring.

There's nothing here, he thought, not so much as a broken branch or twig; and isn't that significant? Surely if Rob Baker had been killed here in the stream, there would have been a struggle of some kind, something that would have left some of those alders smashed or disarrayed. It's cold, and the plants are dead or frozen; if the signs were here a month ago, they would still be here. Even if the man had been hit in the head and fallen backwards into the stream, he would have crushed some of the longer plants draping over the water with his fall.

Only he hadn't fallen here, had he? If he had, his feet would have been pointed toward the path, his headless neck toward the onrushing water. Henry had seen a single hand, sticking out into the crossing. That meant the arm had been outstretched, and the rest of the body upstream.

Could whoever had killed Rob Baker have dumped him a ways farther up the brook, and the water have moved him this way?

Thomas stomped his good foot, trying to bring feeling back into his sodden toes, and assessed his options. The path left the water here, cutting northwest alongside an ancient, narrow field, while the stream went almost straight east. If he wanted to find the place the body might have been pushed in, he ought to step off the right-of-way and elbow his way through the undergrowth.

There was some sort of track along the bank, the sort that sheep or deer might have made. Thomas alternately crutched over the roots and levered himself between tree trunks, staring intently at the undergrowth for any sign of a break.

He was so focused on the bushes that he did not see the man kneeling in a little clearing by the track on the other side of the path. His crutch hit the stranger's knee with a *thwack*, and he shot to his feet with a foul curse.

A foul curse in French. Thomas blinked at the man scowling down at him. How many people spoke French in this parish who weren't Gravenors? This man didn't look much like Kate or Henry, but he and Anne shared the same long face and auburn hair. His was darker than Anne's, and he didn't have much more of a beard than Thomas did himself. He dressed in the same shabby way that Henry and Kate did, with multiple layers obscuring his form.

"My apologies," Thomas said, shifting his crutch to the other side so he could offer his hand. "I didn't see you. I am Thomas Holyoke."

The man looked down at his hand as though it might bite before reluctantly putting out his own. "John Gravenor."

"John Mary," Thomas said, before he could stop himself.

"Yes," was the curt response. "I had better be on my way."

Thomas looked at his hand, and found it was covered in ash, as though John Mary had been digging in a fireplace. "What were you doing?"

John Mary did not meet his eyes, but instead looked over his shoulder. "I'm coming back from the far field. I've had to let it go fallow the past two years, but it will need plowing this year if Kate's to live with me."

None of that explained why John Mary had been kneeling in a clearing in the wood with ash on his hands. Thomas looked around. No trees or bushes grew for four paces on either side of the path at this spot, and the patch of clear ground wore a shaggy coat of dead grass. John Mary had gotten to his feet next to a narrow, sandy depression, and though he had clearly been cleaning away the remains of a fire, Thomas could still see a few pieces of charcoal. Behind John Mary— in fact John Mary seemed to be standing in such a way

as to obscure as much of his view as possible—were
two trees about three paces apart, and if Thomas
squinted he could see the remains of a rope tied
around the leftmost one, as though someone had
erected a tent or hung a hammock there.

"Vagrants?" he asked, nodding at the tree.

John Mary looked so vague that Thomas felt
suspicion rise immediately in his chest. Kate had said
her oldest brother slept in the barn to watch over the
cattle, but was he now camping in the woods for some
reason?

"Bah, je m'en fous," the taller man murmured.

"If you do let vagrants camp on your land, you
ought to warn them that a murderer is wandering
about," Thomas said sharply. "It would be the decent
thing to do."

John Mary's gaze snapped back to him. Thomas
briefly wondered if he had miscalculated terribly. If
John Mary had killed Rob Baker and dismembered him,
then perhaps confronting him alone in the woods was
not the smartest thing Thomas had ever done.

But John Mary only jerked his chin at Thomas' wet
trousers. "You'd best be going back soon. Kate will
have a fit if you make yourself sick."

Thomas shook his head. "I'll keep walking for a
bit." He eyed the alders at the edge of this little
clearing. "I'd like to see where that body was pushed
into the stream."

"There's nothing to see here," John Mary said.

"Maybe the head's still around," Thomas returned.

"You aren't going to find anything," John Mary
repeated, his face going mulish.

"Man, do you realize how much danger you're in?" Thomas exploded.

He realized his mistake a moment too late, as the discordant, familiar notes of John Mary's appearance settled into their proper places in his mind. Abruptly Thomas was back in his anatomy lecture in Edinburgh, listening tensely as Dr. Humphries detailed the differences between male and female skeletons in a bored monotone.

"And as you can see, the brow ridge … is thicker and more prominent … the greater mandibular height …"

John Mary did not have much of brow ridge, though his brows were thick and dark, and his chin was pointed rather than square. Thomas suspected the two waistcoats the other man wore atop each other disguised hips wider than his waist.

John Mary gave him a cold, appraising eye. "No more than you, *man.*"

Thomas sucked in a breath, remembering exactly how close Cousin Daniel was, and how much his future life depended on no one—or no one *else*—discovering his previous one. "Fair enough."

"I told Henry we ought not bring a doctor into the house," John Mary muttered. "But he didn't understand the risk."

Thomas bit back a snappish defense. After all, hadn't he often thanked God for delivering him the least perceptive assistant in existence? Henry had never indicated by so much as a furrowed brow that he suspected Thomas had not been raised as a man, even after living in close quarters with him for seven years, even after carrying him onto the ship that took them back to England, even after—

"Henry understands some things," Thomas said stiffly.

*Kate*, Thomas thought. Kate understands many things. She knew what I was from the moment I came into her house, and I couldn't see it because I didn't see how a woman who lives in the back corner of nowhere would know such a thing. *Men can be very touchy about their relevant anatomy.* Well, she should know, because she was raised with a brother who had every reason to hide his own anatomy.

Thomas spared a thought to wonder about Ophélie and Edward Gravenor, and how they had come to raise such children.

"You really ought to get back to the house," John Mary said.

Kate does not deserve to have so many boneheaded brothers, Thomas thought.

"Did you kill Rob Baker?" Thomas asked.

John Mary's face did something inexplicable before settling back into belligerent indifference. "I did not."

"Do you know who did?"

"Why in this fine green earth under God in heaven do you think I would tell *you* if I knew that?" snarled John Mary.

Thomas felt like a chunk of ice had congealed in his stomach. "To protect Kate and Henry," he said. "To protect your family."

"I am protecting my family," John Mary said. "*Go back to the house.*"

I'm going to help you, whether you want me to or not, Thomas thought, but John Mary had several inches and a significant amount of health on him. If John Mary wanted to drag him away from here, there was very little Thomas could do to stop him. But he wasn't sure he would get another chance to look at this clearing before John Mary removed anything that might connect it to the murder.

That *would* connect it to the murder, Thomas thought.

Thomas bought himself time by the simple expedient of taking a step forward, tripping, and falling heavily. John Mary let out another French expletive, though Thomas landed on his good side, only wrenching his shoulder a little.

Thomas sat up slowly. I'm too old for this, he thought.

"Bordel de merde de putain de vache," John Mary said.

The clearing looked much the same from the ground as it did standing. Thomas put a hand out to steady himself, scrabbling a little into the sand for purchase, and his fingers found several long, narrow slots, frozen into the soil. He frowned a cleared a little of the sand out of the way. It was almost as if someone had carved into the hard soil with the sharp tip of a blade.

His hand closed on something else buried in the sand, a long, flat object, stone or wood or maybe both. His thumb found a pattern carved into its surface, too regular to be the natural effect of wind and time. But before he could look too closely at it, John Mary had an arm under his shoulders and was hoisting him back to his feet.

Thomas shoved the thing into the pocket of his coat.

"Right, too much time outside for you," John Mary said. "On y va."

A flash of red caught at the edge of Thomas' vision, and he jerked his head to see who was watching them, but there was only a black-eyed robin peering down at the two men through the branches.

## CHAPTER SEVENTEEN

"Your lips are *blue*," muttered Kate. "How *could* you?"

John Mary had unceremoniously dumped Thomas on the bed in the kitchen, kissed Kate on the cheek, and vanished again. Kate, who had been heating the morning's milk to start another batch of cheese, took one look at the doctor's white face, pushed the coals from beneath the cheese pot to under the kettle, and applied herself to removing his soaked boots and trousers.

Now she was briskly massaging the foot of his injured leg. His toes were worryingly cold and stiff, and fear tightened her chest and made breathing harder. How many little bits of carelessness had ended in lives lost, in limbs lost? Will had not looked to his footing in the far barn, so he had fallen and broken his neck. Papa had not looked to his footing as he walked along the dam at the mill pond at Roughton, so he had slipped and drowned.

"Everyone in this house is remarkably cavalier about who actually killed Rob Baker," Thomas said through clenched teeth. "I am trying to find out the truth."

"Wiggle your toes," Kate said, glaring at him. She had wrapped him in one of Henry's old coats and several quilts, then climbed onto the foot of the bed and lifted his feet into her lap. "You'll be lucky if all you have is a little frostbite."

"You are not listening to me, and let me remind you that I have years of medical training and experience," Thomas said, glowering back at her.

That, strangely, made Kate furious, more furious than she could recall being. She thought perhaps it was the contrast between this version of Thomas, all officiousness and impatience, and the strange, intimate version of himself which he had briefly let her see this morning, when he had spoken of his past loves. Did he regret taking her so far into his confidence, foolish and common as she was?

"I see," she said. "Then take some advice from a lowly country wife, *sir*. You do *my* work and *my* time a dishonor by treating your own life so cheaply. You are still not strong, and you've no business mucking about in cold water in freezing weather. You would pay me back for nursing you for weeks by catching pneumonia. You might as well—as well—" She cast about the the room for the right comparison, and her eye fell on the pot of milk. "You might as well spit in my cheese," she finished angrily. She was clutching the arch of his right foot now in both hands. His feet were very long and nicely-shaped, she thought disgustedly. Of course they would be; her own were small and stumpy and wide.

"My health is my own concern," Thomas said stiffly, rather as though he were being choked. "There are more important matters at hand."

"And what are those?" Kate snapped. "Proving one of my brothers to be a murderer?" She had not missed the long, hard look Thomas had aimed at John Mary as he rushed out the door.

"Kate," Thomas hissed. "*Stop touching my feet.*"

Kate shook her head, angry tears burning in the corners of her eyes. "If you won't take care of yourself, someone has to. That's what I do. That's what I'm *for.* I take care of—"

There ensued a brief, intense struggle. Thomas leaned forward, wrapped both arms around Kate, yanked her against himself, and then, through some geometrical means she could not quite parse, twisted around so he was lying on top of her.

She had a shocked moment to consider their relative positions; she was now stretched out on the bed, her legs parted so that Thomas' splinted leg could rest between them. He had hitched his good leg up so his calf rested against her thigh. He was not wearing trousers, only the damp small clothes that she had rolled up to his knees, though he still had on a shirt and waistcoat. There were still several layers of fabric between them, petticoats and at least one quilt, and Kate thought dizzily that she would cheerfully take the scissors to her second-best skirt if she could feel Thomas' skin on her skin.

"My feet," Thomas said, his lips almost touching hers, "are ticklish."

Then he kissed her.

I don't think this is a very good idea, said some faraway part of Kate's mind, but she was already past hearing.

Thomas' mouth was still alarmingly cold on hers. Perhaps that was why she put her hand up to touch his head, so she could continue to rub feeling back into his extremities. His ear was certainly chilled as she traced its curve, before lacing her fingers through the hair at the nape of his neck, pulling his face more firmly to her own.

He explored her mouth with tongue and teeth, and then his lips traveled down her jaw and came to rest on her neck. One of his beautiful, long-fingered hands came to her throat and tugged her shawl down so he could apply his mouth to the delicate skin it had covered, kissing and then sucking lightly.

Kate turned her head and bit Thomas on the jaw, too clumsy and too hungry. He lifted his head an inch and looked down at her with glinting black eyes, and she had a half moment to wonder if she'd been too forward, too forceful, before his mouth was on hers again, ravenous, and the hand that wasn't now holding her chin wrapped itself around one of her wrists, pinning her arm to the mattress by her head.

She had missed so much, and she had missed *this*, being anchored securely under the weight of another person half-crazed with wanting. It hurt to remember that Will had ever been like this with her. Will had resented her miscarriages and the stillbirth, but the sickness and depression which had followed had made him furious.

But now Thomas had stopped kissing her, and Kate realized there were tears on her face. He was just looking at her now, not with horror or disgust or even worry, but with a profound, still contemplation.

"Don't stop," she said, or tried to say, but her words came out as a croak. Thomas pressed his face into her hair, inhaling deeply.

Kate realized belatedly that she was still holding the back of his head with her hand. She ought to let go, oughn't she? She stroked her fingernails along his scalp, eliciting a shudder that she felt all through her body. His hair was thick and smooth and cool under her fingers, but his skin was finally warming.

"I want," Thomas said, hoarsely and quietly against her ear, "to take your clothes off and touch you all over."

Kate sucked in a breath. The soft air of his words shivered over her skin. Her stomach felt warm and tight, and the warmth kept moving lower, to where his body pressed heavily between her legs.

This part, Kate thought, this part had always been good, even when she had known to be afraid of what came after, the planting of seed that would never grow.

Thomas can't hurt you that way, her mind said softly. There are any number of other ways he might hurt you, but not that.

"I don't—" she started, but Thomas pulled away from her sharply, a furrow between his brows. That was not at all what Kate wanted, so she strained after him, trying to catch his mouth with her mouth, until whatever she had meant to say was lost again in the warm force and friction of lips. Thomas ran his teeth over her lower lip, and another shudder of heat and hunger moved down her body, thudding between her legs.

I want this so much, Kate thought, dizzy, half-ashamed. She thought she had reconciled herself to her loneliness, but it appeared she had simply been waiting greedily for the insistent, comforting weight of this man atop her in a narrow bed.

"Let me," Thomas said, folding his fingers around her hand.

Then he did something awful and rolled off her, taking his reassuring warmth and weight with him. If not for his leg, Kate would have tried to climb atop him, a thought that made her go pink and hot.

But Thomas' other hand was moving under the hem of the short gown she wore, stroking over her belly and finding the waistband of her skirt. The garment was an old one that Kate had made for herself the first time she had gotten pregnant, but now she was only relieved that it came off easily. Thomas had gone back to sucking on the corner of her jaw, and now he was loosening the ties at the sides of her gown. She had lined and quilted it for warmth, which meant that she didn't usually bother with stays when she wore it about the farm.

"*Oh*," Kate breathed. Hesitantly she drew the hand he was not holding down his neck, his shoulder, to the front of his waistcoat. Of course she had bathed his whole person while he was ill and unconscious, but asking to touch and see him now felt decidedly more personal. She *wanted* to see him. Thomas was considerably more spare of frame than she was; even after several weeks of eating as much bread and fresh cheese as she could bully him into, she could feel the edge of his ribcage through his clothing.

Thomas got his hand beneath her gown entirely, and Kate lost track of what she had been thinking, focusing only on his mouth, lightly brushing her cheek, and the tips of his fingers, exploring her right breast. He stroked lightly, once, twice, only just brushing the very tip of her nipple, before taking her breast in his cold hand. It was maddening.

"You can—" She shouldn't say this out loud, she shouldn't— "You can—harder than—"

She had a fraction of a second to worry if he would be horrified, if he would be disgusted that she knew what to ask for, that she must have learned something from a man not him—

Then Thomas' thumb and forefinger squeezed the tip of her breast, making the nipple tighten in a hard bud of desire, and she sucked in her breath with a sound that was embarrassingly close to a squeal. He rolled her nipple back and forth—like—like—she thought of herself testing cheese curds and let out a little gasp of laughter. Thomas' hand found her other breast, pinching sharply, and her laughter turned into a soft moan. It hurt. "Again, please."

His other hand, the one she had forgotten about, tugged her hand down along her body.

Thomas gently pulled Kate's hand downward, using her own fingers to trace the line of her breast and then her belly. His mind was a perfect, hot, fiery blank of hunger and joy and other emotions he would not name, lest they haunt him in the lonely nights to come. He wished for a dildo like the one he had used with Luisa, so he could rut into Kate, but even without, he

could be inside her, forge some kind of connection
that she would feel even after he was gone.

He liked that she wanted his forcefulness. He liked
it so much that he felt his own body pulsing in
response to hers.

Thomas took Kate's hand and used it to stroke a
path down her side, moving inexorably down her hip,
over her thighs, to the good, lovely, wet place between
them.

"Kate," he said into her ear. "How do you make
yourself come?"

"I—"

He pulled her hand beneath the loose waistband
of her skirt, beneath her petticoat. She was not wearing
drawers. He squeezed her breast, hard, with his other
hand.

"*Kate.*"

"I don't—"

"Here," Thomas said, spreading her fingers over
her own cunt. He ran his thumb over the nub at the
top lightly, once, twice, then used her thumb to do the
same. "This. How do you do this?"

Kate was very red, and her eyes were unfocused.
"I—I mean—Will didn't like—he said it was—he said I
was—not—he didn't like—"

"Will," Thomas said, barely controlling the anger
which surged through his chest, "is dead. The man in
your bed is not, and I want you to touch yourself until
you come."

There was a horrible moment where he wondered
if he'd gone too far—bringing up a woman's dead
husband while his fingers pressed into her cunt was

surely the definition of too far—but then the moment passed, and Kate let out a little moan and tried to press her whole body into his.

"Can't you lay on top of me again," she said, her voice a little desperate. "If you just—"

"No," he said, kissing her neck. "Make yourself come, and then I'll do whatever you like."

"Please," Kate said, turning her face as if she would hide her expression in the pillow.

But under his hand, her fingers had begun to move, tentatively at first, then more firmly. Somehow it did not surprise him that Kate liked a hard, fast stroke, right across the most sensitive part of herself. He loosened his grip for a moment, and she whimpered, but then he pushed two fingers inside her, inside where she was slick and hot and her muscles gripped his hand, and she rubbed herself faster, more desperately as he pumped his hand in her and played with her breasts, pinching and biting them through the fabric of her gown, and then—and then—

And then she was clenching and then relaxing and then clenching again, and he had promised her, so he rolled on top of her, and she spread her thighs so his weight rested solidly on her softest parts. He wore the wooden cock every hour of every day he was awake and most of those he was asleep, and he used it to grind against her. It was not as satisfying as the erect version, but it was hard and he was heavy and Kate clung to him like she was drowning and he was her only hope of rescue. He felt himself approach an edge, and it was so surprising that he bit his own lip until he tasted blood. His core tightened, and he sucked in his breath through his nose and held it until he felt a wave of release shudder through him, starting where he was pressed tight to Kate's wet center.

When Thomas came back to himself, Kate's eyes were closed. She had fallen asleep beneath him, utterly relaxed by two orgasms. He stared at her in astonishment, and then started to laugh.

## CHAPTER EIGHTEEN

The long, flat object that Thomas had found in the remains of the camp by the stream was a whetstone, a gray rectangle of quartz mounted on a piece of darkened wood. A few sinuous lines were carved into the wood which suggested a running horse.

Thomas sat on the old, uncomfortable settee in the Gravenor parlor, staring at the whetstone in his palm, the lithe little horse illuminated by a pale beam of sunlight from the front window. He ran his thumb over it again and thought. Who had left it in that clearing, John Mary or the unknown vagrant?

What had this stone been used to sharpen, and how recently? Thomas thought of the clean slices through Rob Baker's cervical vertebrae, and of the hand-sickle with the twine-bound handle. It had disappeared off the kitchen table sometime in the past few days, and neither Henry nor Kate knew where it had gone. Peter or Anne might have taken it; John Mary almost certainly *had* taken it. Thomas turned that idea over in his head, but it didn't feel quite right.

If John Mary had used the sickle to kill and butcher a man, and he had used this whetstone to sharpen the blade, why had it been buried in the sand? If he had killed Rob Baker, why had he left the body so close to his own farm? If he hadn't, who had made that camp and left the whetstone?

The problem was that Thomas had believed John Mary when he had said he hadn't killed Rob Baker, but he had also believed him when he said that he was protecting his family. Who did he mean?

Kate. Kate. *Kate.* Thomas' hand tightened around the whetstone, and he stared at it without seeing. The days since she had climbed out of his bed had passed in a blur of incoherent, frustrated hunger.

Henry had brought Thomas green wood to make a new, lighter splint for his leg. Then the big man had carefully cut away the old cast using his pocketknife. Henry had a careful and delicate touch, but he could not avoid stretching Thomas' leg in new and unpleasant ways. The boil on his thigh where the edge of the hoof had dug into his flesh had mostly healed, thanks to Kate's assiduous cleaning, but it still ached steadily. Thomas had only managed to get Kate to leave the kitchen by the expedient of threatening to throw himself off the bed and break his leg again. He did not want to know what unpleasant thing might come out of his mouth when he saw the angle his leg had healed at, and he did not want her to know either.

But Thomas could still see her peeking through the kitchen windows every few minutes, and when Henry stood up from beside the bed with a satisfied, "Well!" Kate rushed back in, bearing an armful of silvery willow branches like a small fire-haired, rain-misted goddess. She set to peeling the branches and brewing the bark, before approaching him with a mug in hand and a determined expression.

Thomas should not have let Kate hold the back of his head and tip the smooth hard rim of the cup against his mouth. He was not a child and he did not need coddling and he did not need help, and her fingers tugged ever-so-lightly against the hair on his nape where she held him, making his scalp prickle and a shiver run the length of his spine, and he could feel the grit of the clay in the mug against his still-tender mouth, and he closed his eyes rather than look at Kate's face, her eyes, her lips.

And then, he felt embarrassment enter her body like a cold wind slipping under the door, and the hand holding his head loosened, and she formed his hands around the mug and stepped away from him. He did not open his eyes to watch her walk away from him, but he felt chilled to his very bones.

Thomas could not help but watch Kate, so he crutched his way into the desolate parlor and sat where Kate did not want to be, staring at Edward Gravenor's battered collection of poetry and plays.

After the third day of this, Thomas started taking down books and trying to read. The volumes which had been crammed on the high, ancient mantelpiece had fared reasonably well, the ambient heat wrapping around from the kitchen keeping them dry, but the books in the little writing desk which sat under the leaking window were black with mold.

Kate truly did not like the parlor, for she only ducked in every hour to ask if he wanted tea or toast or some fresh cheese, and she did not linger, especially when she saw a book laid open on his knee. Thomas gritted his teeth and did not follow her back into the kitchen to ask her what she was doing or question her about cheeses or the criminal habits of her brothers. He had tried to ask if there was other family, aunts or uncles or cousins that John Mary might be protecting, but the words had barely formed in his mouth before Kate was refusing.

"We are the very last leaf of the very last branch of Papa's family," she had said, her face twisting in an expression that was like a smile but not very pleasant. "He wrote once to the scion of the name, who I believe lives in Cheshire, and he wrote back to say Papa was a fraud and to stop calling ourselves Gravenors at once."

"And your mother?" Thomas had tried, but Kate confirmed his worst suspicions.

"The flu came to her village, and then the guillotine," she said, very calmly despite how she twisted her apron strings tight around her fingers. "She had no one."

Thomas had not wrapped Kate in his arms and tried to soothe the shadow of desolation of her voice, but his arms and shoulders ached with the desperate effort to keep himself from doing so. This, he thought, was why he needed to confine himself to the parlor and a dusty copy of Coleridge, until he could control himself. He didn't have words for the emotions seething underneath his skin. He had felt a deep tenderness for Luisa, a great affection for Albert Percival, but he could not remember *wanting* another person in this terrified, terrifying, body-consuming way.

He had anticipated each of his assignations with his previous lovers, but when he closed his eyes, Kate's soft body was beneath him and Kate's face was before him, her eyes closed, her lips parted, her glorious hair all around her. It felt like being haunted.

When Thomas had been trapped in his parents' house with Cousin Daniel, a teenaged child subject to unpredictable cruelty, he had craved freedom, *escape*, with his whole being. He had hated the war, with its endless procession of brutalized and dying young men, but the constant movement, from surgery tent to surgery tent, from one city to the next, had suited him, affording a measure of protective anonymity. Few people knew who Thomas Holyoke was in southern Portugal, and none at all knew who he had been condemned to be. The ceaseless change had felt like insurance for his freedom.

Had that been why Thomas had told Henry to leave him to a certain death by infection in Gibraltar? He had not been able to imagine a life without the clockwork of the British Army whirring behind him, giving him legitimacy and respect, the hum of the machinery drowning out any suspicions about who he was or where he might have come from. Like everyone else, he had read the salacious newspaper accounts of female husbands at home in England, inevitably betrayed by their wives to public humiliation and punishment as dictated by the magistrates. The thought of putting his life in the hands of a woman who could destroy him had not been one Thomas could bear. Cousin Daniel had made a point of destroying the trousers and boots, shirts and braces which Thomas had worn around the farm, claiming a brutal intimacy of knowledge: *I know what you really are, and it is not this.* And then he had followed that with more brutality, more insistence that he knew what Thomas' body was and what it was useful for—

Luisa and Percival had both, in different ways, occupied the same shifting ground that Thomas had, Luisa a woman alone in wartime and Percival a queer man in a foreign colony, shifting ground that allowed neither party a clear advantage. The very thought of a good, solid English woman who might wield the same power over him that Cousin Daniel had made the bile rise in Thomas' throat.

And then there is Kate, he thought. Who is already protecting so many people's secrets that I am only one more.

Kate did not make him feel like a terrible, tragic secret. She was an ordinary, gentle woman who was good at making cheese and liked to be fucked, and she looked at him like an ordinary man. An ordinary man who she would like to be fucked by. Kate had only checked on him once today in the very early morning, because she had gone to sell the first of her cheeses at the market in Southbridge. Her absence buzzed against the back of his neck like a mosquito; he kept wanting to rise and go see what she was doing, only to remember that she was not here.

Thomas sighed and turned the whetstone in his fingers, tracing the horse with his thumb. The moanings and mutterings of Coleridge's mariner had no hope of drawing his attention away from this line of thought.

The front door banged open. "Anne's working for Miss James! She's not doing anything terrible for the shilling! Or it might be terrible, but at least it's *respectable*."

Kate yelled this to the whole house before stepping foot inside, but after a minute she poked her head around the chimney into the parlor. "Thomas? Are you there?" Her face was pink with cold, and she clutched her coat and a bonnet.

"Miss James?" Thomas repeated. The name sparked against his memory. "She's the squire's ... cousin?"

"She's Lord Houghton's aunt, and she's *very* particular and peculiar, but she said Anne had been running errands for her and she was a clever girl," Kate said all in a rush, advancing on him. Her blue eyes glimmered with a panicked light. "I don't know why Anne wouldn't just tell me that. But Miss James came to the market in Southbridge today in her pony cart because it was so unseasonably warm, and she bought three cheeses because Anne told her they were French. And they *are* French, Maman was French and she taught me to make them, but I never thought that was a reason to pay extra money, but Thomas, she *did*. A pound of cheese ought to sell for four shillings but she gave me a guinea for three of them. She said they were beautiful cheeses." She seized one of his hands in her excitement. Her cold fingers shook. Her eyes were enormous and so very blue and earnest.

"Don't you have gloves?" Thomas asked, setting the whetstone on his thigh so he could rub her hands between his own. Mentally he was already working out

the value of the cheeses Kate had aging on the top
pantry shelves. The third cow, whose name always
started Kate off singing the same song, had calved this
week, and now she was making two or three cheeses
every day.

"Miss James said I would need a nicer dress if I
am to sell expensive cheese," Kate said, sudden distress
in her voice. "She said she knew she could trust Anne's
word, but other people could not."

Thomas, before he could stop himself, put out a
hand and stroked it over Kate's skirt, feeling the shape
of her thigh beneath. He swallowed hard before
forcing himself to go on. "Did your husband never buy
you new things? I think I've only seen you in things
made over from Henry's old clothes."

Kate's face stilled, some of the wild light going out
of her eyes. Thomas wished he could bite back those
words. He focused on chafing her hands to warmth.

"I think Will thought that one advantage of
marrying a penniless girl was that I couldn't expect
much of him," she said finally, in a tone that sounded
like she was trying to make a joke and failing. "I had a
few more things, but his brother—his brother sent me
out of the house without them."

Thomas' hands closed tightly around Kate's and
stopped moving. "Why would any man be so
uncharitable?"

"He thought it was my fault we had no children,"
Kate said. She slowly sat down on the settee close to
him, as though she were not quite sure her legs would
hold her up. "Well, he would have; that's what Will
thought too." She stared at their clasped hands.

Thomas' hands seemed to be alive with their own intent. One of them reached forward to slide a piece of Kate's golden-red hair behind her ear. He had not thought himself capable of this sort of tenderness. "Pardon me?"

"There were three miscarriages," Kate said, and her words made the cool quiet of the parlor a strange and hollow silence. "And then the baby who was born —was not born. He was not—" Thomas brushed his knuckles across her cheek, and Kate stopped speaking. "I wouldn't let Will touch me for a year after that," she said, in the calm voice of a person who believes herself beyond grief. "And then Will died. So I suppose it is my fault, and his brother was right."

Kate looked very small sitting on the settee; when Thomas glanced downward he saw that only one of her feet touched the ground, and the other swung in the empty space beneath. Her round face did not, he thought, look so calm when he studied her carefully; her lips trembled, and her eyes had a threatening redness at the corners. He looked at down at her small, broad-fingered hands wrapped in his larger ones, and thought of the strength of those hands, the strength of her freckled forearms and the shoulders he had not seen bare in the daylight.

*I am useful*, Kate had said. *It is what I am for.* As though she were a tool, not a woman, not a person.

"Did you ever see a doctor?" Thomas asked. He was not angry, because William Easting was already dead, and therefore Thomas could not beat him to death, and therefore there was no point in being angry.

"Doctors are expensive," Kate said. "It's a natural

process, Will said. I ought to have been able to do it."

Thomas thought again of being trapped in that house with Cousin Daniel, how his notion of his own body had been exploded, warped, ripped open by that man's violation of it. And then that other life forced into Thomas had pushed him out of his own body, made him a refugee hiding in the recesses of his mind, fleeing the horror wrought by an uncaring natural world. *Natural.* All manner of tortures, of suffering, of inhumane cruelty were *natural.*

Why had William Easting not been sent to Portugal, to be blown up for the honor of Britain? Thomas thought.

Kate let out a startled laugh, and Thomas realized he'd said that last thing aloud.

"They had a farm to run, and there was enough money to keep George at home. I don't know how much good a doctor would have done, anyway. You've met Wendell Driver," Kate said. The desperate sadness that outlined her words made Thomas' throat close sympathetically. "The doctor in Copstone before him was worse. That's why Wendell went away to Wolverhampton to apprentice."

"He could have taken you to London to see a specialist," Thomas said, knowing he sounded ridiculous. And then, because apparently he was determined to make a fool of himself, he said, "I could take you."

"You could take me where?" Kate said blankly. She must have misheard him. There was no way Thomas— Dr. Thomas Holyoke—had said what she had thought he had said.

"To London," Thomas said. "I am behind in my reading, but I believe there have been advances recently —"

"With what money?" Kate said. It felt like a great empty place had opened up inside her chest, a hollow spot that perhaps reached all the way down to her womb. Maybe that had been her problem, all along; she had only blank space inside, where she ought to have had organs.

"Your cheeses," Thomas said. "You said you sold three for a guinea, and there must be twelve more on the shelves in the pantry."

"The house needs thatching, and the barn, and John Mary must buy seed," Kate said. "That money is spoken for."

Thomas was still holding her hands, and Kate carefully extracted her own, rather than let him feel her fingers shake. He let her go.

Why couldn't Will have been the one saying this to her, two years or four years or six years ago? Why did she have to find out there was the sliver of a chance she could have been fixed, could have been made whole, after that chance was useless to her?

"There will be more money."

"I can't go to London to see a special doctor as a *widow*."

There was a breath where Kate thought she had ended the conversation, and she was thankful, because her throat felt like it had closed up, and she was not sure she could force more words out without choking on them.

"You might not always be a widow," Thomas said. Kate looked up at him, and the tenderness on his face was too much. She immediately looked away again. She knew, or could guess, the future he was hinting at, because it was a future she had let herself dream of for a few breaths as well.

That was another cruel sliver of hope, and an ember of resentment kindled in Kate's heart. No one would have her in Copstone parish; her family was too strange, and she had a horrible suspicion that Will and George had told everyone in the county by way of the men who drank at King George's Bull that she was barren. The chance that a doctor could bring her safely through a pregnancy was slight, and even if it hadn't been, she could not leave this place. What of Henry? What of all her siblings, and the farm that felt like it might vanish beneath her feet?

At least you know Thomas isn't a man who beds women he despises, Kate told herself. He would not offer this kindness otherwise. But that wasn't enough; it couldn't be enough.

"Who would marry me?" Kate asked, not wanting to hear the answer, but unable to bear Thomas spinning a fantasy that could never be realized.

Thomas drew in a deep breath. "When my leg is healed, I could go alone and set up a practice in London. I have army friends who would recommend me; I think I might make a good living. And then, when I have money—"

"I have no doubt you would," Kate said, blinking back tears. "And I might have a few shillings saved from cheesemaking then, but my family would still need me, and I would likely still be related to a murderer. I'm sure you would find other prospects in London."

There, she thought, that is an ending. He only has to accept it.

But then Thomas reached for her and slid his hand up her jaw, until his middle finger rested in the hollow behind her ear. He did not apply pressure, only let his palm lay lightly against the curve of her face, but the weight of his gaze was so heavy that Kate finally met his eyes again.

"You have not asked what I want," Thomas said. "And I have not yet heard you say what *you* want."

"You have known me for a month," Kate said. She ought to push his hand away, but she could not make herself do it.

"I have known you through your love for your brother much longer," Thomas said. He was not smiling, but there was the barest touch of humor in his voice.

"That—that—" Kate tried to find a rebuttal, but all she could think was *I have known you through your care for my brother just as long.*

Her eyes flicked downward, tracing the outline of an object laying on Thomas' thigh, then flicked back to his face, then immediately flicked downward when a shock of recognition ran through her. "*Oh*," she said. She leaned forward, briefly pressing against him—lord, that felt good—to grab the thing and inspect it. Thomas' hand slid down her neck to her shoulder and off as she moved. She missed his warmth immediately and then scolded herself for the feeling.

Yes, the thing Thomas had been holding was exactly what Kate had thought it was, a blue whetstone mounted on a wooden block, the block carved with a loose representation of a horse. "Oh, where you did find this? I thought it was lost."

"Do you recognize it?" Thomas asked.

"Of course. It was Maman's. I think she brought it with her from France. I thought she took it with her when she—when she—"

Kate swallowed down those last raw words. She had made herself vulnerable enough for one day. If Maman hadn't gone, maybe she wouldn't be here now. Maybe Maman would know what had gone wrong every time with Will. Maybe Maman would know how to protect Thomas, as she had protected John Mary.

"When your mother—" Thomas prompted, frowning.

"I bought a ham bone," Kate said, knowing she was a coward and too tired to care. "I should get the soup started. Henry was ever so careful when he carried my cheeses—not a single one was dented—but the walk to Southbridge and back is ten miles, and he needs a good dinner—*you* need a good dinner, you've hardly eaten for two days—"

She got to her feet and backed into the kitchen, still clutching the whetstone.

# CHAPTER NINETEEN

Peter had just set eyes on the stream behind the Gravenor farm when he heard voices in the trees beside the path. Two voices, both young, talking in low, grave tones.

He stopped walking, and the voices stopped speaking.

Birds chirped in the silence. He squinted into the bushes. Indigo fabric and red hair flickered between the twigs.

"Anne," he yelled. "Shouldn't you be at your new job?"

Silence.

"Anne, if I have to get my nice new stockings dirty to haul you out of the wood, I won't be happy."

The bushes shifted and rustled. There was a whispered conference.

"Whoever you are, I promise I will blame Anne for whatever mischief it is you're up to."

Anne's voice finally came out of the bush. "I only go to the new job on Tuesdays and Thursdays. Peter, what do you want?"

"Who else is back there?" he asked, filing that bit

of information away for later. He pushed a branch aside and craned his head to see. He had not gotten his current position by giving up a chance at any little piece of potentially compromising information.

"If you get her in trouble, I'll set fire to the vicarage," Anne said flatly.

That was very interesting, and it let Peter know exactly who was in the bushes with her. He supposed Daniel Lately was out collecting his rents, and Eleanor had taken advantage of his absence. "Eleanor Lately, what are you discussing with my sister?"

"Don't tell him *anything*," hissed Anne. "He's a monster."

Eleanor stood up from where she had been crouched behind a tangle of hazel and blackthorn. Her thin face was very white, as though she had just received some terrible news.

Peter did not fool himself that he had a vocation for pastoral care. He had blackmailed George Beauford to leave the vicarage at Copstone and recommend Peter as his successor to Lord Houghton because he had not seen a clearer route to protecting his siblings from discovery and exploitation. Maman had impressed the precarity of John Mary's position on Peter from a young age, and as it became obvious that Jake was equally queer, it was clear that *someone* needed to put themselves between the Gravenor siblings and a hostile outside world. While Peter's notions of morality were necessarily idiosyncratic, he never shirked his familial duties.

Gradually slicing away old Beauford's respectable facade to reveal his deep rottenness had been enjoyable, even if it had taken Peter several years to secure hard evidence of falsified wills, money earmarked for charity spent on fine brandy and tobacco, and marriages performed with only questionable consent of the parties involved. He had not found the three years of playacting that followed nearly so entertaining, pretending that he cared about raising funds for a new church organ or the many heart palpitations and backaches of his oldest parishioners.

Perhaps it was that Eleanor's expression right now looked a bit too much like Kate had looked when he had stopped at the Easting farm after Christmas last year and she had told him that though this pregnancy had lasted several months longer than the others, there would be no child.

Peter had sat in the dark parlor of the Easting house, holding his sister's hand, feeling quite numb. He had never believed in God and found people who did almost universally tiresome, but in that moment he would have liked very much for there to be some sort of entity he could lay blame on for this monstrous state of affairs, some spirit he could reassure Kate was accompanying her unchristened infant to a celestial haven. But he had no comfort for someone he would not lie to, so he only held her hand, squeezing it every so often when a sob escaped her.

Eleanor Lately is not your concern, Peter reminded himself.

"Has something happened?" he asked.

"Mr. Gravenor," Eleanor said. "Did you know my parents are not dead?"

"*Eleanor*," Anne hissed.

"Anne told you that?" Peter said, his mind racing to put together all the relevant gossip. He was only seven years older than Eleanor; he vaguely remembered the excited whispering and muttering in Copstone when she had come to live with Daniel Lately. Lately had always claimed she was his ward, implying she was a distant cousin. As soon as he had been old enough to understand how the world worked, Peter had suspected this meant Eleanor was Lately's bastard, but that had never quite felt right. Lately was the sort of man who had no qualms about leaving illegitimate offspring to starve. Peter knew thirdhand of a maid who had been fired from the Lately house who had later delivered herself of a son in Shrewsbury, four months after she was married to a family friend.

"*Don't tell him things*," Anne whisper-screamed. "You think he can't do anything, and then he *does* something."

If Lately *hadn't* left Eleanor in a foundling home, that meant he had good reason for keeping her, which meant he thought the child could either get him something he wanted or he feared legal consequences for abandoning her. Either Eleanor stood to inherit something, or ... Eleanor was his legitimate child. Had Lately been married? If so, where was his wife now, and what had happened to her? Peter had found no evidence of such a marriage in the parish records, which he had combed through with minute attention while he had been in the process of getting rid of Beauford. *What had happened to the marriage certificate?*

The trick with blackmail, Peter thought, was very similar to other sorts of charlatanry; one had to have good instincts and good timing, but hold just enough back that one's target filled in the information one did not already know. He had not had any suspicion of who Thomas might be when he had been looking through the parish records yet again for any information he might turn into a weapon against Daniel Lately, who was so very determined to wrench the Gravenor farm away from John Mary. But the names of the unlucky cousins Lately had inherited his own farm from had lit the barest flame of suspicion in his mind. Kate's and Thomas' reactions to the information had turned the suspicion into a certainty.

"Mr. Lately has not treated you with the kindness that a daughter deserves," Peter pronounced in his saddest, most vicarly voice.

Eleanor's eyes filled with tears, and she hiked up her skirts and stumbled forward onto the path. Anne stood up and crunched over the dead leaves and fallen twigs after her friend, her expression thunderous. She put her arm around Eleanor and glared at her older brother.

"This isn't a game, Peter."

Where was the record of Eleanor's birth, for that matter? Had she had been registered with the parish at all, or had Lately's wife been hidden in some other town? Old Beauford had certainly secreted things away that ought to have been public knowledge, but he wouldn't have destroyed the record outright if he thought it might be useful to him later.

And how had Anne discovered the truth of Eleanor's parents? She had her mysterious job, but she'd had that job for nearly a year. This was clearly new and shocking information to both girls.

"Anne, please allow me to help," he admonished, imitating the silken, moneyed tones of a boy he had gotten expelled in their last year of school for owning a book of pornography. Peter had purchased the book, read it, and then hidden it in the other boy's mattress. "Eleanor, where is your mother? What happened to her?"

Maybe the old man put her in an asylum, he thought uneasily.

Eleanor turned toward the tone, though thankfully she did not try to embrace Peter, which was an unpleasant thing that many of his female parishioners felt called to do in the throes of emotion.

"I don't have a mother," she said, staring past him into some unknown place.

Peter did not quite have time to make sense of that—hadn't she just said that her parents were still alive?—when the sound of footsteps coming down the hill echoed over the stream.

"I'm escorting you both home for a visit," Peter said out of the side of his mouth to Anne. She nodded sharply and squared her shoulders, though she kept a protective arm about Eleanor. "Eleanor's just been scared by—ah—a stray pig. One of Ned Bell's, I imagine."

But when the footsteps—slow, stilted steps, with the clunk of a crutch between them—finally approached the stream, Peter saw that the newcomer was Thomas Holyoke, his dark head bowed to watch his footing as he limped forward, a stick under one arm.

Peter had rather a lot of things he wanted to say to Thomas Holyoke, mostly regarding what the hell he thought he was doing, messing about with Kate's feelings. Peter categorically did not trust men around his sister. She had made her worthless, cruel, and stupid husband seem like a reasonable, upright man for years before the truth became evident, and Peter, who should have known better than anyone that reasonable, upright men rarely were so virtuous at home, had believed her. Before she remarried, because she ought to remarry, Peter was going to interrogate any suitor, under torture if necessary, to find out his true character.

But at this moment, Eleanor's gaze found Thomas. She froze.

Thomas looked up and saw Eleanor. He froze.

Peter looked from one to the other, registering a certain alarming similarity in Roman noses. He thought of the entry he had found in the parish registry of births for April, seventeen eighty-three, for the child of James and Eleanor Lately, *née* Holyoke. *Eleanor.* He thought of Daniel Lately's abandoned bastard in Shrewsbury, and why he had not abandoned this child. He thought of George Beauford and his willingness to marry just about anyone if the right money appeared in his hand.

Peter looked again, hard, at Thomas Holyoke, and he thought of John Mary. John Mary had left the farm once for nearly a year before Peter had finished school, and in the years since Papa had died and Henry and Kate had left, he had continued to disappear sporadically for a week to a month at a time. Peter had always had his suspicions that there was a niece or a nephew who he did not know in another county, and he had quietly resented his brother for not telling him the truth. If his brother had borne a child, Peter wanted to protect that child; if his brother had been taken advantage of by a man, he wanted to kill that man.

Do you think all men like your brother have someone to protect them? whispered the ghost of Peter's conscience.

Dr. Holyoke stopped at the top of the bank and bowed stiffly in their direction. "Eleanor Lately, I presume. Miss Gravenor. Mr. Gravenor." His face was very pale, though his words were measured.

"I—you—" Eleanor stammered.

Anne's arm tightened around her friend again, her knuckles white. She looked like she was considering murdering Peter and Thomas both.

"Why did you leave me there?" Eleanor said.

The grief in her voice was so naked that Peter took a step backward. He looked at Eleanor's face and thought not of Daniel Lately or Thomas Holyoke but of his mother, hunched over his father's sodden body as it lay on the ancient kitchen table. Edward Gravenor had been dragged up from the mill pond by Tom Lawrence, the miller, and one of Ned Bell's sons. Edward must have lost his footing, they said; he always had his head in the clouds, they said. Must have been reading poetry while he walked.

Peter would have sworn on the family Bible that his mother had not loved his father until that day, that she only tolerated him with a kindly contempt born of long familiarity. But Ophélie Gravenor had sat over her dead husband like a ewe with a dead lamb, snarling at anyone who came near her, and whispering to herself when they did not. "Il est tué, on l'a tué." She had not let the vicar or the deacons touch her husband, had instead insisted that John Mary, Peter, Henry, and Jake carry the coffin and do the burying.

Ophélie had hated George Beauford, Peter thought suddenly. That had been the origin of his own decision to destroy the old vicar's life, though it had long been buried under the man's other crimes.

Eleanor's face looked like Ophélie's face, twisted by grief, but also rage.

It could have been different, those faces said. There was no reason for me to suffer what I have suffered. Eleanor's face accused Thomas, the land he stood on, his crutch, the trees holding their breath, all of them complicit in abandoning her to a man who had not been a father.

The stream ran over the rocks of the ford. Birds twittered in the trees, and far away, a cow lowed.

Thomas Holyoke's visage was less painful for Peter to observe. The man's face was drawn tight with guilt and shame, two emotions that Peter did not allow himself to feel. A person made their choices and had to live with them, and he had no patience for those who bemoaned outcomes anyone could have predicted.

Not everyone is given choices, his dead conscience whistled.

The silence that stretched between the banks pressed down on the four of them. It was hard to hear or think, Peter thought, and he wasn't one of the main characters in this play.

"I didn't know you survived," Thomas said, into a silence weighted with eighteen years. His low voice shook the smallest bit. "You came early, and Margaret —the cook—she said there was nothing I could do for you, and she took you away."

"Margaret," wailed Eleanor, that name breaking the dam and letting through a rush of sorrow. Her thin body wavered, as though slammed by an invisible blast of wind. "I—Aunt Margaret! She could have—she *didn't*." She turned to Anne and buried her face in her shoulder.

Anne shot Peter a desperate look.

"Maybe this wasn't the right time for this discussion," he murmured.

The desperate look turned venomous. "She has a right to know," Anne snarled. "Everyone's lied to her for years and years, and she has a right to know. That house ought to be hers, and everyone ought to know it."

That was an angle that Peter had not yet considered, and he suddenly wondered if James Lately had had a will, and if so what it had said and where it was now. Thomas had been the Latelys' only child; surely they had made provision for him.

Thomas had apparently heard what Anne said, and his face contorted as though he were being stabbed. The doctor schooled his features back to neutrality with visible effort.

"I had intended to walk to the vicarage today to speak with you," Thomas called to Peter.

"Then let us all return to my brother's house, for we have much to discuss," Peter said in his most buttery voice, gesturing in that direction with a flourish.

Thomas bared his teeth in an expression that was not a smile.

Eleanor wouldn't look at him. She sat on the lumpy settee in the Gravenor parlor, a piece of jam-smeared bread Kate had brought her dangling from one hand, and she wouldn't look at him.

That's her right, Thomas thought, or tried to think, around the ice filling his head. I don't want to look at me either.

I am a doctor, he wanted to say. I trained at university for three years. I saved the lives of dozens, if not hundreds, of young men at Porto and Vimeiro. I delivered babies in Valletta, and none of my charges were brought low with childbed fever. I improved sanitation in some of the poorest neighborhoods in Cape Town. I have lived a life that was worth living.

I did not abandon you for nothing.

*I didn't know.*

The guilt he had felt when he had set eyes on Eleanor felt like it would rise up and choke him.

Kate, busy wrapping Eleanor's hand around a mug of hot tea, shot a quick glance at him. Had he spoken aloud? It would be strange; he had not been able to speak a single word since entering the house again. The door had been open when they had returned; he had gone to the kitchen, looking for Kate, but the room had been empty, the ancient table bare except for the whetstone he had found by the stream and the twine-wrapped hand sickle which Henry had found in the woodshed. Thomas stared at the sickle, unable to make sense of its presence, then limped into the parlor and sat on one of the rickety old chairs.

When Thomas had set out this morning on the right-of-way behind the farm, he had planned to question Peter more closely about what had happened to the Gravenors' mother. There had to be some reason the whetstone had turned up so close to the stream where Rob Baker had been found. Had Cousin Daniel or one of his hired men stolen the stone, and if so, when? Had they done something to Maman seven years ago, or had they taken it from John Mary?

He had not wanted to question Kate. He had felt raw and strange when she had rejected his ill-considered proposal. Of course she could not go to London with him. It had been foolishness to even speak of it. But he had wanted to give her something, anything, that would soothe the bewildering abandonment of a husband who had been meant to love her and who had not.

Thomas could not protect Kate, as he had not been able to protect Eleanor. Eleanor, his own daughter, a ghost made flesh, was in the same house as he was. Peter followed him into the parlor, then Anne and Eleanor, and finally Kate had appeared, still wearing an ancient coat, clutching a basket filled with early-spring greens.

Margaret must have saved her, Thomas thought. *As she saved me.* But she had not been able to take the child out of that house. How had Eleanor survived eighteen years under the horror of Cousin Daniel? He could not—he would not—

He could not think of what had been done to him

in that house. He could not think of how he had been violated first by that man's entitlement to his body, then violated again by the wrongness of his own body as it grew. He could still feel the thing inside him, sapping his blood, shoving his organs out of the way to make way for itself. He had been convinced he would explode, break open like a rotten sheep full of maggots and spill his guts onto the floor. He had not understood so clearly that he was a man until he knew in his bones that being made to act as a woman would kill him.

That *thing* which had almost eaten him from the inside had been Eleanor, this young woman who looked like his mother and sat on the settee in front of him, looking as bereft as he felt and a good deal more angry. A brutal hand had pulled her through an unwilling doorway made of Thomas' body, and they were both the worse for it.

He could not have stayed in Daniel Lately's house for anyone, not even a child, not even his own child.

They were all talking now in low voices, except Eleanor, but Thomas found he could not make out any words over the pounding of blood in his head. This was why he could not let himself think before, could not let himself revisit those terrible months between his parents' deaths and his escape from Shropshire. If Eleanor remained a ghost, a specter of a dead child, then what had happened to him was not real.

But Eleanor was real, as real as the Gravenors, as real as himself. Kate had brought the girl a handkerchief, a giant white tattered thing, and Eleanor intermittently swiped at the tears and snot running down her face.

And then Thomas thought: Eleanor can't go back to that house, with that man in it. I'd rather kill Daniel myself, in front of a crowd of witnesses, and be sent to the gallows the same day, than let any child, *my* child, be ruled over by that bastard.

This child is flesh of my flesh and blood of my blood, even if the flesh was hacked out of me and the blood was stolen.

"When did the wedding take place?" Peter asked. Thomas realized he was repeating himself. He almost asked *what wedding*, then stopped himself. Of course Peter wanted to know about *that* wedding.

"About a month before Eleanor was born," Thomas said.

"I assume you did not give your consent," Peter said.

Kate made a noise like an angry cat. Thomas looked toward her and found himself presented with a jar of steaming tea. He took a sip and made a face; it was very sweet. He supposed Kate had finally had the ready cash to buy a cone of sugar.

"Drink all of it," Kate said sternly. "You, too, Eleanor. You've had a terrible shock."

Thomas took another swallow, and another. He did feel calmer, though perhaps that was because Kate stood next to him, her hip pressing against his arm. The parlor was very cold, but he could feel her warmth, even through the layers of fabric separating them.

Peter leaned against the edge of the great old fireplace, arms and ankles crossed, though the insouciance of his attitude was somewhat compromised by the grim set of his mouth and brow. "Do you recall the circumstances leading up to the wedding?" he said, after Thomas had drunk more tea.

Thomas stared into his mug, then looked at Eleanor. She was staring at her feet.

"Not well," he admitted. He had spent so much time working not to remember that the memories had become a sort of grotesque shadow play. He knew, more or less, what had happened, but he couldn't place himself in those scenes or remember what it had been like to live them. "I was seventeen. My parents were carried off by influenza early in the spring, and I only just survived it." Perhaps if he hadn't been so weak after the fevers, he could have escaped sooner. "Our family's solicitor contacted Cousin Daniel, as next of kin."

Kate's hand came to rest lightly on his shoulder.

"And did you consent to marry Daniel Lately?" Peter asked sharply.

"I didn't consent to any of it," Thomas snarled. "Not the—" He remembered Eleanor and bit off what he was going to say. "Not the getting of the child, not the marriage. But it didn't matter. He told me he could commit me to an insane asylum for wearing men's clothing if I did not acquiesce, and that my acquiescence was demanded of me by law regardless. I have no doubt he would have carried out that threat."

"He might have," Peter said. "Where was the wedding performed?"

"In our house," Thomas gritted out. "By the vicar Beauford. It was witnessed by Margaret Leigh, our cook, and Cousin Daniel's manservant." Thomas would never, not if he lived for two hundred years, forget the expression of barely contained revulsion that had transfixed Margaret's face, nor how her hand had shaken as she signed her name.

"How very interesting," Peter said, offensively casual. When Thomas looked at him, his eyes were glittering. "Just out of curiosity, what were the terms of your father's will?"

"I don't know. I never saw the will. It hardly matters," Thomas said dully. "Once the marriage was completed, it was all Daniel's anyway."

"Unless the marriage was illegal," Kate said. Her hand tightened on his shoulder, and Thomas had to fight to keep himself from burying his face in her bosom.

His heart twitched with something like hope at the idea that the bond Cousin Daniel had forced between them might be proven null, but he crushed that optimism with the ease of long practice. "You would never be able to prove I was coerced," Thomas said. "Not after nineteen years, and not when Eleanor exists. And in any case, I must be legally dead. I *must* be."

"The coercion couldn't be proven, no," Peter said agreeably. "The fact that the marriage occurred in a house, and not in an Anglican church, between individuals who are not Quakers, would be rather trivial to evidence, though."

Thomas' eyes snapped back to him. "What?"

"The Clandestine Marriages Act of 1753," Peter said. He was now studying his nails. "I would be astonished if the required banns were posted, either."

Thomas' heart clenched. He spoke as evenly as he

could. "Even so. Cousin Daniel is the next of kin; the house and land still rightfully belong to him."

"He isn't your next of kin, though," Kate said, her hand tightening on his shoulder. "Eleanor is."

Everyone looked at Eleanor. Eleanor finally looked up.

"What?" she said, her voice high and thin.

"The marriage was not valid," Kate said. When Thomas started to speak, she touched his hand. "Whether we are able to prove it or not, the marriage was not valid."

The spark of hope which Thomas had tried to smother flickered up into an ember.

Eleanor looked around the room. "Does that mean that—legally at least—Cousin Daniel might *not* be my father?" A thread of hope which mirrored Thomas' own wound through her voice.

"Rot Cousin Daniel and consign him to hell," Anne burst out. "All this is his fault. The body—me being fired—everything."

Kate's head whipped around to look at her sister. "You were *fired?* You said you still had a recommendation!"

"Let us return to the matter at hand," Peter said loudly.

"Rot him to hell, indeed," Eleanor muttered. She covered her mouth with her hands as though she had not meant to say that. Thomas felt the corner of his mouth quirk—it was a sentiment he had constantly repeated to himself at about Eleanor's age, as he shivered in his miserable student accommodations through the damp Edinburgh winter—and for a brief moment he and Eleanor met each other's eyes.

The back door creaked open. Before Thomas could do more than jerk his head toward the noise, Henry's tousled head appeared around the edge.

"Oh—hello Kate—hello Anne—good afternoon, Dr. Holyoke," he said.

"T'arrête-pas là, vas-y, entre dans le salon," came John Mary's annoyed voice from behind him.

"Good day, Henry," Peter said pointedly.

"I don't want to talk to you," Henry said to Peter, a mulish expression coming over his face.

"Henry," Thomas said, exasperation briefly overtaking the other feelings seething under his breastbone. He had spent the first two years of Henry's training as his assistant drilling him in proper manners, chief among them that he oughtn't say that he thought poorly of someone to their face. The British military hierarchy was not one which could or would tolerate honesty.

Eleanor blinked at Henry, and her expression changed from lost to interested. "Oh! You're Henry!"

"Who else would I be?" Henry asked, puzzled.

Thomas knew that if Henry was not answered clearly and succinctly, he would only become more confused and knot the conversation about himself.

But before he could speak, Anne said, "Well, you might look more like Kate."

"You might have been a cow," Peter observed. "Which is the bloody-minded one? Nonnette?"

"Vas-y!" John Mary bellowed from behind his brother's shoulder.

"That's the wrong cow," Henry said.

"Henry and I look a great deal alike," Kate said loyally. Thomas raised his eyebrows at her. "We do," she insisted.

"To no one's credit," Peter muttered. All three Gravenor siblings who Thomas could see turned to glare at him.

John Mary shouldered past his younger brother with a French noise of annoyance. "*Bah!* Ferme la porte, ferme la porte!"

"Are you someone in particular?" Henry asked Eleanor, in his politest tone, as he closed the door behind himself.

Kate let out a little gasp of laughter and covered her face.

Anne made the introductions, while John Mary went into the kitchen and rattled around in ambiguous Gallic fashion. Eleanor stood up and gave Henry her hand. She was an extremely tall young woman, even taller than Thomas, which meant that her eyes were about level with Henry's chin. The two young people stood looking at each other. Henry had clearly forgotten what one was supposed to do with a young lady's hand, so he simply held Eleanor's fingers in his own.

"It's all sandstone out there, you know," he told her. "It makes the soil awfully dry."

Thomas, who had thought he could not possibly feel any more emotions than he was already feeling, sensed a new one blossom inside his chest. He slowly looked up at Kate. She looked down at him, her eyes widening with alarm.

Surely I am misreading this, Thomas thought. He

didn't think Henry fancied women—or men, or really anything that wasn't soil or growing out of it.

"The Staffordshire and Worcestershire canal is cut through sandstone," Eleanor returned. "It's mostly coal going up and down that, though."

I don't think I am misreading this, Thomas thought.

"The matter at hand," Peter said loudly. Henry and Eleanor started apart and looked at him. Peter pushed away from the edge of the great brick hearth and stood in the center of the room. Thomas scowled at him involuntarily. "The matter at hand is that Daniel Lately, approximately eighteen years before present, coerced a young person, currently present, no longer young, into marriage and childbirth, a situation which produced Eleanor Lately, also present. I possess the gravest doubts about the legitimacy of the marriage, which means Lately's legal possession of the house and lands he now occupies is also in doubt."

"Is it?" Thomas said.

"Certainly," Peter said calmly. "If he thought the wedding were legitimate, he would have broadcast it far and wide. But I've never heard a whisper of any previous marriage from anyone in the parish. His claim to Lately House clearly rests on other legal grounds, that is, being next of kin. But if he had been named the benefactor in your father's will, he wouldn't have needed to force you to marry him. Ergo, the will almost certainly made you the inheritor of all your father's earthly estate."

"Why do you care?" Thomas asked, suddenly very tired. "It was a long time ago, and it can't be fixed now."

"I care," Peter said pointedly, "because a man who concealed his cousin's will or forged a new one— forgery being, incidentally, a capital offense, for which one William Booth was hanged but a few years past— might not find himself quite so willing to cast accusations of murder upon members of a family in possession of that knowledge."

The parlor was so quiet that Thomas thought he could hear the beating of Kate's heart.

"You don't know he forged a will, though," Eleanor said.

"Couldn't you look for one?" Henry said, speaking to Eleanor as though she were the only other person in the room. "Does Mr. Lately have an office?"

"I could," Eleanor said. There was a dawning light in her face, as it struck her that she had the power to do something to injure Cousin Daniel. Thomas turned his head away. It hurt to look at her face, so much like his own, but not lined with a thousand disappointments and compromises. It hurt even more because he did not think Peter's proposed plan of blackmail would work. He had no idea how many lives Cousin Daniel had destroyed on his way to wealth, but he would guess it was dozens. Surely, if he could be stopped by knowledge of his crimes, he already would have been.

"Eleanor," he said. He was not sure the girl heard him, so he repeated himself. "Eleanor, don't go back to that house. I don't think you should—"

"C'est quoi?" John Mary bellowed from the kitchen. It sounded like he was yelling at another person, but who else would be in the house? Thomas did not think he could suffer another invasion of cattle. "Qu'est-ce que tu fais? L'après-midi est bien fini et c'est plein de merde!"

"I have to go," Eleanor gasped, looking out the window. "Mr. Gravenor—that is, the Reverend Mr. Gravenor—I'll try to speak with you after Sunday service. I have to go!" She shot Henry one last, fervent look, then disappeared through the unlatched back door.

"*Eleanor!*" Thomas shouted, but there was no way he could catch her.

# CHAPTER TWENTY

"Someone is going to recognize me," Thomas muttered, tugging the collar of his coat higher around his chin.

"I thought you were going to be your own cousin on your mother's side," Kate said out of the side of her mouth. "From Cheshire." She smiled and nodded to a passing housewife.

"She didn't have any cousins," Thomas said disagreeably.

I wanted to come, he reminded himself. I asked to come.

They had arrived in Southbridge in the dim dawn after nearly two hours rattling around in the back of Ned Bell's cart. Ned had been willing to give them a ride so long as no one saw him do it; Cousin Daniel's injunction against helping the Gravenors in any way was clearly still in force. Kate had wanted to sell her cheeses at the Wednesday market, rather than the much busier Saturday one, because they could find a space under the high open arches of the Southbridge Town Hall, a grand, black-and-white timbered building hulking over its brick foundations. Kate did not want to display her cheeses in direct sunlight, lest they start to melt.

Henry had walked behind the cart, carrying the two sawhorses for the cheese table, his brow furrowed in thought. He had been alarmingly contemplative since Eleanor had visited the house the Saturday before.

Well, would it be the worst thing if Henry fancied Eleanor? Thomas thought, before shaking his head to dispel the thought. This was none of his business. Henry and Eleanor would have to figure things out between them, because Thomas could not stay in this place. He couldn't think of Eleanor's future at all without feeling like he might be sick. He had to leave. *He had to leave.* But he also could not leave Eleanor trapped with Cousin Daniel. Kate might escape with Thomas—she might meet him in London in a few years, after her family's affairs were in order—but Eleanor could not stay with Cousin Daniel.

Who very well might have arranged for Rob Baker to be killed or dumped behind the Gravenor farm, Thomas reminded himself. The murder ought to be occupying his full attention, and then he could make plans to get himself to London. The murderer was likely yet close at hand—very close indeed, if it was John Mary—and Thomas didn't know how far Peter's deacon had spread the news that the body had disappeared.

To that end, Thomas had cornered Henry in the kitchen garden earlier in the week and questioned him about what had happened to his mother, hoping to find some connection to Cousin Daniel or another neighbor.

"Kate thinks Maman killed herself," Henry had said, with very little prompting. "She was taken by grief after Papa died." But he did not know why Kate thought so. "Her name was Ophélie," Henry added, but Thomas did not think the power of Shakespearean suggestion would have been enough to convince Kate of anything so dramatic.

They had not found a body. Henry didn't know who had been searching or where they had looked; he had been consumed in those horrible weeks by looking after Kate, who had been distraught. Kate had been relieved that Maman couldn't be refused burial in the churchyard.

"Though, I don't know that Maman would have wanted to be buried in the churchyard," Henry mused. "She didn't approve of God, or Anglicans."

John Mary had remained resolutely close-mouthed about Ophélie Gravenor's disappearance for six years, though he had returned to the farm some few months before her death. Henry thought this was either because of grief—John Mary had been closer to Maman than anyone else—or because he didn't want anyone to know that she had died by suicide.

If his mother had been murdered, would John Mary have had any reason to hide that? Thomas wondered. "Was the farm failing then?"

Henry had hesitated, before saying, "Well, Papa was never very interested in soil. Or cheese. He mostly liked poetry. Maman is the one who ran the farm."

"Did Cou—did Daniel Lately approach your family asking you to sell the land to him while your mother was still alive?"

"Yes," Henry had said, nodding. "He came to tea three times in the year before Papa died."

"Did your father consider selling?"

"No. Where would he have gone?"

"How was my—what was Lately like when he talked to your father? Was he rude? Ingratiating? Threatening?"

"Papa quoted Greek at him until he left. I think it was Aristophanes."

"Then why does Kate think your mother killed herself?" Thomas burst out, frustrated.

"Maman was not well after he died," Henry said, the cheerful equanimity he had maintained throughout the troubling conversation momentarily punctured. His nonexistent eyebrows drew low over his blue eyes. "She said a lot of things which sounded—which sounded like things a crazy person would say."

"Like what?" Thomas prompted.

"She said Mr. Lately had killed Papa. Even though —well—the way Papa died was the way Papa probably was going to die. He didn't ever pay attention to where he was walking." Henry had considered for a long minute before adding, "Maman threw Mr. Lately out of the house when he came to pay his respects after Papa died. She called him a lot of nasty things in French."

Which was a slight Cousin Daniel had probably still not forgiven, Thomas thought now, watching Kate curtsy to another housewife and offer her a sample of cheese on a thin slice of bread. Even if he actually had killed Edward Gravenor.

Thomas leaned against one of the brick pylons holding up the town hall, a few feet away from Kate's cheese table. Henry stood behind Kate, looking bored and uncomfortable. At the first market they had gone to, he had helped her set up, then wandered off to look at the town's ruined earthworks for interesting dirt. Thomas had insisted Henry stay close; he did not want the faintest hint of impropriety to touch Kate for being in company with an unknown man.

The housewife's eyes almost rolled back in her head as the cheese touched her tongue. "It's like butter," she said, sighing.

"It will be even more like butter if you wrap it in paper and let it sit for another week in a cool cellar," Kate said.

"How much did you say it was?" the housewife's friend said, sounding suspicious. "Eight shillings a pound? That's very dear for a cheese."

"It's very good cheese," Kate said earnestly. "Made in the French style, taught to me by my mother, who learned it from her mother in a village outside of Paris."

*Paris* was a magical word. The two housewives leaned together, murmuring, before agreeing to pay six shillings fourpence for a single cheese.

Kate smiled after them, her hands wrapped in her apron to hide their shaking. As soon as the two women walked away, she turned to grin at Thomas, and he felt his mouth curve in an answering smile. His heart stuttered.

That's my girl, Thomas thought, but the words felt like they wedged themselves sideways in his throat.

*She's not your girl.* She doesn't belong to you. None of this belongs to you.

"Henry," he said, jolting away from the brick arch onto his crutch. "I need to take a turn about to stretch my leg. Stay here."

"Oh, but what if you need help?" Kate asked, anxiety folding her brow.

"I'll crawl back," Thomas said, already limping away. *Nothing and no one is yours.*

He crutched slowly south along the high street, keeping close to the shop fronts to avoid wagons and horses. He didn't remember Southbridge very well; most of his parents' business had been conducted in Copstone village, only coming to the market town for specialty items and particular craftsmen. When Cousin Daniel had arrived, Thomas had been confined to the house, and he did not know where the man had carried out his business affairs.

The high street jogged to the right and then began to climb toward the ruin of a Norman castle on the hill. Thomas stopped, rubbing the thigh of his bad leg and thinking.

For the past twenty years, he had not allowed himself to consider what Cousin Daniel had done to him. At first it had been a matter of survival; he had been so furious and terrified and grief-stricken that any little foray down that path had rendered him unable to think or speak or move. And he could not afford to stop for even a moment in those early days of living on his own. As a child, he had dressed himself in boys' clothes whenever he could; but then he had been forced to run, and his very survival depended on strangers understanding him as a man. He had to work continuously, to prove himself as a student and then as an army doctor, a professional above reproach.

But it also meant that there were questions he had never asked himself about what had happened and why. He had never, for example, wondered why his father had left the house and farm to a man Thomas had never met or heard of before his parents' death. Thomas had not talked overmuch with his mother and father about their plans for their estate after they died, but they had never given him the impression that he would need to marry to support himself, never trained him that making a husband happy would be part and parcel of his survival. It was odd behavior for sensible people, if they had known that Daniel would come to possess everything they owned.

Thomas had not known that a marriage needed to happen in a church to be sanctified; he had always thought that the presence of the unctuous, foul little vicar had been enough. But if it hadn't—why had Cousin Daniel forced Thomas into such an arrangement so quickly, when he might have waited, might have battered Thomas into a marriage which no one could question?

He walked slowly up the street toward the castle. About a hundred yards after the jog to the right, there was a neat little shopfront with a black sign hanging above the door. The gold lettering read JONES & SONS, SOLICITORS.

Thomas stood and looked at the sign for a long time. That was the other thing his father had come to Southbridge for: to see his solicitor. Thomas had come with him once or twice; he vaguely remembered the dusty bookshelves and old Mr. Jones' shiny pink head, surrounded by cloud-like wisps of hair.

Would Jones & Sons have a copy of James Lately's will ready to hand, twenty years after his death? If they did, how would he, theoretically a distant relative of James Lately's wife, ask to see it? Could he claim that there had been some small legacy due to him?

What if Mr. Jones recognized him?

Thomas shuddered and turned back toward the town hall.

There's nothing to be done, he thought. No matter how cruel or unfair it all is, it can't be fixed now.

Thomas crossed to the center of the street and through the town hall's arches, passing between a stall selling pickles and a woman hawking a basket of watercress, then froze.

A tall, horribly familiar form loomed over Kate's table. Henry was nowhere in sight. Cousin Daniel, wearing a brown suit, leaned down over the two cheeses remaining on the table. His lip curled back as though he meant to snarl or to spit. Kate's smile looked like it had been painted on, while her shoulders hunched as though she would dive in front of her cheeses.

Cousin Daniel pitched his voice to be heard by the whole market. "Half a guinea for a cheese made in a hovel? That's absurd."

Murmurs radiated out from the nearby farmers and townsfolk. Thomas noticed that the nearest people to Kate's table had begun to inch away from her.

Thomas forced himself forward another step.

He's going to recognize you! his brain screamed. And once Cousin Daniel has hold of you again, you won't even have the grace of a revolver and a bullet.

"It's not two for a guinea," Kate said, her voice high and thin. "It's three for a guinea. Miss James was very happy to pay seven shillings apiece for my cheeses. She said they were as good as any she'd had when she went on her grand tour as a girl."

That statement elicited even more murmurs and a few gasps. Thomas had no doubt that she was repeating Miss James' words faithfully; he didn't think Kate thought very much about grand tours on the continent.

"I can't imagine someone of Miss James' excellent taste saying anything so foolish," Cousin Daniel snapped. He made a motion as though he would jab a cheese with his finger, but Kate shoved the top of the crate the cheeses had been packed in under his hands.

"Sir, you have to pay for that before you eat it," she said. Her voice was shaking, but Thomas thought it was with anger, not fear.

Thomas took another step closer to the table, then another. Walking this slowly, he could get on reasonably well without the crutch, so he held it away from his side. No reason to broadcast his weakness.

I am Doctor Thomas Holyoke, he said to himself. I was a decorated military officer, goddammit. I am Eleanor Holyoke's cousin from Cheshire.

"I demand to try this excellent cheese," Cousin Daniel said. Thomas had always thought he looked like a horse when he pulled his upper lip back in that way.

"I've given away all my samples," Kate said. Her face was very pink.

"Mrs. Easting," Thomas said, and with what he

now knew about Will Easting that name tasted bitter on his tongue. "Do you know this gentleman?"

Cousin Daniel drew himself up and turned slowly, portentously, in a swirl of jacket skirts. Thomas had time to see Kate's horrified expression, before she busied herself tidying her table.

"I am well-acquainted with Mrs. Easting," Cousin Daniel said coldly. "We are neighbors, of a sort. She does not require your assistance, Mr.—" He looked Thomas up and down, contempt in every line of his face. "I'm afraid I don't know you."

It could be a trap, and the glitter of malice in Cousin Daniel's face covered up any trace of recognition that might have been there.

"I am Doctor Thomas Holyoke," Thomas said. "Lately a surgeon of His Majesty's Royal Army. Who are *you?*"

He had a brief moment of joy at the irritation which distorted his cousin's face.

"What chivalry, to involve yourself in the affairs of an impecunious widow with whom you are not acquainted," Cousin Daniel said, marshaling himself. He looked from Thomas to Kate and back again with a sly nastiness. "Or, perhaps, you are very well-acquainted indeed? I understand Mrs. Easting's circumstances are rather straitened of late."

Gasps rippled through the surrounding crowd, ringing outward from Cousin Daniel like water rushing from a thrown stone.

The Wednesday market was nothing like as busy as the Saturday market, and Thomas would wager that everyone in the surrounding five parishes would know that Daniel Lately had called Kate a whore by sundown.

"Mrs. Easting and her brother have been my kind hosts for six weeks," Thomas barked. At least the anger burned through his fear. "Henry Gravenor was my surgical assistant for seven years in Portugal, Valletta, and Cape Town. He is an honorable man, from an honorable family."

Cousin Daniel's eyes narrowed. "Henry Gravenor, the idiot?"

The fear which had iced Thomas' veins and made his heart sluggish melted and went to steam. Thomas' hands balled themselves into fists, but before he could shove one into his cousin's midriff, Henry appeared in one of the arches at the other end of the market, jogging and panting. Onlookers who had only inched away at the sound of raised voices now dove out of the way of the enormous, red-faced man.

"Kate!" Henry gasped. "I've found a man who will sell us enough straw to thatch the roof! John Needham, his name was. We've only to hire a wagon and horse to get it home. And—" Here he triumphantly held an object, or rather two objects, aloft.

The two baby goats trumpeted their displeasure at suddenly being eight feet in the air at the top of their lungs. "Look here! Kids!"

"*Henry,*" Thomas and Kate said, almost in the same exasperated tone.

Thomas turned back to Cousin Daniel to tell him to move along before Thomas helped him do so with his fists, but the man had already backed away and was threading his way through the crowd.

There escapes our doom, Thomas thought, his skin crawling.

# CHAPTER TWENTY-ONE

Kate unpinned her hair and untwisted her braid. She stood in her parents' bedroom. Usually she washed in the back bedroom, but there was a warm beam of late sunlight coming through the window, and she needed the ancient spotted mirror to be sure she'd scrubbed off the last splatters of mud from the road.

Her back and shoulders ached, and her head hurt even more fiercely. Numbers raced through her mind, crowding and jamming against each other like branches in a flooded stream. She had sold seven cheeses all told, making two pounds and sixpence. She had given a young housewife a discount on the one she had dented while protecting it from Daniel Lately's grasping fingers. The load of straw for the roof had cost half her profits, and another quarter had gone to hiring the horse and wagon for the rest of the afternoon. John Mary hopefully still had a few friends he could barter with for the labor. She hadn't been able to find out how much the goat kids, both little does, cost; Henry insisted he had paid for them himself, and it had been a very good deal.

Kate wondered with resignation what untoward

thing Henry was doing for extra money.

"Goat milk makes very good cheese. We had it often in Portugal," he told her earnestly, then set about building a pen for the kids in the corner of one of the barn stalls. It was warm enough now that the cattle only came into the barn for milking, so Henry had blocked off the back half to store the thatching straw. John Mary had gone somewhere without telling anyone.

Kate had wanted to ask Thomas about the goat cheese on the continent, but she had also felt overwhelmed and sad and dirty inside and out, so she had retreated upstairs to collect her feelings.

Those goats won't be ready to be bred until late this fall, Kate thought, and they won't kid until next spring. Henry thinks we'll make it until then. She swallowed hard at that thought, and her hands briefly stilled on her hair. She could claim that Henry didn't have any sense, but that wasn't true; it was that his sense was nearly all reserved for farm matters, with little to spare for other people.

And if the farm is still running, I will still be here, Kate thought. Thomas will have certainly gone to London by then, but I am needed here. I don't know if I can go back to the market at Southbridge, after the accusations that Daniel Lately made. He's a wealthy man, and a lawyer himself; people might decide it's in their best interests to believe him and not me.

She wondered if Miss James would still buy her cheeses, if she thought they came from the hand of a loose woman.

Well, if Kate had to go all the way to Telford to

sell her cheeses, she would do so. No one knew of the Gravenors and their troubles in Telford. She wondered if how she had felt alone behind her cheese table, Daniel Lately leering while everyone around pretended they couldn't see, was how John Mary had felt for the last eighteen months, as Lately had tried every method to push him into selling the farm. It was a terrible, isolated, helpless feeling.

Thomas knows the truth of how it is here, Kate thought. I am not alone.

Thomas will leave soon, she reminded herself. He has to, for his own safety. And that is fine. I will be fine.

Slowly she picked up her comb and began to work it through her hair. It was a relief to have it down; her scalp ached with how tightly she'd wrapped the braid to make sure it would stay neat through the entire market.

"Kate?" That was Thomas' voice.

"Yes? Is everything all right?" Kate had turned and was halfway across the room before she had realized that for his words to be so clear and distinct, he must be standing at the top of the stairs, and if he were standing at the top of the stairs, he would be able to see her in her undergarments. She had taken off her stiff dress—not new, but made over from one of Maman's old skirts—scraped the mud off the hem, and hung it up, along with her nice petticoat and the stays she only wore to go off the farm. Now she wore just shift and stockings, the shift so worn it was practically transparent.

He's already touched your unmentionable bits, Kate told herself.

Yes, but he didn't *see* me while he did it, she

retorted to herself, feeling slightly hysterical.

"Are you all right?" Thomas asked, levering himself into the front bedroom between the newel post and his crutch.

"You should be more careful of your leg," Kate said.

"You're not my mother," Thomas said, laying a hand on her waist.

Kate thought at first he was trying to steady himself, and she took hold of his elbow and his waist also, but his weight did not come to rest on her. A flush crept upward from the top edge of her shift toward her cheeks.

"You should sit," she said, trying to sound authoritative and not managing it.

"Only if you sit as well," Thomas said.

They sat on the edge of the big bed which Kate's parents and grandparents and great-grandparents had slept in.

"The walk back from the market was hard for you," Thomas observed.

"It shouldn't be," Kate said, embarrassed.

Thomas gave her a look. "And?"

"Yes," Kate said, too tired to prevaricate. "It's hard for me to walk very long. I get exhausted. I used to bleed if I overexerted myself, but that's mostly better now."

"Anemia," Thomas muttered, briefly pressing two fingers to her wrist as though he would take her pulse. "Some of the money from your cheeses needs to go to buying beef."

"Yes, Henry needs—"

"Beef for *you* to eat," Thomas said sharply. "Thin blood is common among young women; I have no doubt that your lost pregnancies made it worse for you. The treatment is red meat, eaten several times a week."

Kate swallowed hard. "Would that have made a difference, to me keeping those—to me being able to —if I had—"

"No. It would make a difference *now*. Listen to me." Thomas turned to her and took Kate's face in his hands. "A human body is wonderful and fearful, but if we are made in God's image, then God is lame and broken."

His fingers curled under her jaw, and his thumbs rested against her cheekbones. Kate could feel tears welling in her eyes, so she closed them and concentrated on the feeling of his hands.

"I operated once on a soldier who had been shot five times in the back. Every bullet had missed an organ or a bone, and enough of the whiskey had left his system to crack jokes by evening. He died in the night from a heart defect he'd been born with." Kate heard the bitter smile in Thomas' words. "I know because I was so angry I did an autopsy, though I could little spare the time or effort."

Kate put her hands over Thomas'. "Sometimes I worry that God was punishing me, because of Maman and Papa being the way they were," she whispered. She had never said this out loud to anyone. Henry would not understand, because what was wrong with the way Maman and Papa had been? John Mary would be angry at the insult to Maman. Peter would be enraged by the idea that God was real or had any business judging his family.

Thomas fell silent, and Kate could not open her eyes, in case she had disgusted or annoyed him.

"I used to think," he said slowly, "that the way I am must be an offense to God, an offense to the natural order of man and woman. It didn't matter to me," he said, breaking off with a short, harsh bark of laughter. "I couldn't survive as what the world would have me be. Cousin Daniel taught me that. But I thought that I was choosing survival in this life at the price of my soul, and I decided that was a fair trade."

Kate's eyes flew open, and she scowled at Thomas. "That's stupid. Why would God punish you for being the way he made you?"

Thomas stared at her, and his eyes crinkled very slightly at the corners. He slid one hand away from her cheek and brushed his fingers over her lips. "Let me finish."

"All right," Kate said, feeling mutinous. She did not approve of Thomas, who was possibly the best and most perfectly formed man she had ever met, questioning his own existence, but she supposed she could tell him that later.

"I studied in Edinburgh, and I enlisted in the army as soon as I'd had my training," Thomas went on. "I was in Portugal, then in Malta, then in Cape Town. I met thousands of men, and a few women." He took a deep breath, a shaky one. "And there were people who knew. I didn't let myself see it then, because the notion that I wasn't passing unnoticed terrified me, and I couldn't work if I was afraid. But at every stage of my life, there has been at least one person who looked at me and saw who I was, and said nothing, because they believed me."

Kate took the hand that had touched her lips and pressed a kiss into the palm. "Henry knows."

Thomas quirked an eyebrow. "He told you that?"

"No," Kate said.

Thomas laughed again, but this was a much kinder sound.

"So far as I can tell in this hellish modern age, God can only work through the hands of his people. I do not think that if God found me to be an abomination, the kindest and best men I have known would have let me be," he said. "Nor the kindest and best women."

Thomas stroked his hand over the back of Kate's head, caressing her ear. She let out a small, desperate laugh of her own, and pressed her face against his shoulder.

"I do not think God punishes us by not making us perfect," he said. "I do not think God wants perfection or even understands it. I think we are meant to understand how God is from how we are."

Very lightly, Thomas tugged at Kate's hair, gently pulling her head back. When she turned her face up to him, he pressed a kiss to her mouth. His lips were chapped, rough, and she wanted to run downstairs and bring up some butter to smooth over them.

"I am not so good as you," she whispered.

"Don't be foolish," Thomas said, kissing her ear and then biting it.

He lay back on the bed and pulled her with him, and Kate let him do it. She kissed the column of his throat, bared by the open neck of his shirt.

"I would like to see you," Thomas said, hooking a hand behind her knee and drawing it up the back of her thigh a few inches.

Kate swallowed hard. "I—"

She took a deep breath, looking hard into his great dark eyes, and then she ducked her head into the neck of her shift and scooted it over her head. It caught beneath her hip, but Thomas' hand was the there to ease the fabric free.

"There," Kate said, lying back down and rolling to face him. "A farmwife in repose."

Thomas looked at her, his eyes moving slowly up and down her body, resting briefly on her heavy thighs and breasts, her silver-marked soft belly, then coming back to her face. Kate recognized his expression with a jolt deep in her core. His eyes were almost black with greedy desire.

His hand went first to the marks on her belly, evidence of what had almost been, and he ran his fingers up and down the deep tracks. Kate almost cried, and then did cry, because what else could she do? It was not as if Thomas didn't know the pain she had gone through.

Thomas kissed her face and kissed her mouth and sucked on her lower lip, and as he did his hand moved to her hip. "I want to try something," he murmured against her neck. "You'll have to move a bit, because of my leg, but I think the bed is big enough."

Kate went very pink, imagining what the bed might be big enough for. Her early sexual education had consisted of watching the ancient bull, Sylvester, mount the cows. She would not necessarily mind Thomas mounting her, though she would worry for his splint—

But Thomas was urging her with his hands and soft commands to lie on her side across the top of the bed, her head resting at one edge and her legs pointing at the other. She was short enough that her feet only hung over a bit as she faced him. He lay on his stomach in the proper direction one normally lay in and raised himself on his elbows. Then, with the same greed burning in his eyes, he put a hand on her ankle, bending her top leg, and pushed her knee up, baring her to the light of the late afternoon and the cool air of the bedroom. He bent his head and kissed the inside of her thigh.

Kate, who had until this point been a little mystified and a little amused by all this geometry, understood.

"Oh," she said. "*Oh*. Are you sure? What about— what about your dignity?"

She did not say, What if I taste bad? But Thomas, who portioned his smiles out like they were the last drops of laudanum on a battlefield, grinned at her. The touch of his hand was firm as he traced her outer lips and then the inner ones, then barely dipped inside with a knuckle. Kate let out a little gasp at the sensation, then another when Thomas brought that knuckle to his mouth and sucked it clean. Suddenly the cool air of the room did not feel so cool.

Then he bent his head and nipped at her inner thigh again, before taking one of her hands and entwining it in his hair. This took several minutes of experimentation—when Thomas sucked at her nub or shoved his whole face into her cleft or did something else that felt particularly good, she unthinkingly yanked on his hair, which he at first took to mean that he should stop, and she did not want him to stop.

Surely his tongue was not so large when he put it in my mouth, Kate thought foggily. Her hips rocked against Thomas' face without her meaning them to, but when she tried to still herself Thomas gripped her buttock and pressed her back against his mouth. She clenched, and he gripped her harder.

It took a long time. Kate had thought she preferred a brusque, forceful coupling—and maybe she did—maybe she had told herself she did—and she liked when Thomas used his teeth, running them along her slickness, liked when he used his fingers to press inside and give her more friction—but it seemed she also liked that he took his time, alternating softer touches with harder ones.

The room was shadowy when Kate's stomach tightened, tightened again, pulled her back into an arch that Thomas encouraged with his hand, and then skin-lifting sparks radiated outward from where Thomas worked in her cunt, waves and waves of them. Kate gasped for air.

Thomas pressed his wet face to her belly, pushing her onto her back, and she dragged her hand through his hair.

"I should," she started.

Thomas growled. The vibration sent an aftershock through her soft parts.

"But," she said, and her mouth seemed to be

producing these words without her mind's input, because they were slightly slurred and confused. "I should be of use—"

Thomas turned his head toward her, revealing a malignantly slitted eye, and growled again.

Some time later, when the room was fully dark and they had crawled under the tattered coverlet together, Kate pressed her still-naked body against Thomas. This time he rolled on top of her, pushing his hips down between her thighs, and put his lips to her ear, speaking so softly that she did not think someone outside the bed could hear, let alone someone in the next bedroom. And he spoke of things she had not imagined, things he could do to her and with her with the proper objects and preparations, and she shuddered beneath him and clung.

# CHAPTER TWENTY-TWO

When Kate woke, the bedroom was dark. From the icy chill of the room, she thought it was probably an hour or two after midnight.

For a long time she did not move, only felt. She was still bare, though she could feel her discarded shift bunched beneath her hip. A leg lay between her legs, and a heavy arm was draped over her breasts. She lay on a softer mattress than the one on her own narrow bed, though this one smelled of dust and damp.

When she turned her head, she found a face jammed against her neck. Kate breathed in deeply. She was too tired to say what Thomas smelled like, only she thought that she would dream about the scent for years. She touched his nose lightly, feeling the bump at the bridge of his nose, then his thick eyebrows, then his lips. He sighed heavily in his sleep.

I am lying naked in my parents' bed with my lover, Kate thought. Thomas had unfolded the coverlet at the end of the bed and draped it over the two of them, but he had not drawn the bed curtains. When Henry had come up to bed, he had almost certainly seen them. What had he thought they were doing? She didn't want to worry him. Was she setting a poor example for Anne? Surely Anne knew better than to model her life after Kate's, at this point.

Kate rubbed her face in the darkness. What had awakened her? She was still exhausted, and she didn't want to be alone with her thoughts.

A sound came from the window, and she froze. Someone had closed the shutters and drawn the curtain —more evidence that Henry had walked through on his way to bed—but one had a loose hinge, listing to one side and letting sounds filter through from the yard in front of the house.

The sound of crunching slid faintly through the window, regular, rhythmic. Steps, and they had to be in the front yard, or the sound wouldn't carry through the second-floor window. A deer? A dog? No. It sounded like a person.

It could be John Mary, Kate thought, sitting up. Thomas flopped back onto the pillow, still asleep. He grunted. Kate got out of the bed and pulled her shift over her head, shuddering at the cold night air. She went to the window and eased the shutter open.

The footsteps paused, as though they sensed a listener. Then they started again, passing the house, crunching on gravel and then dry grass, and went onward, toward the barn.

It could be Anne, Kate thought. She ought not be out, but it was clear that she had been doing a lot of things she ought not be doing in the past year. The connecting door to the back bedroom was closed but not latched, and Kate pushed it open with only a small squeak of the hinges. She fumbled across the wall, feeling for the pegs where her clothes were hung. She took down a dress. Henry shifted and snorted in his bed.

The footsteps did not belong to John Mary or Anne; she knew that as deeply as she knew the feel of cheese curds between her fingers. She pulled the dress over her head and hunted for her boots on the floor, her heart pounding.

The person outside could be a neighbor or a stranger who meant no one any harm.

A decapitated body had been found in the stream a little more than five weeks ago. There was someone out there in the night who meant only harm.

"Henry," she whispered, bending over her brother. "Henry, I need you to wake up and get dressed. There's someone outside."

"Huh?" he mumbled.

"Yes," she whispered. "Someone I don't know. Meet me downstairs. Please be quiet."

"Whunh?"

"Henry," Kate said, raising her voice slightly. "Wake up and get dressed." She turned and felt her way back into the front bedroom. She hesitated for a moment beside the bed, listening to Thomas' deep breathing. Should she wake him? It might be nothing, and then—

A piercing scream rang through the night.

"FIRE! FIRE! *FIRE!*"


Eleanor felt decidedly unwell. She was not in the habit of running anywhere, and she was especially not in the habit of jogging long distances. Running nearly two miles in the cold April night in the dim light of the moon, over fields littered with rocks upon which she stumbled and through prickly hedgerows which snatched at her hair and clothing, was perhaps the most unpleasant thing she could imagine doing, and yet here she was, her throat sore from panting and a sharp pain in her side, thumping steadily onward. She thought she could see the dull gleam of the stream behind the Gravenor farm through the trees, and she briefly allowed herself to hope she would arrive in time.

This particular jog had started with a fall from a window, because when Cousin Daniel had returned from collecting rents on Lady Day and found that she was not in the house, her lessons with Miss James had been peremptorily canceled and she had been confined to her room. When Cousin Daniel had found Eleanor in his study two days later, reading one of a stack of letters she had found stuffed in the bookcase, a hard, open-handed slap and a locked door had been added to her confinement. She had not been able to make her meeting with the vicar. In the normal way of things, Eleanor might have tried to wait out his displeasure; Cousin Daniel invariably grew bored with tormenting his ward—

I'm not his *ward.* I'm his *daughter.* Eleanor stopped, clutching her stomach as she sobbed for air. She felt like she might be sick, and she could not say if her nausea was from the running or the repellent knowledge that Cousin Daniel shared more than a house with her.

I have to get away from him, Eleanor thought. He knows that I know. I don't know how he knows, but

I'm sure he does. I am not safe in that house.

If Aunt Margaret hadn't come to the door and told her what she had heard Cousin Daniel say to Zachary Walpole, Eleanor might have fallen into another night of restless, fevered sleep. As it was, she had climbed out her own bedroom window, letting herself down on the wisteria that grew up the south side of the house. She had missed her handhold in the dark and had fallen the last four feet. Her bones still felt rather loose.

Zachary Walpole was one of Cousin Daniel's hired hands, who did much the same sort of work about the farm and the parish that Rob Baker had done. Zachary was not as smart as Rob had been, but significantly meaner. Unlike Rob, Zachary had never pinched Eleanor or made kissy faces at her, but after she had seen him dispatch a litter of kittens with a mattock, she had made a point of never being in his line of sight.

Zachary had gotten a head start while she pried open the catch on her window and climbed down the outside wall, but he was not a local man and hopefully would be taking the long way round by the proper roads, walking at a normal pace. No one was expecting him at the Gravenor farm, after all. Eleanor was running and cutting cross-country. She had debated taking a horse, but at least one of the hired men slept over the stable, and she did not think she could saddle one without waking him, and she doubted she could ride bareback without falling off.

It had taken Eleanor four minutes to decide what to do after Aunt Margaret had told her through the locked door what she had overheard. The cook had

been standing under the open window of the study
when she heard Cousin Daniel tell his man to *deal with
them*. Margaret felt eavesdropping on her hated
employer was not only her right but her Christian duty,
an attitude Eleanor had appreciated but not quite
understood until meeting Thomas.

*Why* hadn't Margaret told her about Cousin Daniel
and Thomas? Why had she left Eleanor to think she
was an orphan with no parents?

Cousin Daniel had any number of personal
grudges and had threatened several of his neighbors,
but Margaret had heard the words *doctor* and *cheese*, as
well as several other words which she would not repeat
to Eleanor that had convinced her of Cousin Daniel's
ill intent. Margaret didn't know what he had told
Zachary to do, but she was frightened.

As she stood in the trees above the ford, it struck
Eleanor that this was not the first time Aunt Margaret
had sent a young person running from Lately House in
the middle of the night. She wished—well, she wished
a lot of things. She wished she could have brought
herself to tell Margaret about Thomas. He had made it,
all the way to the continent and back. Margaret ought
to know that.

There was nothing Eleanor could do about it now.

Eleanor crept forward, unpleasantly aware that the
rushing of the water would cover the sound of anyone
else moving about in this night—anyone, for example,
like Zachary Walpole. She did not want to be caught by
Zachary in the darkness.

Aunt Margaret knew I would do my best to warn
the Gravenors if she told me what Cousin Daniel had

done, Eleanor thought, dragging her skirts up above her knees to wade through the stream. The water was already higher than it had been a week ago, soaking her stockings to the knee.

She knew. She *knew*, Eleanor thought. Margaret thought her much braver than she knew herself to be. Eleanor swallowed. Things could not be the same after this night. What would Cousin Daniel do to her? There was no hope of her returning to her locked room without being discovered. Would he throw her out? Would he pack her off somewhere? She had not been able to find any records of his relationship to her or Thomas in his papers before she had been discovered. She was not sure they still existed, if they ever had. There had been a small stack of letters from the old vicar George Beauford, written in a most insinuating and presumptuous tone, but none of them *said* anything, only implied that Cousin Daniel owed him money.

I could run away and start a new life. I could marry Henry Gravenor. The thought stopped her in the middle of the stream for a long minute, before she shook herself and sloshed forward. She was not sure precisely how marriages were contracted, but she was fairly sure it took more than some indecorous thoughts on her part and some hand-holding on his.

Eleanor crested the hill behind the farm. She could see the dark bulk of the house now. There was something wrong with the scene, and it took her a long moment to understand what it was. The house was not lit by the faint moonlight, but by a red glow from somewhere behind it. A red glow like—

"FIRE! FIRE! *FIRE!*" she howled.

She began to run again, though her ribs felt like they would split. Blisters had formed on the backs of her ankles, and they alternately stabbed and throbbed with pain.

"WAKE UP!" she screamed. "WAKE UP! *FIRE!*" Her lungs hurt so much she worried she might vomit.

The fire must be in the barn. Of course, she thought, horrified; the Gravenors' cows would be in the barn. Without them, there would be no milk, no cheese, and no money. She pelted down the last curve of the path and around the house.

Eleanor ran into someone, an enormous someone who let out a soft *oof* at the impact. A pair of large hands seized her shoulders. Her heart felt like it would slam through her breastbone with fear. There was a scream in the distance, suddenly cut off.

"Let go of me!" she squawked. She tried to kick whoever it was in the shins, but misjudged the distance and almost tripped and went sprawling on the path.

The large hands steadied her and kept her from falling.

"Miss Lately?"

Eleanor gaped. That was undeniably the grave, polite voice of Henry Gravenor, which meant that the large hands must also belong to Henry Gravenor.

"I—yes—he's—he's—" She forced herself to take a deep breath. "He's setting the barn on fire!"

"The goats!" Henry sounded truly horrified. Suddenly he was no longer holding her, but racing away across the farm yard. Eleanor stumbled, then gathered up her skirts and ran after him. Her stockings were wet from the stream, and her aching feet squelched with every step.

Her mind raced. There were goats in the barn, too? That must have been the scream she heard. She thought of Zachary and his mattock and felt sick.

"The straw! The new straw for the roof! It's all in the barn!" That was Kate's voice from closer to the house, rising in a heartbroken wail.

Then a voice spoke which sent a painful chill of recognition through Eleanor. *Thomas*. Her—her father. Her other father. "We'll worry about the straw as soon as we put out the fire. We'll set up a bucket line from the well. Where's Anne?"

"Yes! Buckets!" That was Anne's voice. Eleanor tried to remember where the well was; she thought it was in front of the house, close to the drive leading out into the lane. Her heart sank. She didn't think the Gravenors could cross that distance without running, and Thomas couldn't run.

"The cows—" Kate started.

"The cows are all out in the wood! It's only the straw!"

"Did you hear me?" Eleanor yelped. "Zachary— that is, Cousin Daniel—he's here—*somewhere*—he's got a mattock!" That didn't sound as frightening as it was, and she wasn't sure they understood. "He kills things with it!" She pushed past Kate and Thomas, straining to see more. The barn was a low building some little distance from the house, built up against the side of the hill. Red light illuminated the low open doorway, which was then blocked by a huge form ducking inside of it.

"*Henry!*" Eleanor yelled. "*Don't!*"

"The goats!" came an answering yell.

"What's he doing?" Anne demanded.

"He bought two kids at the market," Kate said, her voice laced with despair.

"*Henry!* Don't be stupid!" Thomas bellowed.

Eleanor picked up her skirts and ran toward the barn, after Henry.

"*Eleanor!*" Kate screamed.

Time felt like it had slowed to the pace of treacle flowing over snow. Tongues of fire ate through the thatch and licked up into the night, casting demonic shadows. The fire was at the far end of the building, opposite the low entrance with its stone lintel. Smoke poured out from under the eaves and the open doorway.

There was another little scream; now Eleanor could hear the vibrato that marked it as coming from a young ungulate throat. There was at least one terrified goat kid still alive inside.

It was a small building; why hadn't Henry already grabbed his goats and escaped?

Feeling increasingly sick, Eleanor ducked her head through the door and held her arm over her face, coughing. She couldn't see more than dim shapes moving around in the fiery interior. It was punishingly hot inside, and the air wavered in front of her eyes.

Wait. *Shapes.* There were two man-sized shapes moving through the barn, one huge and towheaded, one shorter—one shorter and raising a long shadow over his head—

She filled her lungs with burning air and shrieked.

"HENRY! BEHIND YOU!"

The goats screamed. Zachary Walpole, who was apparently even more foolish than she had thought, surged out from one of the cattle stalls and swung his mattock at Henry. But Henry was suddenly not there, and the mattock cut a path through empty, smoky air.

He won't leave without the goats, Eleanor thought, her stomach a riot of terror, but I can at least keep him from getting his head bashed in.

"OI!" she shouted, putting her hands on her hips. "*Walpole!* I see you! You'd better come out of there right now, or I'll have the constable on you!"

Zachary turned toward her voice, the fire reflected in his eyes. Eleanor watched a simple calculation happen behind his hard stare. She was the only one here who knew definitely who he was. Arson was a crime he could hang for. Cousin Daniel would not forgive her defection to the Gravenors. Zachary might still get his money from his employer even if he killed Eleanor.

She turned, ducked through the low barn door, and ran.

Or tried to run; her legs seized painfully, and her throat burned from breathing smoke. Eleanor tripped, half-fell, struggled to her feet, and tripped again. A hand grabbed her hair and she screamed.

Two piercing goat cries rang out in response.

"*Eleanor!*" More than one voice was yelling her name, but she couldn't figure out who or where they were.

"Help!" she yelled, or tried to yell, but it came out as a choked garble of coughing.

"Give me that," Henry said nearby, also coughing. There was the sound of grunting, as though the two men were playing tug-of-war.

Eleanor did not see what happened next, but Zachary's grip loosened, and then no one had hold of her at all. She fell ignominiously into the churned-up mud of the cow pen. When she looked up, she saw Henry looming over her, two small goats under one arm and Zachary's mattock in his other hand. A shadow flitted away in her peripheral vision, but the fire was too loud for her to hear anything else.

Henry turned his head to cough into his shoulder, then crouched next to Eleanor. "I'm sorry," he said.

Eleanor opened her mouth to say he didn't need to be sorry, but then he dropped the mattock and scooped her up in the arm that wasn't holding the kids.

# CHAPTER TWENTY-THREE

Thomas offered up several prayers of thanksgiving that the barn was not any closer to the house, with its ancient, dusty, flammable thatch. The fire had grown too much to be put out, fueled by two roofs' worth of straw inside the building and atop it. The Gravenors were reduced to pouring buckets of water all around the barn to keep it from spreading. Thankfully it had been a wet spring, so no sparks caught in the grass or trees.

None of the neighbors came to see about the fire or the screaming, though Ned Bell was only a quarter-mile away and Fred Halverton only twice that. Thomas wondered if Cousin Daniel had warned them off, or if the discovery of the headless body had been enough to make all the surrounding farmers decide they wanted nothing to do with the Gravenors. Either way, the solitary crackling of the fire filled him with foreboding. It should not be like this. There should be people coming to help.

Kate was weeping steadily as she ran back and forth from the well to the barn, her grief over the lost straw and barn and terror over the safety of her twin burning through her composure. One of the cows—Georgette?—appeared out of the woods and stood by the front door of the house, lowing indignantly at whoever passed. Henry carried Eleanor and the goats inside the house, but when he reemerged, Eleanor followed a few paces behind him, looking frayed and very determined.

Where would the arsonist run to? Thomas wondered. Eleanor had shouted something about Cousin Daniel—about another hired hand—but would the man go back to the Lately house immediately or lie low for a while? Would Daniel's man hang about, waiting for a chance to do the Gravenors more mischief in the darkness, or would he flee the parish altogether?

Thomas' bad leg sent daggers of pain lancing into his hip and lower back as he limped back and forth. They did not have enough buckets, so he was using Kate's cheese pot to carry water. He needed to sit down, but he would not leave Kate to face the wreckage of her farm alone. Would the arsonist try again? And now that Cousin Daniel had shown his hand so plainly, what would his next move be? Clearly he had meant for the fire to happen in the night, with no witnesses; he had not reckoned on Eleanor following his man from Lately House and raising the alarm.

But John Mary usually slept in the barn, Thomas thought. Why hadn't he raised the alarm?

A cold thread of fear wrapped itself around his heart.

"Kate," Thomas said sharply. "Where is your

brother? Where is John Mary?"

Kate stopped and stared at him blearily, rubbing her eyes with the back of one hand. "I don't—Henry. Henry, do you know where John Mary is?"

Henry dumped another pot of water into the barn moat. "No," he said. "He was gone when we got home from the market."

Kate opened her mouth and let out a little cry. Thomas, suddenly uncaring that her siblings could see him, limped toward her and wrapped both arms around her. She smelled like smoke and sweat and fear; he was sure he did as well. Kate buried her face in his neck and sobbed.

Over Kate's head, Thomas saw Eleanor tentatively tug on Henry's sleeve. "What—is—does—" Her voice was raspy, and she started to cough again.

"The loft where John Mary sleeps was over the pile of thatching straw," Henry said bleakly. "I didn't see—but I don't know."

Eleanor looked up at him, her face a mask of horror. Anne stopped moving mid-step, her face blank, her mouth slightly open.

Kate shook in Thomas' arms. He pressed his lips to the top of her head and closed his eyes.

They kept sentry over the burning barn until the fire had died down to smoking embers and the clear, miserable light of dawn stretched over the eastern sky. When the five of them filed back into the house in battered disarray, they discovered the two goat kids sleeping in the center of the parlor settee. The legs of all the chairs bore new teeth marks, and the animals had pulled down a book of Greek tragedies from the ancient writing desk in the corner and eaten most of it. The cows refused to come out of the wood, and periodically a deafening *moo* pierced the still cold air.

Kate was too exhausted and too sad to make breakfast, so Thomas helped her upstairs and laid her down in the bed where he had made love to her the evening before. He meant to go down and examine Henry and the others to assess the damage the smoke had done to their lungs, but somehow he ended up lying next to Kate on the bed, his arms wrapped tightly around her. He dimly heard several pairs of footsteps pass through the room, but saw nothing; the room was still dark in the middle of the day when the shutters remained closed. He wondered if Eleanor was sharing a bed with Anne or Henry, and then realized he would now worry where Eleanor was and what she was doing for the rest of his life. He hoped she was with Henry, who would at least do what Eleanor wanted.

Eleanor's testimony would give the Gravenors clear grounds to pursue legal action against Cousin Daniel. He was a tricky old monster, and would likely seek to discredit her—his *daughter*, goddammit—or them through any means he could. Thomas supposed this was why he had so publicly cast aspersions on Kate's character at the market. But if he could not discredit them—well, he had shown he was open to other methods of getting what he wanted. In some ways, knowing that the barn fire was arson put them all in more danger than if they thought it was a terrible accident. But if Eleanor had not come—

Eleanor had run two miles in the dark to warn them. She had gone into the barn after Henry.

Thomas had not raised Eleanor; he knew he had no right to feel pride in her defiance or her bravery. And, yet, something like pride was unfurling in his chest, a strange, warm feeling. He ought to feel only despair in this hellish situation. His doom drew ever closer, tangled up with the fate of this family who had cared for and sheltered him.

I am alive, holding the woman I love, and the child I thought was dead is alive, sleeping in the next room, Thomas thought. Things will be terrible soon enough. I can be forgiven for having the smallest amount of hope in this moment.

When Kate woke, Anne was shaking her. Late afternoon light angled through the window.

"Kate," she whispered. Her face was very white. "Kate, you have to get up."

They've found John Mary's body, Kate thought. She was going to be sick.

"It's not what you think, but it's bad," Anne said, reading her expression.

"Thomas?" Kate said, her voice thick. Exhausted as she was, she didn't think she could have slept at all if Thomas hadn't been holding her, and now he was gone.

"He's outside, looking at it," Anne said grimly.

"It," Kate repeated.

She had slept in her clothes, so it took relatively little time to force her feet into her boots and stumble downstairs.

Eleanor sat at the kitchen table, her face very white, her dark hair a cloud around her face. Someone had placed a slice of buttered bread and a cup of tea in front of her. She had clearly touched neither, but only stared into space.

"She's already seen it," Anne said, tugging Kate along. "Come on. The back door is faster."

Henry had made a new pen for the goat kids out of chairs and twine in the corner of the parlor. They bleated in suppressed rage as the women passed them, and Anne reached down to fondle one of their little heads.

Anne led Kate out the back door, past the kitchen garden, and up the path that went toward the stream. The day was windy and misty, the sky overhead iron gray, and she wrapped Henry's old coat more tightly around herself. Halfway up the hill, Thomas stood in the middle of the path, looking down at something, a grim expression on his face. Henry stood a ways off the path between two cows, his gaze fixed on the sky.

Kate came to stand by Thomas. She swallowed hard.

He was inspecting the headless body of a man, sprawled gracelessly in the middle of the path. It was not John Mary; this man was much shorter and broader and wore unfamiliar laborer's clothing. A cow pat obscured the stump of his neck. It looked like he had been cut down fleeing from the farm.

Thomas turned toward her. His face did something when he saw her, his brows drawing low and his jaw working. For a moment Kate thought he would take hold of her, but he only stared intently into her eyes, before jerking his head toward the corpse. "Eleanor said this is Zachary Walpole, the man who burned down your barn last night. She recognized his clothing."

"What—" Kate looked at Anne, then at Henry, then at Thomas. "What does this mean? Who could have done this?"

"He's still stiff," Thomas said. "He was probably killed a few minutes after he escaped the barn."

"Leave it for Peter to deal with," Henry suggested, tugging on Antoinette's and Nonnette's horns to guide them back down the hill. "He's good with dead bodies."

"That's not—Henry, we can't," Kate said. "We have to—" She stopped, staring at the corpse, then looked up helplessly at Thomas. "What can we do? People will think—they *must* think—"

"We had to have killed him," Anne said. "He burned down our barn and tried to kill our cattle. If I didn't know none of us had done it, I'd be sure we had."

"Where is John Mary?" Thomas asked abruptly.

Kate's stomach dropped, and the world wobbled around her.

"No, Kate, stop," Thomas said, and suddenly he had hold of her again, squeezing her upper arms with his hands, "Think. Walpole didn't behead himself, and I don't think he fell down dead of fright."

"You think John Mary cut off his head?" Anne said, poking the dead man's boot with her boot.

"John Mary wouldn't do that," Henry announced. "He'd make sure the cows were safe before he murdered anyone."

"I think when the fire has cooled down enough to

dig through the ashes, we're not going to find any bones in the barn," Thomas said. His eyes were very intense, as though he were trying to will Kate to believe him. And oh, she wanted to believe him, wanted to believe that her oldest brother was not dead, horribly smothered in smoke and flames. Thomas' fingers tightened briefly around Kate's arms, until she swallowed hard and nodded at him. He released her, though reluctantly, and he did not step away. "I don't know where John Mary was or what he was doing last night, but I think once we know that, we'll know what happened to *him*." He jerked his head toward the body. "And presumably what happened to Rob Baker, too."

"Right," Kate said weakly. "So we just have to find John Mary. How do we find him?"

"I think we should hide the body," Anne said. "I mean, put it in the woodshed, until we can figure out what to do about it."

They all looked at the body again, except for Henry, who had gone farther into the trees in pursuit of another cow.

"That's sensible," Kate allowed. "I think."

Thomas looked like he might object, but then he sighed and rubbed his face. "Very well. I suppose there's no point in asking questions none of us can answer yet."

"I'll get a sheet, and we can wrap him in it and carry him down," Kate said, turning back toward the house.

She had reached the back door before she heard the sounds of an altercation inside the house. The wind whipping her hair around her ears had covered the sound while standing on the hill, or maybe she had unconsciously assumed any cries were from the goats in the parlor. Perhaps she was simply too tired for words to penetrate; she felt like her head was swaddled in a thick gray blanket.

But now Kate was sure there was yelling, and she yanked up the latch and rushed inside. There was no one human in the parlor, but the goat kids hurled themselves at the walls of their chair pen and bleated at the top of their lungs. The front door stood open.

One of the voices was Eleanor's. "Let go! *Let go of me!*"

"Eleanor!" Kate cried. She grabbed a poker from the fireplace grate.

Daniel Lately's curricle, two matched bays stamping between the shafts, stood in the yard, and Daniel Lately himself stood in front of it. Kate realized with horror that she had taken the sound of the wheels on the gravel for the crackling of leaves in the wind, so she had lost precious minutes in intercepting the man. Lately looked more disarrayed than she had ever seen him, his cravat half-untied and a lock of white hair falling in his face. Kate hoped that Eleanor had tried to claw his eyes out. He had hold of Eleanor by her wrists, and every few steps he stopped to shake her.

"—ungrateful—horrible—worthless—child—"

"Daniel Lately!" Kate shouted, standing on the front step. "You leave Eleanor be!"

He stopped and turned his cold gaze on her. "Whore," he spat. "You have no business telling me what to do with my own—ow!"

Eleanor had stamped on his foot.

"You have no business lying about me in Southbridge market!" Kate screamed. "You have no business harassing my brothers! You have no business sending an arsonist to my house! *Henry!*" She almost called for Thomas, too, but a sudden surge of fear ran through her: whatever horrible thing Daniel Lately meant to do to Eleanor, what worse thing might he do to Thomas?

Instead she screamed again, "HENRY! *Henry!*"

Daniel Lately stared at her. Then, slowly, coldly, he turned to Eleanor and slapped her. The blow was so hard that the girl sagged in his grip. Then he turned back to Kate.

"That is a slanderous statement," he said. "You will hear from my solicitor."

At that moment Henry appeared around the side of the house, his face brick-red, having clearly sprinted from the wood upon hearing Kate's cry. He paused for a moment, taking in the scene, then charged forward like a white-blonde bull.

Daniel Lately's eyes bulged, and he dragged Eleanor into the curricle and mounted the step. There was the crack of a whip, and the vehicle wheeled into the road. Henry ran after it, but the whip cracked again, and again, until the curricle pulled away.

## CHAPTER TWENTY-FOUR

And the terrible thing has arrived, Thomas thought.

Anne was staying at the farm with the cows, though she had argued ferociously that she should be allowed to bring the herd to Lately House and let them wreak havoc inside. Henry had absorbed his sister's report of Eleanor's abduction in silence, then disappeared and reappeared bearing a mattock and a determined expression. Thomas wondered where he had gotten the mattock; it looked newer and sharper than any of the Gravenors' other tools.

Kate had insisted Thomas use both of his crutches while they walked cross-country.

"You'll need to conserve your strength," she insisted. "It won't do if your leg gives out halfway." She also insisted they all drink a cup of strong tea before departing.

"I don't know what we're going to do," Thomas repeated. He had thought of, and discarded, a new plan every hundred yards closer they came to Lately House.

Eleanor is *my child*, he thought. I have every right to make sure she is safe and treated well.

And I can't prove it without sacrificing everything I am and everything I've worked to become.

"We have to do something," Kate said. She kept saying this, again and again. She swayed slightly when she stood in one place. Thomas had wanted to argue that she must stay at the farm with Anne so she could rest, but she was still clutching the poker and looking mutinous.

"We'll steal Eleanor," Henry said helpfully.

"Eleanor is her own person," Kate said severely.

"We'll help Eleanor steal herself," Henry amended.

"We'll bluff, while Henry finds Eleanor and takes her away," Thomas said, knocking aside a branch that had fallen into the right-of-way with one of his crutches. It was the plan he kept coming back to, the plan which, for all its many flaws, he felt had the most chance of working. "Then we'll go to the vicarage, and Peter will …" His voice trailed off. Hopefully Peter would have found something, something real and written down, that they could use to stop Cousin Daniel. But until then: what could they threaten him with? The accusation that he was not actually the owner of Lately House? The fact that he had sent men to violently harass his neighbors? Or, the fact that Thomas suspected that Cousin Daniel had arranged the murders of his own men to cover up his crimes?

*The problem is,* Thomas thought, *that Cousin Daniel doesn't care about any of that. He's gotten to where he is by being the coldest-hearted bastard in several counties.*

The mattock swinging by Henry's side caught his eye.

We can't just murder Cousin Daniel, Thomas thought. That's … that's …

How many innocent men did you see go down under cannon fire? a voice at the back of his mind asked softly. How many civilians did you see maimed by soldiers having fun in their off-hours? What cruelties did you see dispensed to the natives of Cape Town, for the sin of having their land stolen by a greedy empire?

It is one thing to witness atrocities and know that there is no reason or order to the atrocity, Thomas thought. It is another to decide that you are allowed to commit atrocity yourself.

Besides, we've already the one body to dispose of.

He sighed and shook himself.

Kate touched his shoulder, and he met her painfully blue eyes.

"I don't know if it will be all right," she said, very quietly. "But I am glad to be with you in this."

If Cousin Daniel threatens Kate, I am going to bash his head in, Thomas thought.

"Yes," he said out loud. "Yes."

Lately House was newer and more modern than the Gravenor home. It had been built by Thomas' grandfather in the first decade of the last century, with a tiled roof and symmetrical glass windows flanking the front door. Thomas remembered that there were four rooms on the ground floor and four on the second, and a large kitchen in the back where Margaret the cook had reigned supreme. The square farm yard with the animals and equipment, granary and barns, was laid out behind the house.

The house faced southwest. The sun was low in the sky, and the red light glimmered off the panes of the windows. Thomas wished he knew how many men Cousin Daniel employed, and how many were engaged specifically for threatening his neighbors. He wasn't sure how much land his parents had owned, but there had always been people taking horses and cows in and out of the yard, and in the fall they had hired several dozen young men to cut all the wheat. He remembered a few—old Lawrence, and Adam Bell, who he supposed was cousin to the Gravenors' neighbor—but he would be surprised if any of them remained. If they had to face a dozen, or even six, men who believed that Cousin Daniel was in the right, they'd have no chance of getting out of here with Eleanor.

Henry, Thomas, and Kate stood in a tight cluster in the shadow of a hedgerow. Thomas made a note to thank Kate later for insisting he bring both crutches; his bad leg ached, but he suspected he would be crawling by now if he'd tried to walk the last two miles without aid.

"I don't suppose he'll let us in," Kate murmured, her eyebrows drawing together.

"No," Thomas said. "But we won't be asking him. We'll go around the back."

Walking around the back meant more time in the open where someone might see and stop them, but Thomas limped forward as though he belonged here— as though, in fact, the house belonged to him.

*Not to me,* he thought suddenly. *To Eleanor.*

The kitchen was a large brick room which stuck

out of the center of the back of the house, a half-story lower than the rest of the building. A door opened directly onto the yard, so the cook could send a girl across the way for milk and eggs with all due haste, or run herself if the girl was out sick.

Thomas, his throat suddenly tight, knocked on the door. He was thankful for Kate's quiet presence at his side and Henry's looming one at his back.

He had barely put his hand down when he heard a voice muttering from the other side. A familiar voice. His heart clenched. The door swung open a crack.

"If you're delivering my order from Grisham's, you're a day late," snapped a hoarse female voice. "And if you're anyone else, I don't care to see you."

"Margaret Leigh," Thomas said quietly.

"Yes, you know my name," she responded testily. "Good job to you. Now go away. I've had a terrible long day."

"I've come about Eleanor," Thomas said.

There was a long silence, and then the door opened another few inches. This side of the house was in shadow, but Thomas saw a pale sliver of Margaret's face. Her eye was rimmed with red, as though she'd been crying.

"What about Eleanor?" she said.

"She can't stay here," Thomas said.

"She should have never been here," Margaret said, her voice full of bitterness. "I should have kept running with her until I got to France. But what could I do, once that awful man came to fetch her back? He's her father. And anyway," she added, suddenly stern, "what business of yours is this, young man? Who are you?"

Thomas opened his mouth, but nothing came out.

"I'm Catherine Gravenor, ma'am," Kate said, pushing close enough to him so that Margaret could see her face through the door. "And my brother Henry is with me. Eleanor is my sister Anne's particular friend. She—she came last—"

The door suddenly swung all the way open, and Margaret beckoned to them furiously. "Come in," she hissed. "Come in right now. Keep your voices down. Did she get there in time?"

Margaret looked very thin and very old. Thomas had thought she was thin and old when he had known her as a teenager, but he realized now that she had probably been middle-aged and no thinner than Eleanor. Now she looked skeletal, her fingers gnarled with arthritis, and her hair had gone white and thin.

"Henry saved the goats, but the barn burned," Kate whispered.

Margaret closed her eyes, an expression of defeat creasing her face. She took another deep breath, and then her eyes snapped open. "Is everyone safe, then?" she demanded. "That man he sent is a bad one. I've seen him—well, never you mind what I've seen him do. He hasn't been back here yet today, but I expect he's lying low."

Kate and Thomas exchanged looks. "I don't think he'll be returning," she said carefully. "We haven't been able to find my brother John Mary since the fire, but we're not sure—we're not sure what happened."

Margaret shook her head, her lips pressed tightly together. She looked at Thomas, her eyes narrowing.

"And you? You're that doctor fellow, aren't you? I heard you cut Rob Baker up after he died to see what happened to him. Why involve yourself in this? It's an ugly business, and it will only get uglier."

Thomas stared at her. His mind was a perfect blank.

Why I am here? he thought.

Because I had to run away.

Because you gave me money and clothes, so I had a chance.

Because you kept Eleanor alive.

Because Henry saved my life, when I didn't particularly want to live.

Because I love Kate, and I thought I wouldn't be able to love anyone.

Because I don't want Eleanor to suffer what I suffered.

Because Cousin Daniel is a monster.

He swallowed and scrubbed a hand over his face.

When he looked back at Margaret, her face had changed, and he knew that she knew.

"My God," she said. She put a shaking hand over her eyes and lowered herself into a chair by the window. "My God."

"I've—" His voice sounded rough, so he cleared his throat and tried again. "I've as much right to see that Eleanor is looked after as anyone."

Margaret lowered her hands to her lap, clutching her skirt. She nodded, first slowly, then decisively, almost angrily. "So you do."

"Which room is Eleanor's?" Kate asked. "We thought—it's not much of a plan, but we thought we

would talk to—to him—while Henry went and got
Eleanor and took her away to the vicarage. My brother
Peter should be able to do something for her."

"The room on the north corner of the house,"
Margaret said dully. "But he's locked her in, I don't
have a key."

"My room," Thomas said, feeling rather sick.
Suddenly he hated Cousin Daniel so much that he
wondered that he had ever thought any choice but
killing him was the right one.

"I've got a mattock," Henry observed. "It's very
sharp."

Margaret looked as him at though she had not
noticed the six-and-a-half foot, fifteen-stone man
standing in her kitchen. She looked at the tool in his
hand, and then back up at his face. "That looks like
Zachary Walpole's mattock."

"Not anymore," Henry said.

Margaret, apparently making up her mind, got
back to her feet. "He'll be expecting his dinner soon,"
she said. "He takes it on a tray in his study. I'll bring it
in to him, and you'll come right behind me. You'll have
a minute or so to get up to Eleanor's door," she told
Henry. "I'll drop the tray or somesuch to make a loud
noise, and you open the door then and go out the
kitchen door with her as fast as ever you can. She's—
she's—" Margaret took a deep breath before
continuing in a higher voice. "She's likely a bit woozy
yet, as he boxed her ears a fair bit after they returned
home. You hold her steady."

"I will," Henry said.

"Is there anyone else in the house? Any more

servants?" Kate asked in a low voice.

"He had only his man Jordan, and he's been dead for six months," Margaret said shortly. "No one else."

"No one else?" Thomas repeated. "But—"

We might be able to do this, he thought, wondering.

"He's tight with his money, *Mister* Daniel Lately is," Margaret said, her voice laden with contempt. "There's that boy sleeping over stable, Bingham or Binley or something like that, and there will be a few day laborers in the morning."

A bell rang from the front of the house. Margaret bared her teeth, and Thomas felt himself make the same expression. "There he is." She yanked a tray out of a nearby cupboard and started slamming items down on it.

Kate stood on her toes, and Henry obligingly bent his head so she could kiss his cheek. "Be careful, Henry."

"I will, Kate."

Thomas wanted to demand that Kate kiss him and tell him to be careful, too, but he did not.

The bell rang again, this time longer and more loudly. Margaret muttered under her breath as she sliced bread and ladled stew into a bowl. When Thomas looked at her, he saw her cheeks were damp.

"I should have done it," she whispered. "I should have done it. I've the stuff for the rats, and I could have done it slow-like. But if they'd caught me, where would she go? Where would my girl go?" Her words had an incantation-like quality, as though these were thoughts she'd had so often that she said them to herself in her sleep.

The bell rang once more, this time for a full minute.

Margaret hoisted the tray, murder in her eyes.

"Follow me," she said.

# CHAPTER TWENTY-FIVE

Daniel Lately's study was on the southern corner of the house, as far from Eleanor's room as it was possible to be. Kate very much hoped this meant that the sound of her brother chopping the lock off the door would be somewhat muted.

Thomas looked haggard, as though he'd just received news of the death of an old friend.

If we get through this, I am going to cut him a slice of my best-aged cheese, Kate thought, burying her free hand in her skirt, and then I am going to kiss him and kiss him, and then I am going to hold him until he sleeps and his face doesn't look like that.

The hallway of Lately House was carpeted, and the walls were paneled in dark wood. Kate felt very thankful for the carpet, as it muffled the sounds of two extra sets of footsteps following Margaret Leigh down the hall with her heavy tray.

The cook stopped before the last door on the left-hand side of the hall and glanced behind her. She met Thomas' eyes, then Kate's, then nodded sharply. She leaned against the door, pressing the handle open with her elbow, and went in.

"It's about time, woman," Daniel Lately's voice snarled from inside the room. "Are you deaf?"

"No, sir," Margaret replied woodenly. "You have visitors."

"I certainly do not have visitors at this hour. Tell them to leave."

Thomas took Kate's hand for the briefest moment, squeezing it in a painful grip, before he strode into the room.

Kate followed as closely behind him as she could.

Daniel Lately paused, a pen in his hand. The fire in the room was banked; the only light came from a single candle on his desk.

"What is the meaning of this," he barked, looking from Thomas to Kate. Then he looked from Thomas to Kate again, and a horrible thing happened.

He smiled.

"I expect," he said, "you've come to make a deal with me."

Kate filled her chest with air. "Yes. Eleanor—"

"Shut up, you little whore," Mr. Lately said. His eyes were fixed on Thomas. "I meant you, *Doctor* Holyoke. Or should I say—"

But Mr. Lately did not get a chance to say the name, because at that moment Margaret upended the tray over his head.

"I give notice!" the cook bellowed.

Kate heard a crack of wood overhead. She prayed Mr. Lately didn't hear it too.

"You old bitch!" roared Mr. Lately. "I'll show you notice!" He fumbled in his desk drawer, soup dripping down his hair and onto his shirt, as he grabbed for something.

Margaret skipped backward, surprisingly nimble for an old woman. But then she stopped moving, her eyes fixed on a single point.

Mr. Lately had reached into his desk and pulled out a pistol. With ostentatious precision, he pulled back the cock and set his finger on the trigger.

"I don't know what you all think you're playing at," he said softly. He pointed the gun at Kate, and her heartbeat picked up speed. "But I think I'm done playing. Catherine Gravenor, you will write a letter telling your brother to sell his farm to me—at a very reasonable price, given that your life will be included in the bargain. You will be my guest until he consents. Margaret Leigh, you are dismissed henceforth. You will have no reference. If I hear of you anywhere within Shropshire, I will have you arrested and whipped for vagrancy."

The barrel of the gun swung toward Thomas. "As for you," Mr. Lately said. His eyes glittered. "It's pleasant, isn't it, to have these loose ends tied up after so long?"

"I am not a loose end," Thomas snarled.

"You are an abomination before God," Mr. Lately thundered. "I should have had you committed to an insane asylum the first time I caught you putting on trousers. The fact that bearing a child did not cure you bears witness to your persistent madness. You will certainly go to an asylum now, and society will be saved from your perversion of the natural order."

Kate felt sick. She could not tear her eyes away from the pistol. She wanted in equal parts to beat

Daniel Lately's head in and to throw her arms around Thomas and comfort him.

She considered the distance between the door and the desk. She was not especially fast, and she was not sure she could bring the poker she still held in the folds of her skirt down on Mr. Lately's head hard enough to knock him out.

There was a thump from overhead. *Henry.* Henry might yet get Eleanor away from here, if they could stall long enough.

"Give me a pen," Kate said abruptly. "I'll write the letter now."

Daniel Lately turned his sickening smile on her, but his pistol stayed pointed at Thomas, who he seemed to think was the most dangerous of the three of them. "No, I think not. Why rush such an important matter? I think it would be better if you had a few days to think on the wording, and your brother had some time to consider the implications of your loss, before sending it."

"Why on earth did you behead them?" Thomas burst out.

"What?" Mr. Lately said.

"Rob Baker and Zachary Walpole," Thomas snapped. "I understand why you killed them, or had someone else kill them. But why on God's earth go to the effort of beheading them?"

Kate swallowed hard. She had thought the idea that Daniel Lately might have killed his hired men nonsensical, but the gun he was now threatening them with lent the idea some credence.

The smile dropped from Mr. Lately's face, and he

stared at Thomas. His face twitched, as though he were struggling to keep his expression neutral. Finally he said, "Do not attempt to confuse me. Rob Baker is no longer in my employ. Zachary Walpole took leave to visit his family in Cheshire."

"They did not," Thomas said coolly. "Both of them have gone to their final judgment. We found their corpses close to the farm. Did you think if no one recognized them, you wouldn't be connected to their murders?"

Kate met Margaret's eyes across the room.

I've got the poker, and I'm younger and stronger, she thought. I think it's down to me.

She began to ease herself toward the bookshelf at the side of the room. Daniel Lately's full attention was on Thomas now, and he didn't seem to notice. She wasn't sure if Thomas believed what he was saying, but she hoped desperately that this line of questioning would keep Mr. Lately angry and distracted.

"There were no murders," Mr. Lately hissed. "If a man who used to work on my property died in an accident, it's nothing to do with me."

"*Beheaded*," Thomas repeated. "Beheaded, with a sharp blade, by someone who knew what they were doing. I suppose that rules you out."

Kate quickly revised her prayer to include not making Mr. Lately so angry that he shot Thomas.

"You *are* mad," Daniel Lately said, in a tone of mock-wonder. "Completely, absolutely, spectacularly mad. Coming into my study late at night, raving about murders and beheadings. The constable will of course understand that I was forced to defend—"

No more time, Kate thought, and dived toward the desk, swinging the poker in a wide arc. She would have tried to hit Daniel Lately if she had been a few steps closer, but she would settle for making it impossible for him to aim truly at any of them. The tip of the poker sent the candle flying across the room before slamming into the wood of the desk, sending vibrations up and down her arm. Kate did not turn her head to see where the candle landed, but suddenly the room was very dark.

The gun went off with a tremendous *bang*, at the same moment, Thomas roared and Margaret howled, and two bodies hit the floor a moment later. Kate barely contained a sob. Had they both fallen? Had one of them been killed?

"You're all mad!" Mr. Lately yelled. There was a crash, as though he had shoved away from his desk and knocked his chair to the floor, and then another crash that sounded like him throwing his gun away. A drawer rattled, and Mr. Lately snarled, "I've another gun, and I know where are you are, you little whore."

Margaret Leigh let out a soft moan from the floor. Kate swallowed against the terror closing her throat and clutched her poker more tightly. She could see only the darkest outline of the man in the shadow, but he did, indeed, seem to be aiming the gun at her.

"Drop that damn poker or I'll shoot you," Mr. Lately said. "You have five seconds."

"You won't get my brother's farm if you kill me," Kate pointed out, in what she felt was a very reasonable tone.

"*Do it,*" Mr. Lately hissed between his teeth.

"You've no right to that farm anyway, you slovenly, half-French mongrels."

There was a laugh from the hallway. It was a low, soft laugh. A woman's laugh.

Kate did not turn around; she did not want to take her eyes from Mr. Lately's second gun for even a moment. But her spine prickled all the way up to her hairline. She had not thought of the open door of the study at her back, nor the hallway that was now black with the new night. Now it was all she could think of.

"Oh, God, Eleanor," Thomas moaned. "You were supposed to get away."

"That's not Eleanor," Kate said. Her hands were very cold. She would not have thought until this moment that there were quite so many flavors of fear, nor that she could feel so many of them simultaneously.

The laugh came again. This time it was so close that the laugher must have been standing just outside the door.

"You!" Daniel Lately called. "You in the hall! I am armed! Do not test me!"

He's very frightened, Kate thought. I wonder if he recognizes that laugh, too.

The laugher spoke, so softly Kate had to strain to hear. "Fils salaud de putain salaud, do you think I am afraid now? You have one bullet left."

Kate closed her eyes. She could not help herself. A hand grabbed her ankle and yanked her urgently toward the floor; a half-second after she crouched down, another shot rang out.

"Don't come any closer!" Mr. Lately screamed.

The room was completely dark and still, though the two shots so close together still rang in Kate's ears. The air smelled of smoke and gunpowder.

Thomas' hand slid up Kate's leg and squeezed her calf, and she had to fight back a little cry. He was alive. He was *alive*.

"Are you there?" Daniel Lately demanded of the silent room. "Are you there?"

No one responded.

"Foolishness," he snapped. His voice shook. "Foolishness and games. You think you can frighten me? Nothing frightens me."

The steps which passed by Kate were so quiet that if a bare foot hadn't nudged her midriff, she would have thought she imagined the whisper of a sound.

There came the sound of Daniel Lately fumbling in his desk, presumably to find another candle. "All this for nothing," he said angrily. "I suppose I'll have Oliver drag them out when he comes in the morning." His chair squeaked, and his shoes clicked across the floor. There was a soft crunching, as of the banked coals being disturbed, and then a light flared as the wick of the candle caught.

Daniel Lately stood and turned back to the room to survey his handiwork.

And so, he was able to look Ophélie Gravenor in the eye for a single moment, before she swung her sickle around and cut his throat.

"*Maman,*" Kate said, sitting up. A thousand questions battled on her tongue, but the first one to escape was, "Where have you *been?*"

# CHAPTER TWENTY-SIX

John Mary leaned on the stone wall and glowered down at what little of the pigs he could see in the light from the little tin lantern. Maman had returned only four months ago, and he had already spent more time in the company of these pigs than he had with his own sister. It was enough to put a man off bacon for life.

Of course, he thought, using a billhook to turn what was left of the headless corpse over so the sharp-toothed animals could get at the rest of it, perhaps if he hadn't been hiding that Maman was both alive and responsible for more than one violent death, he wouldn't have been so nervous about talking to Kate. Henry was safe enough; if John Mary pointed at a bank of soil and asked a question about it, Henry would so be intent on relaying all the information he knew about that specific sort of clay that John Mary would not need to say anything more for an hour. But Kate was perceptive. Kate knew when things were wrong. She had almost had the whole truth out of him the first week she had returned, and he had only put her off by going into great detail about the villainy of Daniel Lately.

John Mary rubbed his face and sighed. He had suspected from the first that Maman had not killed herself, in spite of the clothing she had left artistically twisted in the waterlogged roots of a tree close to where their little stream met the Severn. First of all, Maman believed that bad things should happen to other people, not to her or her children. Second of all, Maman thought that Daniel Lately had pushed Edward Gravenor into the millpond and left him to drown, and she certainly wouldn't die before she revenged herself upon her enemy.

Third of all, and most importantly, John Mary would have *felt* it if Maman had died. He and his mother had been together almost every hour of his life since his birth; she had carried him through events she could only describe in French and terrors she could not speak of at all. John Mary knew that Rob Baker was not the first man she had killed, nor the second, nor the third. She had done many things to escape France as a young woman with an infant, in a time when many men felt they had been given carte blanche to act as they would in the new world revealed by the revolution.

John Mary had been very small, but he remembered the smell of blood.

He had unwillingly understood why she had left after Edward passed. Her husband was the center of the difficult new life she had built for herself in this cold, hostile country. Edward read beautiful poetry about love and wrote his own awful verses about cows and clouds; he was good with children and terrible with account books. Edward had never imagined a world where he might have to kill another human being to defend himself. He had thought his wife was the most beautiful woman in the world, who made the best cheese in Europe, and he had adopted John Mary without qualm. Ophélie had not respected Edward, but she had loved him with the angry love of someone who has lost everything else. Without him as her anchor, Ophélie could not stay grounded here.

John Mary had not known where she had gone, but he had had his suspicions. Five years had passed while she did whatever she needed to do wherever she had gone, and he had pieced together a living from farming poorly and doing some other things rather well that he did not care to tell his more law-abiding siblings about. He thought Peter would understand, but Peter might also blackmail him.

And then Daniel Lately had approached John Mary and made his offensive offer to buy the farm. And then there had been the business with the bull, and Anne's job with the Telfords, but more importantly there had been men waiting for John Mary outside a public house in Wolverhampton, and he'd only just gotten away from them with a broken nose and a few broken ribs. John Mary could not go to a doctor without risking discovery, so he could not risk being injured. Suddenly he could only sometimes sneak away to do his real job. He had found himself relying more and more on the farm for cash, just as the farm's income diminished from *some* to *almost none.*

He had not known how to contact his mother, but he had suspected. She had sold cheeses to Miss James, Lord Houghton's evil-tempered maiden aunt, but they had also spent time together, more time than a squire's relation and a poor farmwife had any reason to pass in each other's company. After the beating, John Mary had approached Miss James and asked if she might pass on a letter to their mutual friend. He had found it very curious that she had invited Anne to Bassenthwaite House, and more curious still that she paid Anne so much for so little work. Anne had no doubt imagined her movements were a secret. But then, John Mary had always been the one who accompanied his mother to the markets in Southbridge, and perhaps the only one of her children who knew Miss James before Ophélie's disappearance.

John Mary sighed and dipped the lantern low. The corpse was … well, still recognizably a corpse, but he didn't think it would be for too many more days. This was the very back of the narrow strip of land where old Dennis Irons kept his animals, and he only ever fed them at the front. If the pigs ate quickly, nearsighted Mr. Irons would never notice there was something odd at this end of the pen.

It had been Maman's idea to just throw Rob Baker's head to the pigs. With a few expert hacks of the sickle, he had become a faceless corpse, unidentifiable. John Mary would have argued with her about the body, but that was the same week that Kate and Henry had moved back into the house, and he had been too busy to figure out where exactly she'd put the rest of the fool man. Then, after Fred Halverton and Wendell Driver had found the body, it had taken her a few nights to get into the woodshed unobserved. She had woken him up early in the morning with a sack of body parts for him to carry.

John Mary wished she could have butchered this fellow up as well; it had been a nasty bit of work to drag him this far.

He didn't think his mother's determination to behead her enemies was entirely sane, but then, who *was* entirely sane, or had a right to demand sanity of others?

John Mary had finally been able to get away to do his business when Kate was at the Wednesday market. It had taken much longer than intended, and he hadn't arrived home until the dark early hours of the morning. John Mary had tripped on this newest dead body while mulling over how he might obfuscate where he'd been and what he'd been doing. He wasn't sure which one this was; he thought it was probably either Zachary Walpole, a particularly vicious specimen from the next county, or Will Riggs, a man who had done work for Daniel Lately in Birmingham. John Mary was quite sure Riggs was responsible for his broken nose and Walpole at least one of his broken ribs, so he didn't feel particularly bad for whichever one this was.

The barn was a total loss, but he had watched Anne herd all eight cows and three calves around the yard in a circle from the cover of the trees before he started dragging the body back toward the hungry pigs. Kate and Henry and the doctor were gone. John Mary would have been more worried about this, except Maman was gone from her most recent camp as well. He suspected the doctor was too smart for his own good; he'd very nearly caught John Mary out while he was cleaning up Maman's last camp by the stream. But Kate was sensible, and Henry would do whatever Kate told him to do.

And Maman would not let anything bad happen to her children. A competent, angry woman could accomplish a great deal; a competent, angry woman who everyone thought was dead could accomplish even more.

## CHAPTER TWENTY-SEVEN

"You're lucky, though I know it doesn't feel it," Thomas told Margaret, his voice carefully even. "The bullet only grazed your arm. If it had hit the bone, I'd be amputating it right now."

He finished tying a pad of linen over the injury, which he'd washed out with a decanter of brandy he'd found on the shelf, and stitched with thread he had taken out of Margaret's own sewing basket in the corner of the kitchen. He thanked every single soldier whose bullet wounds he had bandaged for the fact that his hands did not shake. Margaret's bones were intact, but she had lost a great deal of blood. She was very white and very silent. She had downed a glass of brandy before he started sewing her up, but the pain would still be intense.

Thomas lifted his eyes, briefly met the stunned, dead stare of Cousin Daniel, then lowered them again. At least Margaret had not lost *that* much blood. Kate had lit every candle she could find in the room and stoked up the fire so he could see to work, with the unpleasant side effect that he could see the corpse of his cousin all too clearly.

"Where is Henri?" Kate's mother asked. "Cat, where is Henri?"

I am not thinking about this, Thomas thought, giving the bandage another twist and tucking the end under. I am not thinking about the fact that Kate's mother—*Kate's! mother!*—has apparently been going around the county cutting people's heads off. Deserving people, certainly—but also no. *Cutting people's heads off.*

He poured a few fingers more of the brandy into a glass and gave it to Margaret. "Here. Have a bit more."

"Henry is taking Eleanor to the vicarage," Kate said. "Maman, aren't your feet cold?"

"Bah," the older woman said, shrugging. If not for the bloody sickle in her hand, Thomas would have taken her for any other poor laboring woman; she wore an old-fashioned bodice and skirt and several shawls knotted about her neck, and she wore no shoes. She looked quite like Anne, though her face was thinner and graver, and a few wisps of coin-bright hair stuck out from beneath the cloth she had wrapped around her head.

The sickle, Thomas realized, with a jolt of cold recognition, was the same one Henry had found in the woodshed, with the twine-wrapped handle and unusually sharp edge. Of course.

"Why the vicarage?" Ophélie had switched to French.

"Peter is at the vicarage," Kate said patiently. She had sat back down on the floor; he could see her hands shaking when she lit the candles. Her beautiful blue eyes were red-rimmed, and her god-like hair had come loose all around her face.

"He is not," her mother said. "Or, he should not be."

Kate threw her mother an exasperated look. Thomas suspected that Ophélie Gravenor was in the habit of being cryptic. "Yes?"

"I have left him a letter," Ophélie announced. "He will be here shortly."

"Mother, Peter won't check for the post until morning," Kate said.

"He will. I have tied the letter to the neck of a cat."

"*Mother*. A cat?"

"A black-and-white cat. He looked very respectable."

Thomas covered Margaret again with her own jacket, now torn and stained with blood, and frowned at the two women. "Is she serious? And why is Peter coming?"

"He is my son," Ophélie said, ignoring his first question and wiping the blade of her sickle on her skirt. Her English was still heavily accented after decades in the country, he noticed.

"You have several sons," Thomas said, getting to his feet and fighting his temper down. "Why this one?"

"Erm," Kate said.

"I thought he would help me kill Daniel Lately," Ophélie said calmly. She took off one of her shawls, knelt by Margaret, and wrapped it tightly around her shoulders. "But now he can do the papers."

"I don't—" The papers? Thomas thought. "What papers?" He looked to Kate, but her expression was baffled. She looked very small sitting on the floor, her knees drawn up to her chest. He wanted to——he wanted to——

"*Kate*. There you are. I suppose I should have known——MOTHER. You——Good God. Well."

Peter stood in the doorway, a leather case in his hands, his jacket, breeches, and white stockings as pristine as ever. He took in the scene with a small grimace, his gaze lingering on Cousin Daniel's cut throat. Thomas supposed that even as practiced a killer as Ophélie Gravenor needed more than one swipe with a razor-sharp sickle to behead a man.

"Well. I suppose this all makes sense, after a fashion." He sighed and laid the leather case on the table. "Dr. Holyoke. Is the lady on the floor unconscious or dead? Merely resting? I see. Mother, I confess I had hoped we might meet again under more auspicious circumstances."

"Help me take this lady into the parlor, where she can rest without the face of that trou-de-cul staring upon her," Ophélie commanded her son. "And then we will talk about papers."

She and her son lifted Margaret between them and bore her out of the room. Thomas held out his hand to Kate, who took it and struggled to her feet. She still held the poker, a fact he felt rather than saw as he pulled her small, soft body against himself.

You could marry Kate, his mind said.

He froze in place. *You could marry Kate. You could marry Kate.*

*You could* ... Cousin Daniel was dead.

Don't get ahead of yourself, Thomas thought.

Kate squirmed in his grip, and he released her, embarrassed. "Thomas? Are you all right?"

Thomas passed a hand over his eyes. "I don't know how to answer that."

Cousin Daniel was dead. Dead. *Dead.*

"It was rather—" Kate made as if to look back, then shook her head. "I suppose it was rather a surprise."

I am free, Thomas thought, only just restraining himself from grabbing Kate and kissing her. They were both so tired that he thought they might fall down, and he thought Ophélie might kill him as well if he touched her daughter.

Kate did not look like she felt the same relief Thomas did. She looked, if he were perfectly honest with himself, devastated. Ophélie or no Ophélie, he took her hand and twined his fingers through hers.

Peter and his mother had taken the dust cover off the chaise and arranged Margaret upon it when Thomas limped into the parlor, clutching Kate's hand. Peter went back to the study and fetched his leather case, and Ophélie produced a lap blanket from another room in the house and tucked it around Margaret. She had fallen into unconsciousness, and Thomas hoped she would awaken again after her body had repaired some of the damage.

"I've been very busy," Peter announced, taking the floor like an actor delivering a monologue once his three audience members had arranged themselves on the settee, Kate in between her mother and Thomas. Thomas noted, with a new stirring of panic in his gut, that silent tears had started to roll down Kate's face.

Then he saw that Ophélie had taken her daughter's other hand and was clutching it quite as tightly as he was.

"Busy doing what?" Kate asked, her voice only a little choked.

Peter opened the case and flourished three pieces of paper of different sizes. "I have been hither and yon, thither and everywhere, sister, attempting to find out the truth of the late—the extremely late, one could argue—Mr. Daniel Lately's entanglements." He must have caught Thomas' grim stare, because he continued in a more normal tone. "Well, firstly, the dead fellow in the next room isn't Daniel Lately."

"*What*," hissed Thomas and Kate together. Ophélie only narrowed her eyes and tapped her lips with her fingers.

"First I went to visit our old friend Mr. George Beauford," Peter said, baring his teeth in a frightening parody of a smile. "He's taken up residence on the other side of Birmingham, did you know? I had been through all the records he had left in the parish, including some he would have been wiser to have destroyed, but I found it very curious that there was no record of the marriage Dr. Holyoke witnessed or the child which followed shortly thereafter, when the presumed Daniel Lately had gone to such trouble to procure both."

"Peter," Kate said warningly. "I know this is a good story, but I won't be held responsible for falling asleep."

Thomas thought of Kate falling asleep, curled on his shoulder, and briefly wished that they could put off all these revelations until the next day. But no. He needed to know.

"Yes, dearest sister," Peter said, sounding mildly chastened. "Well, Mr. Beauford, upon being pressed, found that he did in fact recall the events to which I referred, and he in fact retained his own personal records of both." He held out the first piece of paper, which Thomas saw was a page cut from a church registry book. "Do you notice anything?"

Thomas couldn't look. His eyes found the date, but they would not read the names that came after it.

"That says Daniel Lackley," Kate says, sounding puzzled. "It's got the right witnesses, but—"

"Yes, I thought that was very odd, as well," Peter said. "Beauford liked to indulge in his wine, the miserable old bastard, but I don't think he would have made quite such a glaring error. And so I went from his home to Birmingham, to the street where our deceased friend claimed to have had his premises as a solicitor. And what do you think—"

"*Pierre*," Ophélie said sternly, at the same moment that Kate said, "*Peter.*"

Kate's hand tightened briefly around Thomas', and he forced himself to take a breath.

"Yes, yes, of course," Peter went on breezily. "It seems that Daniel Lackley *did* operate as a solicitor on Dale End."

"Daniel Lately, you mean," Thomas said. He suddenly felt so tired he might vomit, or lie down on the floor and sleep there.

"Daniel *Lackley*," Peter said. He was clearly enjoying this far too much. "He had a ratty little office a street over from Daniel *Lately's* bookshop, who died of consumption about two months before your parents' solicitor came to Birmingham looking for your next of kin following their deaths." He paused, waiting for this to sink in.

"Keep going," Thomas said bleakly. "He's already dead, so it's not like I can kill him again."

"I don't know how he thought of the scheme," Peter continued. "My suspicion is that Beauford was involved, frankly. The Lately family solicitor was from Southbridge; I don't think he had any notion of what a little shit Beauford was."

"Can't you ask him?" Kate said.

Peter took a long moment to examine the papers in his case, carefully not looking anyone else in the face. "George Beauford was unexpectedly taken by a severe stomach ailment and has shuffled off this mortal coil, I fear."

"What?" Kate gasped. "When was that?"

"About an hour after I left him, I should expect," Peter said.

Thomas glanced at Ophélie. She had said nothing in response to this story, but a thin smile curved her lips.

Kate closed her eyes. "Oh, Peter."

"I also checked with a barrister who I happen to know," Peter went on, pacing across the carpet. "There was no way the marriage *Cousin Daniel* forced on Dr. Holyoke was legal; it took place at night, and not in a church. The marriage code bars both of these things. I have written to the Archbishop to check if he acquired a special license, but the chances are vanishingly small.

Mr. Lackley was not the sort of man who had an acquaintance with the Archbishop. I then went back to Southbridge and spoke with a certain Mr. Jones."

"My family's solicitor," Thomas said. God, he was so tired.

"His son," Peter said. "He was still a clerk in his father's office when this scandal occurred, but it made his father so angry that he remembered the details well. The purported Mr. Lately acted in ways he found highly suspicious at the time. It did not, for example, escape his notice that the fellow demanded to have all copies of the late Mr. James Lately's will given into his possession, nor that Mr. James Lately's only child disappeared under rather mysterious circumstances immediately thereafter, leaving *Cousin Daniel* the legal steward of their lands."

"But Mr. Jones didn't give every copy to—to—" Kate struggled for a minute before she gave up trying to refer to the dead body at the end of the hall. "Did he?"

"He did not," Peter said, holding out the second piece of paper.

"Read it," Thomas said, rubbing his eyes. "I can't."

"It is what you'd expect. It would have all been yours."

Is that what I would expect? Thomas wondered. I don't think I've known what to expect for twenty years.

"So—so—so—" Kate stammered.

"It is time to let Pierre do the papers," Ophélie announced, her resonant voice filling the room. "And right many wrongs which have been committed in this house of evildoers."

"So your *solution* is to forge a record of Eleanor's birth, have *me* forge a false medical report that says Cousin—Lately—Lackley—whatever the hell his name is, or was—died of a heart attack, bury his body quickly, and hope no one notices he had his throat cut?" Thomas demanded.

"You've forgotten altering Mr. Beauford's record of your marriage to one Daniel Lackley to make it look like it happened in Birmingham and a forged record of your former self's premature death in that same city, so that Eleanor may inherit free and clear," Peter said, still preternaturally calm. "Of course, we've no record of Daniel Lackley's death, but as he hasn't been heard from under that name in over twenty years, that shouldn't be a problem."

"It wouldn't work if anyone liked Daniel Lately," Anne said.

"I think dozens will come to the funeral to make sure he's dead," John Mary said darkly.

All the Gravenor siblings currently in England gathered in the Lately parlor in the early light. Kate felt somewhat guilty about this; she had fallen asleep when Peter had started to explain his plan last night, and apparently no amount of shaking would waken her.

When she was finally woken by a thin sunbeam sliding through the curtains to touch her face, John Mary was sitting in a chair by the bookcase. Maman, Thomas, and Margaret Leigh were nowhere to be seen.

Kate had immediately burst into tears and hugged her older brother, but before she could demand explanations there was a cacophonous mooing from behind the house, interspersed with earsplitting bleats. She rubbed her eyes clear of sleep and raced back to the kitchen, where she peered out the door.

Anne stood in the Lately farm yard, surrounded by cows, a small goat under each arm.

"I gave you the whole night to figure it out," she announced in a carrying tone. "Now Antoinette can deliver justice."

Kate opened her mouth to inquire about her sister's knowledge of French history, then closed it. "Justice is ... in process," she said carefully, hoping she was not lying. "And don't let Antoinette into the house." The last thing they needed, she thought, was for the cow to start eating the corpse.

A search of the house had revealed Thomas in an upstairs bedroom, spooning hot broth into Margaret's mouth, but no trace of Maman. She had not even left the shawl she had wrapped around Margaret the evening before.

Kate had felt tears rising again, so she busied herself with fussing over Margaret, bringing her more blankets and pillows and cups of tea. She had briefly let herself think—let herself hope—that she would finally be able to talk to Maman. She had so many questions. What had happened when Maman had disappeared? Had she survived an accident or staged her own death? Where had she gone in the intervening years? Who else had she killed? Were there people looking for her?

But Kate found that she most wanted to ask her mother an entirely different set of things. How had Maman kept the gray mold off her cheese? What did she think of Henry's idea to make cheeses from goat milk? How had Ophélie decided she could trust Edward, after everything she had gone through, and would marry him? Had she ever lost a baby? How had she survived it?

Why had she left when Kate still needed her?

But Maman was gone.

Margaret was very weak, but as yet showed no sign of fever. Every few minutes she querulously demanded to know where Eleanor was.

The difficulty with this, Kate thought, was that Peter had already been to the vicarage and back this morning, bringing the alarming news that there was no trace of Eleanor or Henry on the premises. Kate planned to be extremely worried about this, just as soon as she was done worrying about the crimes being committed in front of her.

Now four Gravenor siblings and Thomas stood around the desk in the study. The body of Daniel Lately—Lackley? oh, she couldn't keep this straight— had been wrapped in a sheet—several sheets, in fact, as he kept leaking—and taken down to the cellar to keep cool.

"Don't be prudish," Peter said crisply. "Thousands of soldiers' files passed through your hands during the war. Not a single one was compromised or rushed in any way?"

A strange look passed over Thomas' face. "Not to my knowledge," he said.

Kate looked at Thomas; his eyes, gloriously burning as ever; his imposing brows; his defiant nose and chin. She glanced down at the desk, where he had braced himself with his beautiful, beautiful hands, his careful, strong, delicate surgeon's hands.

She looked at him, and longed for him, and felt her insides riot with desire and fear. What would this man, this beautiful man, want with her and her crazed family? He had left England so that he might live an honorable life, a useful life, a life of dignity and service; and now he was surrounded by her family, who were all homely, homicidal, or both. She loved them to her marrow, but how could she ask him to do the same?

"I'm sure you can find that your morals will stretch to making sure none of my family hangs for murder," Peter said.

"Even the ones who are murderers?" Thomas snapped back.

Kate's insides stopped rioting and froze. She could not look away from Thomas' face.

"Especially them," Peter said. He put his hand in his pocket.

Kate suddenly found her voice. "Peter," she said. "If the thing you are about to take out of your jacket is either a knife or a pistol, *no it is not*. We are all friends here."

Peter gave her a look that was very similar to the look he had given her for tattling on his recurring theft of strawberries from the Halverton garden at a much younger age.

Thomas, however, was not amused. "Friends," he repeated. He sounded disgusted. "*Friends*."

"May I remind you—" Peter began, in his friendliest, most terrifying voice.

"I WILL PERJURE MYSELF IF I MUST, BUT I WILL NOT BE CONDESCENDED TO," Thomas roared. "GIVE ME THE DAMN PAPER."

"Thomas—" Kate started, pushing forward.

"Not now," he said sharply, writing quickly, loosely, on the piece of parchment which Peter had procured for him. She glanced down at what he wrote. *Apoplexy.* He signed the paper and and slammed down the pen. "There. There's your death certificate."

Kate's heart sank toward her heels, and she backed toward the bookshelf.

Thomas clutched a bundle of papers in cold fingers, his heart thrumming in his throat. Peter had written several letters describing the dastardly deception of the false Mr. Daniel Lately, four in the most lurid language addressed to newspapers printed in Birmingham, and one in the stateliest of terms to Mr. Llewyn Jones, Jr., Solicitor, Castle Street, Southbridge. He thought Peter had meant to post this last himself, but he had snatched it off the desk on his way out of the room.

I have perjured myself, he thought; I have been an accomplice to murder; I have let a murderer walk free. He had not been able to look at anyone else in the room after he signed his name to that lying piece of paper, especially not Kate. Apparently Thomas was as susceptible to bullying as the next man. He could not but feel a shiver of disgust at his own easy complicity with Peter's plotting.

But the man—*that* man—is dead, Thomas thought. Daniel is dead, and he will never touch me again. Eleanor is safe from him, and the Gravenors— the Gravenors—

Cousin Daniel was really, irrevocably dead. Before they had bundled the body down to the basement, Thomas had spared a moment to jab at the slice through the man's neck with a penknife left on the desk. The trachea and esophagus were fully severed, along with the vital arteries. The only thing keeping the head from falling off was the spine. Whatever his name, whatever his ancestry, the man would never terrorize anyone again.

Thomas limped through the house, down the kitchen stairs, and into the yard. Pain lanced through his leg, and he leaned against one of the stable's doorposts, his vision briefly doubling. He needed to get to Southbridge, and there was no way he could walk. Cousin Daniel had kept a curricle, though, and at least two horses. Thomas hadn't driven in a long time, but his mother had assumed that he would have need of the skill, so shortly after he learned to ride he had been set to steering a pony-cart around the paddock. If the animals weren't too wild, he could set them on the road and they would carry him to Southbridge by day's end.

The two bays he found in the stable were skittish but not poorly-trained, and both geldings allowed themselves to be harnessed and guided between the poles of the curricle. Thomas stood for a long moment with his hand on one gelding's withers, waiting to see if fear would seize him; the last time he had been so close to a horse, it had shattered his leg and his life. But no fear came. This stable belonged not to the army, not to Cousin Daniel, but to the shadow of his mother and her creatures.

Thomas hooked each harness to the poles,

struggled up onto the seat of the curricle, and picked up the traces. The two geldings were only too happy to proceed at a slow walk, so Thomas stared at the side of the road and struggled not to fall asleep.

These horses will belong to Eleanor, Thomas thought, though he was so tired that the steps to achieve that end refused to line themselves up in his head. This house will be Eleanor's. Eleanor will be safe, whatever happens to me.

I have perjured myself, Thomas thought; but then he thought of the letter Henry had written for the soldier being blackmailed for buggery, using his signature. Did he regret that?

Did Thomas regret the hundreds—thousands—of letters he had signed with the name he had given himself, which no legal authority would recognize?

If it came to that, Thomas thought, do I regret walking at the back of the murder machine which is His Majesty's Royal Army for more than ten years? Do I think I am blameless for what horrors were wrought in Portugal and in Spain, simply because I was not at the front of the line?

People will know, a voice in his head whispered, a voice that had chased him from continent to continent. If you stay here, people will *know*. People will find out who you really are.

Thomas stared into the still-bare fields. I know who I really am, he thought. I am Thomas Holyoke, medical doctor. I have a daughter. We have both survived, against all odds—

No, he corrected himself. Not against all odds. With Henry and Kate and Anne and John Mary and yes, even and especially Peter and their terrifying mother all sitting on the scales, pulling for all they're worth. I am in this with them, because they have thrown their lot in with me.

Thomas had taken a few sheets of paper from Cousin Daniel's desk, with the idea that he might write to the Army Medical Board and ask for a letter of recommendation, or at least the addresses of doctors who had worked with him in the field. He thought Frederick Neal was still in Malta building his small maternity hospital, and Pieter van Heuren was still in Cape Town arguing for closed sewers, but there had to be other medical fellows who remembered him. He had spent nearly twenty years creating himself, Thomas Holyoke, and if Daniel *Lackley* had proven anything, it was that what mattered was what people believed, not what actually was. The more evidence Thomas had to shore up his position here, to solidify the idea of a retired army doctor in people's heads, the safer he would be.

Thomas stared at his hands holding the reins, then looked up to watch the prickly brown stubble of wheat fields roll past. For some reason, Kate's fierce voice came into his head, enunciating carefully: *The marriage was not valid.*

There is a truth to things, Thomas thought. Whatever the law is, there is a truth to things that we are all pursuing.

I *must* marry Kate, he thought. I *will* marry Kate.

But first he would go to his family's solicitors and deliver the damning letter that Peter had written, the letter which established that Cousin Daniel was a dead liar and Eleanor should inherit everything.

The leftmost horse shied toward the center of the road, and Thomas clicked his tongue and whistled. The horse continued to pull away from the ditch, and the other horse began to turn with him. Thomas could just see a lump of something in the bristling brown grass at the side of the road, something that shivered slightly in the breeze, as though it were covered in fabric. He sighed and reined the animals to a stop. His mother's lessons were not so fresh in his mind that he wanted to fight two scared horses. He could get out and walk them past whatever lost bit of wind-shaken laundry had upset them.

It was only when he set his feet on the damp ground that the lump unfolded into a tall human shape and stared at him with pale cold eyes.

"I am going west," Ophélie Gravenor said.

She swung herself up into the curricle before Thomas could say anything and tucked her bare feet beneath the rug on the floor. He supposed she did not know how to drive, because she did not reach for the reins, only stared at him as he clambered back into the vehicle after her and picked them up himself. Now that the distressing shadow in the grass had been removed, the bays were perfectly happy to walk forward.

I wonder if she means to kill me, Thomas thought, and then, nonsensically, But she *can't* kill me. I have to marry Kate. And secure Eleanor's future. *And marry Kate.*

"I have to marry Kate," he said out loud, slapping the reins lightly against the rumps of the horses. They sped up from an amble to a stroll.

"Why? It isn't as if you've gotten her pregnant," Ophélie said.

Thomas glanced at her, trying to see if she meant to be cruel, but Ophélie's face was unreadable.

"I have to marry Kate," Thomas repeated, as much to savor the words as to explain himself.

Ophélie stared at him, unimpressed.

Thomas sighed. "I love her and want to protect her, and it would be easier if I married her."

Ophélie pointedly looked away from him, out into the fields.

Did you tell John Mary he would never be able to marry? Thomas thought angrily. Never be able to trust anyone? He gritted his teeth. He desperately wanted to rescue exactly one Gravenor sibling; the broken hearts of the others were not his affair.

"It is not easy to be a widow," Thomas tried again.

This time Ophélie did look at him, her pale eyes flashing like sickles. "I know."

Thomas swallowed, thinking of the drowned Edward, and Henry's descriptions of his mother's grief. "I know you know. But you are—you are a different sort of woman than Kate is. It is very hard for her to be alone."

"It is better to be alone than with a bad man," Ophélie said flatly.

Those sharp eyes skewered Thomas and pinned him to side of the curricle, some strange, frightening combination of grief and rage burning in their depths.

Thomas thought of Will Easting, of the abuse he had aimed at Kate, who had been so desperate to please. He thought of his own hatred for a dead man, his idle dreams of digging the fellow up and pissing on his bones.

Thomas thought of the woman who sat beside him, a woman who had wandered alone in the world, cut from the normal bounds of society by a brutal past, an intimate knowledge of death that few acquired outside of war. Thomas thought about what Ophélie might have done to survive the birthing of a new France, what she had been willing to do to bring a small child safe and whole to refuge in England.

He thought about what she *had* done, when her son's inheritance and livelihood had been threatened. He thought of Rob Baker's cold, headless body lying in the stream, and Zachary Walpole's decapitated corpse stretched out across the path. He thought of Cousin Daniel's sightless eyes.

Henry had told Thomas that Will Easting had fallen to his death from a haymow in one of his barns. Henry had heard from a neighboring farmer that Will had smashed his face and broken his neck. Will shouldn't have been up in the haymow, Henry had said gravely, which Thomas had taken as a indictment of his former brother-in-law's intelligence. It had not occurred to him at the time that Henry had been commenting on a certain peculiarity around the man's death.

Thomas looked out at the brown fields, then down at his own hands, then again at Ophélie, who was still watching him closely. A divot had appeared between her eyebrows.

Inexplicably, Thomas thought of his own mother, tall and dark-haired, calling out instructions as he sat atop his first proper horse, her black eyes as sharp as the gaze piercing him now.

Love makes one unspeakably brave, Thomas thought.

"You are not going to tell Kate," Ophélie said, her words falling into the silence like lead plumb lines into the sea.

"No," Thomas said.

"I did what needed to be done," Ophélie said.

"I know," Thomas said.

"*You* will do what needs to be done."

"I will," Thomas said. And then, because he felt he had to make the attempt, even if he was sure it would fail, he said, "You should come back to the farm. Your daughter—your family has missed you."

"No," Ophélie said. "Not yet."

They drove in silence the rest of the way to Southbridge. When the ruins of the castle atop the hill came into the view, Ophélie jumped down from the curricle and disappeared into a patch of trees on the right side of the road.

## CHAPTER TWENTY-EIGHT

That was that, Kate supposed. She had left the Lately house alone after the most important papers had been forged and signed, arriving back home just before sunset. She had slept the sleep of the desperately grieving and had woken into a world where her mother and the man she loved were still gone. Now she was washing her hair, because she couldn't think of anything else to do. She wondered what Thomas had been doing all today, and then rebuked herself soundly. That wasn't her concern anymore, if it ever had been. He was doubtless making preparations to go to London, to start his life anew.

Thomas did watch your mother kill a man, she thought, wringing out her hair into a bucket. And inspected two other men she had killed. And ... well, Kate didn't especially like to think about it, but she was sure Thomas was considering the fact that Maman had dispatched Rob, Zachary, and Daniel very competently. One might almost suspect that they were not the first to fall under her sickle. A less conscientious man than Thomas might balk at letting such a woman walk free, and Thomas was a very conscientious man. She had seen the expression on his face when he had signed the false death certificate, and it had looked like revulsion.

All this time, Kate thought, staring into the steaming pot of water on the hearth. All this time, she's been alive. The horse whetstone hadn't been lost; she had had it with her. All this time.

She blinked back tears, and then, when that was not enough, she pressed the heels of her hands into her eye sockets to suppress the flood.

I needed you, she wished she could have said to Maman, when she had been falling asleep on the Lately settee while listening to Peter explain the entire plot. I needed you when I lost the first baby, and the second, and the third, and the fourth. I needed you when Will hardened his heart against me. I need you *now*, when the man I love has left, and I can't even blame him for leaving. I am not enough. I need you, Maman, and you're not here.

Kate stood in front of the kitchen fireplace in her shift, scrubbing her scalp. She thought she might burn the dress she had been wearing when they had gone to rescue Eleanor. She wasn't sure that Mr. Lately's blood had actually splattered onto her, but it made her skin crawl to touch it.

She rinsed her hair in hot water once more, then began to comb it, starting from the ends. Her hair wasn't so long, only halfway down her back, but it curled terrifically, and as a consequence tied itself into knots at the least provocation.

Anne had stayed at Lately House with Margaret Leigh. John Mary had rounded up the cattle—Kate thought with a pang of the milking she'd missed, but she thought the calves would likely have had second and third breakfast and consider themselves very lucky —and herded them off somewhere, though whether to one of the Gravenor fields or a likely-looking Lately field, she wasn't sure. Peter had given Anne the little pistol he had been keeping in his pocket before he rushed off to post his letters, in case any of the Lately help showed tendencies in the line of Rob Baker or Zachary Walpole. He thought it likely that once it was publicly known that Cousin Daniel had been a vicious fraud, any other toughs he had paid would slink off to find new employment.

Anne had exhorted her to stay, to not exert herself, but all Kate could think of was falling asleep between Maman and Thomas, both of them holding her hand, and waking up without either.

I will be fine, she thought. I have always known this would happen. I will be fine.

I have to be fine.

She had walked back, and a distance that she would have normally covered in an hour took her almost three. She kept needing to stop and cry. Every part of her body hurt, including her heart. She had not awakened this morning until an hour when she would normally be preparing lunch, and even the most mundane of cheese chores were exhausting.

Kate guessed it was near three o'clock now, from the light coming through the windows. She wondered whether John Mary would come home tonight. She wondered where he had been when the barn burned. He had been lying for Maman; but he had been lying about something else too, and she was not sure what.

She wondered where Henry and Eleanor were. She wished she hadn't told Henry to take Eleanor to the vicarage; she should have known that his dislike of Peter was stronger than his desire to make his sister happy. She wished she could make Henry understand that Peter's attempts to control his brother came from desperately wanting to protect siblings who he knew the world would ravage; she wished she could make Peter understand that the more he tried to control Henry to keep him safe, the farther away he drove his brother.

Once Eleanor was fully awake, Kate had no doubt that Henry would follow her instructions to the letter, but she wasn't sure what Eleanor might ask Henry to do. There had been something very tender in the way they had stared at each other when introduced in the Gravenor parlor, but … surely … *surely*, the child wouldn't jump straight to marriage from there, would she? Kate thought of Will, of what she had believed of Will and how he had failed her, and felt a little sick.

But Eleanor might. Henry was kind, biddable, and very tall. Eleanor might fancy him quite a lot, and given that she hadn't been allowed to fancy anyone before in public, it would likely take her whole person by storm. Cousin Daniel, her erstwhile guardian and false father, was now dead and wrapped in multiple layers of sacking in the Lately House cellar, so it was not as if anyone stood in her way.

Kate finished with one section of her hair, put it over her shoulder, and started combing the next.

She was so lost in thought that she did not hear the footsteps in the yard, nor their distinctive, uneven cadence. When the front door opened, Kate let out a little shriek, and dropped her comb.

"Oh—rot—"

Thomas closed the door, turned around, and froze.

His eyes skimmed over her from head to foot, and then returned to her hair. His mouth formed an O.

"Lord almighty," he said. "Give me grace."

"I had to wash it," Kate said defensively. "I was all covered in smoke. And blood. And—"

Thomas limped closer, but he did not grab her, only stared. Finally he said, "I'm not going to kneel, because I don't think I can get up again."

"What?" Kate said. "Why—why would you—"

"I've been to my father's solicitors," he said. "I gave them Peter's letter, and explained that I am Thomas Holyoke, cousin to James Lately's wife. I gave them a great deal more detail about my mother than I think they cared to have, but at least they believed I knew her." He shook himself. "Eleanor and Henry went to Bassenthwaite House last night. Eleanor left a letter with Miss James, which Miss James then left with my father's solicitor. Apparently she's taken them both in the Houghton family coach to stay with a friend in Ipswich."

"Oh." Kate took a long moment to digest this. "Well, it's not Gretna Green, at least."

Thomas raised his eyebrows at her.

"If Eleanor wants to marry Henry, then I am delighted for them both," Kate told him. "I just—I don't want her to feel that she is forced into anything. She has choices. She *must* have choices." She swallowed hard.

Thomas stared down at her. "She will have many choices, yes. The Lately estate is nothing like so grand as——*he*——would have had everyone believe, but there's a hundred acres, and shares in a coal mine."

"Shares in a coal mine," Kate repeated weakly. She looked around for a stool; she needed to sit down.

Thomas stayed close behind her, but not touching her, as she settled on the nearest seat, tucking her shift around her legs and shoving away twinges of embarrassment about her bare calves. It wasn't her fault that Thomas had come in while she was undressed; he hadn't told her what time he would be coming back, if at all.

"I think Eleanor would happily make you a gift of new thatching straw, to replace what was burned," Thomas said quietly.

Kate scowled at him. "I won't have her feel beholden. If——if she could *loan* us a pound, I will pay it back as quickly as possible. Oh, I need to make cheese today." She let out a little gasp.

Thomas just looked at her. Then he asked quietly, "May I touch your hair?"

"I——" Kate pinkened. "If you would like, yes."

"I would very much like." Thomas moved behind her, and suddenly she felt his fingers on her scalp, tracing delicate patterns between her locks. He ran his fingers through from roots to tips, sending waves of tingling down her neck and spine.

He wrapped both hands in hair and gently tugged her head backwards until she was looking up at him.

Kate swallowed.

"When I first woke up in your house," Thomas said, "and saw you, and saw the sunlight on your hair, I thought that this must be what God looked like to Moses."

"I think that might be blasphemy," Kate said, in a small voice.

Thomas turned her head and kissed her, pressing his lips very lightly to hers.

"It is not," he said against her mouth. "It might be the only true thing."

He pulled back far enough for her to focus on his eyes, then let go of her hair and began to pull his hands away. Kate let out a reflexive whimper and clapped both her hands over his.

"I—you—I—" She could feel another wave of tears coming on.

"I didn't mean to be gone a whole day," Thomas said. "Mr. Jones saw how exhausted I was, and bid me rest in a chair in his office; when I woke up it was too late to set out again, and they stabled the horses for me."

"I thought," Kate said, barely swallowing a sob, "that you would not come back. Because you saw—you saw who we really are." Who I really am, she thought.

Thomas went very still, then said, "I have known who you are for a long time."

"You aren't beholden to us, either," Kate said, and the sob broke through.

Thomas leaned forward and rested his lips against hers until her breathing had slowed, and then he leaned back.

"You have choices, too," Thomas said. He unlaced

one hand from her hair, but he kept hold of her fingers, using them to stroke her neck. He took a deep breath, as if steeling himself. "I will write to the officers I served under throughout the last twenty years and get recommendations, but I imagine it will take a while to establish myself in private practice in Southbridge. I have even less in the way of ready cash than you." He gave her a half-smile.

"That's—I'm very happy for you—"

"Peter will marry us," Thomas said, steel in his tone. "If I had to perjure myself on his say-so, then he'll damn well post the banns for us and do the service without a fee." Suddenly unsure, he shot her a sideways glance. "If that is what you want. I understand if, after all, you do not wish to be married again—"

Kate pushed forward and kissed him. "If I have a choice, then I choose what I love, and I love you, I love you very much, but oh, are you *sure*, because you shouldn't trap yourself for my sake—"

"*Kate*," Thomas said dangerously.

"Because—I can't—I can't have children, you know I can't, I can't—" She could hear herself, and she sounded like she was nearly in hysterics, but then Thomas' grip on her hair tightened again, and he kissed her until she was breathless and a little dizzy.

"We have both been robbed of the children who ought to have been our own," Thomas said into her hair. "I love you. I do not need anything from you but your love in return."

They kissed until it was fully dark in the kitchen, and then Kate lit a candle and got down the cheese she had been saving, the first one she had made from

Antoinette's milk, and she cut a thin slice and carried it to Thomas and placed it on his tongue. He chewed slowly, smiling, and then he kissed her palm. "It's very good."

"Yes," Kate whispered. He turned and wrapped his arms around her, and they stood together in the dark kitchen, one candle burning on the table.

## Acknowledgments

*(from J. Winifred)*

My house is too small to have this many cows in it.

## Acknowledgments

*(from Sharon)*

This book could not have happened without the help of many incredible people. First, I would like to thank Rose Lerner for talking me through the plot in the very earliest stages, when my brain was too scrambled to think how cheese and murder might coexist in a manuscript. Terry Kieferling did a sensitivity read for transmasculine representation on an early draft, and his feedback made the resulting book stronger, more coherent, and more deeply-felt. Jen Prokop, my developmental editor, gave me invaluable feedback about the pacing and the emotional arc of the romance, and I am deeply indebted to her genre expertise. Felicia Davin did a sensitivity read for infertility issues and also suggested some more period-appropriate alternatives to my 21st-century French. Aleksei Valentín did a second read for transmasculine issues and delivered very welcome encouragement.

One person did so much to help me through the

first and second drafts of this book that I am not even sure how to begin thanking them. Kari Dru Muether helped me with multiple check-ins a week during the months when I was writing and editing, advice about plot snarls, and innumerable discussions working through characterization and representation. Without them, I would not have been able to finish writing this book at all.

## About the author

J. Winifred Butterworth is definitely not elderly goblin Juniper Butterworth wearing a doily on her head. Both of them bear only a passing resemblance to Sharon J. Gochenour, a writer and illustrator living in Massachusetts. They've all visited a few places and consumed a few dairy products.

Links to more writing, artwork, blogging, and news can be found on sharonjgochenour.com.